UNLEASHED

UNLEASHED

a REWIND *novel*

CAROLYN O'DOHERTY

BOYDS
MILLS
PRESS

AN IMPRINT OF BOYDS MILLS & KANE
New York

Boyds Mills Press
An Imprint of Boyds Mills & Kane
boydsmillspress.com

Printed in United States of America
ISBN: 978-1-62979-815-8 (hardcover)
ISBN: 978-1-68437-897-5 (eBook)
Book data is on file with the Library of Congress.

First edition
10 9 8 7 6 5 4 3 2 1

The text is set in Janson MT.
The Carson Ross narratives are set in Century Gothic.

To my mother, who always believed I would write a book one day

01 ◀◀ *CARSON ROSS*

CARSON ROSS STUDIES THE BODY CRUMPLED IN THE corner of the basement: white female, mid-twenties, brown-haired, wearing jeans and a grimy T-shirt with *Just Do It . . . Later* printed on the front. Blood pools on the floor around her head in a sticky lake. She has contusions on her cheek, a sizable gash on her right temple, and lacerations on her face and arms, the latter presumably from the broken window through which she's most likely been shoved. The woman's head is twisted back at a sharp angle, as if she's looking over her shoulder to see who caused her fall. Despite the gruesomeness of her condition, she's noticeably pretty.

She's also noticeably dead.

"The office manager found her an hour ago," says the deputy hovering at Ross's elbow. His eyes are bright, and his acne-flecked cheeks are flushed with eagerness. Ross's jaw twitches. It should be the coroner giving him this background, or at least a senior officer. Saddling him with a kid barely out of the academy is typical of the department's lack of respect for time agents.

"The printer ran out of toner," the deputy continues, "and he came down to the basement to get a fresh cartridge." The deputy shuffles a little closer. "Do you think it could be a Sikes killing? Chief said he always places his victims in a spot where they can't be found until it's too late to rewind the crime."

There is no way this is a Sikes killing. After chasing the elusive thief/murderer for six years, Ross knows his MO better than anyone, and this death does not fit the pattern. Sikes uses more failsafe methods to kill his victims than a bash on the head: a slashed throat, a well-placed bullet. He's also too smart to rely on chance, and the basement of an active business is hardly the kind of place one can count on to be empty of people for the seventy-two-hour time frame beyond which most rewinds can't be sustained. Not that Ross is going to tell the deputy that, or anyone else for that matter. The clues that led him to uncover Sikes's real identity are Ross's secrets, ones that, for now, he intends to keep locked up tight. Sikes's arrest will be a bombshell, and Ross has every intention of saving that revelation for the perfect moment—the one that is most likely to advance his career.

Ross pats the eager deputy on the shoulder, using the movement to put some space between them.

"It *could* be Sikes." He flashes the kid his trademark smile, the charming one that shows all his teeth. "Let's find out, shall we?"

The deputy stares at Ross with the kind of openmouthed wonder usually reserved for movie stars. Ross's smile widens to dazzling. This deputy isn't a bad kid, really. Even though this isn't a Sikes crime, it will be satisfying to show a new recruit the ease with which a seasoned time agent can solve a murder.

Ross turns and beckons to the spinner who's waiting by the concrete stairs on the other side of the room, her face carefully averted from the twisted corpse. She's a delicate-looking teenager, with long dark hair falling over the shoulders of her regulation maroon Crime Investigation Center shirt. Ross struggles for a second to remember her name—Cookie? Yummy? Oh, right.

"Yuki," he calls. "Will you come join us?"

"Yes, sir." The girl sidles over, managing to approach without actually looking at the crime scene.

Ross quashes a sigh. Alex, his former spinner, was never squeamish. Plus, he's told Yuki three times she should call him Mr. Ross. She's not going to be of any use to him if the two of them don't bond, and no one bonds with people they call *sir*.

Yuki stops in front of him and holds out her left arm. The metal band clasping her wrist gleams dully under the single overhead bulb.

"What's that?" the deputy asks.

"It's called a leash." Ross pulls a key from his pocket and unlocks the three-inch-wide bracelet. "Spinners wear them whenever they leave the Center. It emits electromagnetic waves that prevent them from accessing time."

The leash falls away and the deputy backs up a few steps—a ridiculous precaution. What threat does this kid think a little girl like Yuki could possibly pose? The propaganda built up over the centuries to make people fear spinners was as illogical as it was effective.

Ross leans toward Yuki, speaking to her with both gentleness and respect.

"Are you ready to freeze time?"

Instead of answering, the girl places two fingers on the back of Ross's hand with a touch as light as a butterfly's. She takes a deep breath, gathering herself for what appears to be a great effort, and closes her eyes. The hush of the basement solidifies into absolute silence. The doe-eyed wonder on the deputy's face transforms into an unmoving mask. The faint breeze from the building's upper floor vanishes. Light dims as the bulb's rays are stopped dead in their tracks. Every thing and everyone freezes as this single moment of time locks into place.

Almost everyone.

"Nicely done," Ross says.

"Thanks." Yuki removes her fingers from his skin and starts fiddling with a stack of red plastic bracelets that circle her right arm. The clacking they make in the frozen silence is harsh.

"Can you start the rewind?" If this were Alex, Ross wouldn't have to ask.

Yuki closes her eyes again. Ross waits. And waits. The only reason he doesn't tap his foot is fear of breaking her concentration, which, judging from the deep line in her forehead, is taking all her energy to maintain.

After months of working with Alex, Ross has forgotten how rocky other spinners' rewinds are. When Alex rewound time, the images were pale but crystal clear. Yuki's efforts, once they finally begin, are smudged and hazy. Ross watches as what looks like a film starring blurry ghosts spools out everything they've just done in reverse—his shadowy replica bending to speak to Yuki, his hand reclasping the leash on her arm. A faint rendition of the deputy moves forward. The Yuki of one minute ago detaches herself from the real girl and drifts backward toward the steps. Sound follows the ghostly images: words, all played in reverse, create incoherent gibberish, mingling with the ambient noises also being replayed backward—traffic passing outside the building, the faint hum of electricity. Ross massages his temple. He always forgets to bring earplugs to block out the irritating jumble.

The rewind lurches, the speed of the passing minutes rising and slowing in random bursts. A handful of shadowy officers back down the stairs, their wavering outlines passing right through Ross as they move toward the body. Radios squawk meaningless noise. Cameras flash and then click. Notes disappear from pads.

Ross prods the body with one toe. Alex once told him that rewinding time felt like reeling in strands of invisible silk. Yuki seems to be hauling in a massive fishing net, one that's slippery and heavy with knots.

"How are things at the Center?" Ross asks, when the pace of the rewind finally settles into something resembling a rhythm.

"What?" Yuki's eyes fly open. The rewind stutters, and she just manages to catch hold of it before it stops altogether.

"The Crime Investigation Center," Ross says. "It must be a bit tense there these days."

The look she gives him is as blank as the corpse's.

"I just meant it must be hard to have four spinners disappear overnight like that," Ross amends.

"They didn't disappear," Yuki says. "Dr. Barnard told us they got sick."

Ross studies the girl's expressionless face. The Center's director has a reputation for scientific brilliance, but his interpersonal skills are hardly warm and fuzzy. Does Yuki really believe the story Dr. Barnard told them? Spinners are raised with the lie that time sickness can strike its lethal blow at any moment, but losing four on the same day is extreme. Wouldn't Yuki have heard rumors? From

5

what Ross has been able to discover, Alex and her friends escaped in the middle of the afternoon. Surely someone saw something odd.

"It just seems strange so many kids got sick all at once," Ross suggests.

Yuki looks confused. Stupid child. Ross turns back to the body. A man who must be the office manager lets out an eerie scream before leaning over the victim to check her condition. Ross tips his head to better see the man's face. It's startlingly unclear. He sighs. It's going to be a real pain when the killer shows up and has to be identified from these bits of mist.

"Can you speed up the rewind?" he asks Yuki.

It's hard to tell if she succeeds. The basement's few windows are blocked by a line of ornamental shrubs, so clues to measure the passage of time are sparse—no duplicated sun spinning through the frozen sky, no rush of cars or passing pedestrians. Ross jingles the change in his pocket. The instant in time that he and Yuki occupy expands by some immeasurable amount. The past spools out around them, tedious and unchangeable. Ross yawns. He picks out a quarter from the rattling coins and traces the shape of the face detailed on its surface.

"What do you think happened to the victim?" he asks Yuki.

She shrugs. Her gaze is unfocused and sweat beads along her upper lip.

Ross turns the quarter in his hand. "Any thoughts about who might have done this?"

Yuki's eyes flick over the body, and then away again, as fast as if they had been stung.

"Isn't that why we're doing the rewind?" she asks.

"Right."

Ross takes his hands from his pockets and walks over to sit on the stairs. He misses Alex. She was a perfect spinner, especially once her true skills had emerged. Alex cared about solving crime, and she listened to all his theories with such seriousness. She was particularly devoted to the Sikes case—even more so once she learned that Ross's former police partner, Sal, had been one of Sikes's victims. Ross sighs. Life is so unfair. He'd been smart enough to find a great police partner and then a great spinner and both of them had been snatched away from him.

Ross studies the step beneath his feet and sees a crack running through the gray concrete. It's narrow, but deep—the kind of flaw that over time can lead the entire staircase to fail. He puts his foot over the miniature chasm. He made a mistake with Alex; he can see that now. He should have kept her from seeing him kill Austin Shea. He thought she would understand that since Shea worked with Sal's killer, his punishment was deserved, but the girl's idealism, so helpful in some ways, turned out to be an unexpected weakness.

Ross rubs his foot over the crack, feeling the slight bump it makes beneath his shoe. The whole situation is horrendously unfair. One tiny mistake and the plan he'd spent years painstakingly stitching together unraveled in an instant. What really stings is Alex's lack of gratitude. Before he became her agent, she was just a dying child forced to perform time tricks for a police force that barely tolerated her. It was *he* who gave her purpose; he who took her off the drug, Aclisote, so her real powers would emerge; and he who presented her with the truth. It was outright selfish of her to take all those gifts and use them for herself.

Something flashes in the corner of his eye. Ross looks up and sees the misty shape of a tumbling body rising up to the gaping window. It's moving so fast he misses the moment it passes through the glass.

"Stop the rewind!" he shouts.

Yuki, who has been staring off in the opposite direction, jumps.

"Hold time right there," he tells her.

Ross races up the stairs and out the building's main door. The air outside feels heavy, the dark of a rewound night layered like fog over the morning's natural light. Ross ducks under a band of yellow crime-scene tape blocking the entrance and makes his way to the side of the building. Plants mask the broken window, though right now, shadowy images of them are yanked to one side. The victim's body rests on the ground in the gap between them. Her face is still battered, but the slashes to her flesh have not yet occurred. Beside her kneels a man, his hands gripping her shoulders as he prepares to ram her body through the window's shattered glass.

The guy definitely isn't Sikes. Sikes—real name Matt Thompson—is an average-height, middle-aged white male. This killer, while also male and white, looks nothing like him. Ross steps closer, scrutinizing the blurred face. Young, he thinks, though he's basing this more on the man's outfit than any identifiable features: baggy jeans, dark hoodie, shaved head, and a pair of those rings in his earlobes that open a hole wide enough that Ross is pretty sure he could fit his quarter through it. The guy's clothes—like his victim's—are cheap and worn. Ross's nose wrinkles in disgust. These two are not going to turn out to be some of Portland's finer citizens.

Ross walks a quick but thorough circuit of the surrounding area, searching for any other potential suspects. The building is on a corner lot, and the street in both directions is clear of any

8

remembered visitors, as is the parking lot at the back of the building. The only possibly suspicious item is a rusty metal pipe behind the dumpster, which Ross carries back in case it proves important.

"Keep rewinding," he calls down to Yuki when he returns to the broken window, "but do it slowly."

Time shifts backward again, setting the scene in motion. Even accounting for the awkwardness of watching someone in reverse, the killer's movements are clumsy. Perhaps he's distraught. The man pulls the body away from the window. When it's clear of the surrounding greenery, the woman's head and shoulders abruptly leap into his arms—a drop in reverse. The killer drags her across the lawn, an action that looks particularly strange since he's leaning away from the body in counterbalance as he appears to move forward. When he's ten feet from the building, he turns and lowers her to the ground. He remains on his knees beside her, hands wrapped over his bald pate as he rocks back and forth, emitting a strange, high-pitched wail.

Ross lowers himself so he's next to the pair and studies the ground around her head. Just beside the gash on her temple is an area of tamped-down grass and dirt. Superimposed over this is the ghostly image of a sharp rock, the top corner of which is partially embedded in the woman's head. So much for his pipe theory. Ross runs his fingers through the disturbed earth. It's wet from last night's rain, but there's no rock. Distraught as the killer seems now, he must have had the wherewithal to get rid of the cause of death, plus some luck, since the rain has erased his bloody trail.

The rewind flickers, and the movements grind to a halt. Ross drops the meaningless pipe and gets to his feet.

"You doing OK, Yuki?" he calls.

"Yes, sir," she answers, though her voice is faint, and Ross would bet money it's more from strain than distance. He suppresses a sigh.

"Just a couple more minutes. Keep rewinding."

There's a pause before the scene grinds back into motion. It's moving faster now, with Yuki presumably rushing to cover some ground before she loses her hold. Ross feels another pang of loss. This whole business was much more pleasant with Alex.

The killer lurches to his feet. The woman on the ground twitches, then follows the same trajectory, rising in a quick surge to collide with the solid mass of the man's fist. Ross dusts his palms against the front of his pants. Involuntary manslaughter, ten to sixteen months in prison. It's hardly even worth convicting.

The ghostly couple engages in an exchange of violence. His fist bursts away from her face; her nails remove gouges in his cheek. The air is rent with angry squeals that even in their muted form are clearly shouts. Ross can't make any sense of the words, but given that no object of value ever emerges, the disagreement is almost assuredly interpersonal. Jealousy. A loan gone bad. Broken promises.

Ross snatches the pipe off the ground and hurls it at one of the building's upper windows. There's a deafening crash and glass rains down in a glittering shower. The rewind abruptly halts, but Ross doesn't care. He's seen enough. What a waste of his talents. He is worth so much more than rewinding grubby murders of irrelevant people. Ross glares at the glass's cruel edges. When he was a kid, his favorite movies were the ones about men who took justice into their own hands and never worried about collateral damage. These were his heroes, and it was how he envisioned police work. The real job proved disappointing, a tedious mess of rules and paperwork that turned justice into a mismanaged

10

bureaucracy that set criminals free and gave victims no resolution. A lesser man might have become disillusioned, but not Ross. He paired up with the brilliant Salvador Rodriguez, and together the two of them fought through the bureaucratic haze to achieve an impressive arrest record. After Sal's murder, when the police chief pulled him off the Sikes case and reassigned him to the unpopular time squad so he could "recover," Ross used his own intelligence to unearth the true potential of the spinners. With their skills under his control, he would be able to finally fulfill his childhood dream: Carson Ross, defender of right, by any means necessary.

The vision was so perfect, the fantasy just starting to turn into reality, when Alexandra Manning ran away and ruined everything. Ross kicks at a stick lying in the grass, sending it hurtling across the lawn. It hits a parked car with a loud thud.

"Mr. Ross?" Yuki's voice warbles up from the recesses of the building. "Sir? Is everything all right up there?"

Ross wipes a hand across his face.

"Everything is fine," he says.

He walks over to the window, broken glass grinding beneath his feet. Yuki peers up at him through the bushes. Her face looks pale and strained in the basement's dim light.

"You can let time go," Ross tells her.

The girl's features relax, the world around them blurs, and the next instant, everything returns to how it was when she stopped time. Ross again stands next to Yuki, the victim's body at his feet, and the spinner's fingers resting on the back of his hand. The deputy completes his shiver of anticipation. Outside, the rusty pipe is back in its spot behind the dumpster, and the upper window it had shattered is now intact.

"We're back," Ross tells the deputy.

The younger man's eyes bug out of his face.

"Did you recognize him?" he asks. "The killer?"

Ross hesitates for only a second.

"The rewind was a bit blurry," he says, "but I have a pretty good idea who did this."

The admiration in the deputy's eyes soothes some of the burn in Ross's heart. He might as well make use of the rewind. A rewound murder charge is hard to fight, and there's no point wasting it on the dumb schmuck who actually killed her. *He*'s not a serious threat to public safety. Ross mentally runs through his list of known criminals, the ones who deserve to be arrested but have so far managed to avoid conviction: Mercer Lee, Fred Watson, Joseph Sully. One of them won't have an alibi for last night. Even if the crime isn't exactly the one they committed, putting them behind bars means one more scumbag off the streets.

Ross takes out Yuki's leash and reattaches it to her arm. The arrest will be a small gain, nothing like the scope of what he could accomplish if he had a personal spinner working just for him. Yuki rubs her forehead, making no effort to hide what the rewind has cost her. Ross turns away. How will he find someone new? He runs through the roster of qualified spinners still living at the Center: Raul, Angel, Aiden, Simon. Not one of them has a reputation for any particular spark, and the fifteen Youngers will take too long to train. Finding a quick replacement for Alex was always a slim hope, and this mission has crushed it.

He heads up the stairs, Yuki trailing behind with a forlorn shuffle that grates on Ross with an irritation close to pain. Somewhere out in the city, Alex is hiding—scared, confused, and completely unprepared to survive in the real world. It's only a matter of time before the girl does something to expose her location. When she does, the wipers—the Center's private security team—will find her and ship her off to the Central Office. There, they will snuff out all her potential with a quick, quiet death.

Ross's pace quickens as he marches down the hallway. He won't let it happen. Alex is too valuable to throw away. If the wipers can find her, then surely so can he. Ross reaches the front door and steps out into the unfiltered sunshine. Alex has spent three days cowering in fear. Ross is confident that once he finds her, he'll be able to convince her to work with him again. After all, he knows her weaknesses. He knows everything she loves and fears. He will get her back.

02 ◀◀

THE WOMAN ON TV IS CRYING. CAMERA CREWS PRESS their lenses into her grief, soaking up her loss and confusion in the name of increased ratings. *Why me?* her teary eyes beg. *Why him?*

I turn my head, only to be confronted with ten identical images pummeling me from an entire wall of TVs. An electronics store is not the place to go if you want to avoid seeing Portland's hottest news story of the week: Young, pretty Emily Shea came home from a visit to her parents to find her husband in bed, alone, with his throat slashed. He'd been dead three days. The cops said the Shea's side-door lock had been jimmied, but the burglar alarm never went off, and none of the neighbors saw anything suspicious. The one set of fingerprints the police found in the house had no records attached to them. The crime is surrounded by mystery.

A mystery to everyone but me. I can tell them exactly what happened that night because those unidentified fingerprints at the Shea house are mine.

"Alex." Jack nudges my shoulder. "What about getting one of those?"

Mrs. Shea's eyes follow me when I turn away from the screen to see what he's pointing at, making me snap at Jack with an extra dose of irritation.

"What would we do with a giant speaker back at the squat? Victor won't even let us have a radio."

Jack stares hungrily at the box. "We could plug headphones into it," he says. "Or look at those! I heard that brand is the bomb."

Jack starts off toward a locked cabinet full of speakers ranging from the size of a toaster to a matchbox. I grab the back of his T-shirt.

"We came here to get cell phones," I whisper. "That's it. We are not going to go around stealing a ton of stuff just for fun."

Jack shakes off my hold and crosses his arms. "Let me see if I understand. Taking stuff is OK if *you* want it, but when I want something, it's called stealing?"

I sigh. I couldn't have managed the last few days without Jack, but that doesn't mean the guy doesn't drive me crazy. When we left the Center, I'd been exhausted and still staggering from a car crash. It was Jack who carried KJ out of the clinic, Jack who convinced Shannon to come and nurse KJ, and Jack who found us a place to live. Jack also taught me how to use the bus system, and I have to admit his company makes me less anxious on the endless errands that keep us alive. Still, if it were KJ out here, he would be helping me figure out a long-term survival plan, instead of trying to convince me that taking stuff from a faceless corporation doesn't count as stealing. KJ would be calm and responsible. KJ would not be trying to impress that loser Victor.

"This isn't about stealing stuff in general," I say, choosing my words carefully in an effort to come off as sympathetic yet firm. "It's about how some things are necessities and others are luxuries."

Jack makes a disgusted noise and marches off to check out a display of something called sound bars. I glance back up at the TV screen. Mrs. Shea has been replaced by a reporter standing in front of what looks like a small lake, talking about flooding in Puerto Rico. Behind her, a tall man is herding a group of about a dozen children off a wooden rowboat. I'm about to head over to the cell phone section when I notice the words *Four Spinners Found Dead* scrolling across the bottom of the screen. Prickles erupt all over my skin.

"Jack?" I call, but either he's too far away to hear me, or else I'm whispering. It's hard to tell because my ears feel like they're stuffed with cotton. I step closer to the TV, straining to catch the reporter's voice through the haze in my brain.

"The survivors," she says, "were removed from Puerto Rico's only Children's Home early this morning."

Children—spinner children—stagger off the boat. The prickles on my skin feel like a thousand needles stabbing me from every direction. The spinners range in age from about four to eight, too young to start work at a Crime Investigation Center, and they're all staring at the camera with bewildered expressions.

"Doctors," the reporter continues, "say the deaths occurred when rising flood waters cut the Children's Home off from critical supplies. A worker with the Red Cross said the Home had not been marked as a priority location in the city's rescue plan."

Not a priority. I put a hand on some shelving to steady myself. Did the spinners starve to death? Or did the Children's Home realize they had to ration their supplies and chose to do it through a convenient outbreak of "time sickness"? My vision blurs. The faces on the screen morph, the young strangers transforming into the friends I left behind: Aiden, Raul, Yuki, Simon, Angel. I shudder. I have to get them out.

The reporter says something about checking in with people's reactions, and a shot of a bunch of protestors waving signs flashes on the screen. Angry yells burst from the speakers. The words are lost under a roar of boos and jeers, but in my head, the accusations all point out my failure: of the twenty-four spinners living at the Center, I only rescued four.

My mind scrabbles for the scattered shreds of survival strategy I've managed to put together over the past few days. Phones. We need cell phones so we can communicate when we're not together.

The guy at the phone counter sports a neatly trimmed beard and an earnest expression behind his square plastic glasses. I fiddle with a few of the fancy models on display, pushing random buttons as if I have a clue how the things work. Earnest Guy keeps pace with me from the other side of the counter as I move along the row.

"How's your day going?" he asks.

"Fine." My palms are sweating, but I'm afraid I'll look suspicious if I wipe them off. This turns out to be a bad call since the next time I pick up a phone, it promptly slips out of my hand.

"Oops," I mumble. The phone, attached to the display case by a thin wire, bounces against my knees.

Earnest Guy places his hands on the counter. "Can I help you find something?"

"Yeah, um . . ." I glance over at Jack. I'm regretting that I annoyed him so much he's ignoring me. Jack is good at talking to salespeople. "I want a phone . . . two phones, actually . . . but not a contract. Isn't there a way to just get a temporary one . . . I mean, aren't there . . . ?"

My voice trails off. I can feel the heat of a blush spreading up my cheeks. Am I making him suspicious? Any normal sixteen-year-old would know all about cell phones. Earnest Guy cocks his head. My heart starts beating so hard he can probably see it throbbing beneath my sweater.

"You mean a pay-as-you-go model?" he asks.

"Yeah." I offer him a weak smile. "That's what I meant. I just forgot the word." Maybe he'll just think I'm scatterbrained.

Earnest Guy reaches under the counter and pulls out a phone nestled in a plastic box. He starts rattling on about buying minutes and programming the phone. I nod as if concepts like texting and web surfing are things I know about in any context besides TV. It doesn't help my concentration that the whole time he talks, Earnest Guy's eyes keep sliding around my face. I try to picture what he sees: a girl with straight brown hair dressed in jeans and a plain blue sweater. Nothing to justify any heightened interest. OK, except maybe the two Band-Aids my bangs don't do a very good job of covering up and the fading bruises decorating one cheek. I smooth my hair down over the back of my neck—no sense in letting him see the larger bandage hidden there.

"Thanks," I say, when he finally finishes. "I'll think about it."

I start backing away. The sales guy puts out a hand to stop me.

"Hey," he says, "is everything OK?"

The enormity of the question leaves me momentarily mute. Is everything OK? The institution I'd called home turned out to be poisoning me with Aclisote, a drug I'd always been told was the only thing that kept me from going insane. My best friend, KJ, was given so much Aclisote he's now semicomatose. We are living illegally in a warehouse. And, oh, yeah, I watched Carson Ross, the person I admired most, murder Austin Shea three days ago and then threaten to frame me for the crime unless I promised to work for him. So, no, nothing about my life at the moment is what you'd call OK.

Not that I can tell Earnest Guy any of that. I force myself to smile. "Yeah, sure."

The guy frowns. He seems nice enough. Maybe he has a sister who's my age. Or a kid. He glances toward the TV section, then leans toward me.

"That guy you're with," he says. "Your boyfriend? I saw you arguing." His gaze flickers over my bruises again. "He didn't hurt you, did he?"

He is so completely off base, I almost laugh. Jack might be annoying, but he's also a spinner. We spinners stick together. We have no reason to hurt each other. The rest of the world takes care of that.

I shake my head, point toward my face, and tell him the truth. "I was in a car accident. I'm fine now."

Earnest Guy looks like he wants to say more, and when I walk away, I can feel him watching me. Great. Here I am trying to be anonymous, and some goody-goody helpful dude decides to take an interest. I search three aisles before I find Jack in the place I should have checked first. He's back in the music section, standing in front of a bin of CDs, headphones draped over his dark hair, sampling tracks from an album called *Greatest Hits of 2010*.

I wave a hand in front of his face. "We've gotta go."

Jack starts singing a flawless imitation of Bruno Mars's song "Billionaire." A pretty girl in a red hoodie, the only other person flipping through the CDs, lifts her head to watch him.

"Come on." I reach for the headphones. Jack dances out of my reach. He starts singing more loudly, his hips gyrating to the rhythm. Hoodie Girl nods her approval.

"Jack!" I lunge again. The headphones reach the end of their tether, and I manage to snatch them off his head.

"OK, OK." Jack holds his hands up in surrender, laughing as he backs away.

"We don't want to draw so much attention," I mutter, as I put the headphones back on their hook.

"Speak for yourself." Jack winks at Hoodie Girl, who grins.

I clench my jaw so hard my teeth creak. Jack is medium height, well muscled, with a smile that's charming, but not quite trustworthy. Yesterday, he buzzed his hair so short it sticks up all over his head. I think it makes him look like he's trying really hard to be cool, though clearly Hoodie Girl doesn't agree with me.

"Do you have any sense at all?" I hiss at Jack. "We're going to rob this place, so it's better if no one remembers we were here. Not to mention that we're fugitives."

"Always with the melodrama," Jack whispers back. "It doesn't matter if people notice us. We won't be here when the stuff disappears. And we're not fugitives. The Sick hasn't announced we're gone."

I grip Jack's arm and yank him toward the exit, not bothering to argue. *Of course* the Sick—what we call the Crime Investigation Center, or CIC—hasn't *publicly* announced that we ran away. To do that, Dr. Barnard would have to admit that four of his spinners are freely mingling with the public, a fact likely to cause nationwide panic, given how much Norms fear us.

"Chill out." Jack tries to pull his arm out of my grasp. "You're going to rip my arm off."

A muscle in my neck spasms. I let go of Jack's arm and massage the sore spot with two fingers. Not that it helps. Ever since we left the Center, I've felt like I'm a string pulled so taut that I can practically feel myself vibrating.

We head for the store's main entrance, passing by Earnest Guy, who is watching us from behind the phone counter, a frown creasing his brow. I smile at him. He doesn't smile back. I pick up my pace. *We're just normal teenagers*, I tell myself, *shopping on a Thursday afternoon.* My hand creeps up to touch the bandage at the back of my neck, a twin of the one Jack wears. The slice where Shannon cut out the trackers the Center used to monitor us is still tender. I drop my hand back down to my side. *Normal teenagers*, I think again, *just normal teenagers.*

We're nearly at the exit, when two men step into the store. They're walking in tandem and sporting predatory glares that mark them as security. Their eyes sweep across the busy space and lock onto me and Jack.

We both stop. We're standing at the lip of an aisle, hemmed in by racks of home security systems. The guards separate. The first moves toward us, while the other circles around toward the back, clearly intent on preventing our escape. My chest tightens so much that blood no longer reaches my brain, forcing my thoughts into a single terrified loop: *If the guards catch us, they'll take us back to the Center. If we go to the Center, Dr. Barnard will put us back on Aclisote. If we go back on Aclisote, we'll die.*

Jack grabs my hand. "Come on, Alex. Do it."

I watch the guard walk toward us, paralyzed. He's five feet away. Four. He opens his mouth.

"Excuse me. Can I ask you . . . ?"

Jack's hand tightens around mine and everything freezes. The man's words stop mid-sentence, leaving a silence so absolute my heart thuds like a drumroll. The guard behind us hovers with one foot off the ground, the other barely touching it, so he balances on an impossibly small piece of his instep. Near the entrance, two cart-wielding shoppers stand perfectly still, their pasty faces stuck in expressions of disapproving curiosity. No one stirs in the entire store. Nobody—except me and Jack—so much as breathes.

I slump against a piece of shelving. The threat of capture has turned me shaky and hollow, like my stomach decided to take a vacation to visit my feet. Jack glares at me with a decided lack of sympathy.

"Why didn't *you* freeze time?" he demands. "You know mine's useless." He squeezes my hand again, crushing my fingers. "Come on, I'll melt right now and you refreeze."

I shake my head. "We can't."

Jack flings my hand away like it's a piece of trash. Jack's right that his freeze is not going to get us out of this mess and mine could. Two weeks ago—a couple of days after I stopped taking Aclisote—my skills changed. Now, unlike any spinner I've ever heard of, anything I do during frozen time stays that way after time starts again. Which means I can do lots of things without getting caught—like steal expensive electronic equipment. Or avoid getting nabbed by threatening security guards. Or give Carson Ross the opportunity to murder a defenseless man sleeping in silver-gray pajamas inside a locked house.

"If we run away in frozen time," I say, "everyone will see us disappear into thin air."

"So? You did that when you got away from Dr. Barnard."

"That was different. He was going to kill me. I didn't have any other choice."

"And we have a choice now?" Jack points toward the semi-floating guard.

My stomach hurtles back into place, landing in my middle with a sickening lurch.

"We still can't just disappear. There are too many people." I wave my hand to include all the shoppers paused in their pursuit of new acquisitions. Normal people going about their unremarkable day.

Normal people who believe spinners are lower than maggots. "Think about how much the Norms already hate us. If they find out we can change things while time is frozen, they'll freak."

"Let them freak." Jack kicks at a box of surveillance cameras, denting a hole into the cardboard. "Why should we hide what we can do?"

"If the Norms freak," I say, "every spinner back at the Center will be sent to the Central Office. Our photos will be broadcast on all the news channels. We'd be caught within days. And given how much Aclisote Dr. Barnard gave KJ, I don't think we'd live very long once we got back."

An image of how KJ looked when I left him in Shannon's care this morning, an image I've taken great pains to repress all day, flashes into the forefront of my brain: His long body stretched under a pile of blankets, skin so washed out its natural warm brown appeared gray. Even his lips hung slack. I held his hand, whispered his name, and got no more response than if he'd been a turnip. Just a few nights ago, I'd kissed him for the first time, and we'd planned a future so perfect I should have known it would never come true.

I wrestle all my fears back into the box called *denial* and focus my attention on our immediate disaster. The electronics store is near the end of the mall's central hallway. I peer past the guard through the open doorway. Statue-like shoppers stand among padded benches and ceramic planters. Stores line the space around them, their wares spread out in colorful displays—here a mannequin in artfully shredded jeans, there a basket overflowing with fruity bath gels. I chew on a thumbnail, a bad habit I've picked up lately. We can't stay and get arrested. We can't just disappear.

"What if we run," I say. "In real time, I mean. You let time go, we run until we find a place to hide, and then I'll freeze and we can disappear."

Jack kicks a bigger hole in the box. "Where do we run to?"

I point down the hallway. "Over there."

Just beyond a discount clothing store stands a furniture outlet. Its glass windows hold two large mahogany dressers and an oversized bed with so many pillows there's no room left to lie down.

"Fabulous Furnishings," Jack reads off the gleaming green-and-black sign.

"That place is jammed with stuff. It will be easy to get lost." I lick the rough edge of my thumbnail. "The problem will be outrunning the guards."

Jack narrows his eyes at our twin pursuers. "We can use this."

He stalks over to a display rack and gives it a hefty shove. Controllers fly in all directions, bits of plastic splintering off them as they hit the ground. The rack itself smashes against the closest guard, knocking him to the floor. In the quiet of the freeze, the sound is apocalyptic. I stare down at the wreckage. This is not my first choice for an exit plan, but we're so far from my first choice of anything at this point that I barely waver.

"It's worth a shot." I take a breath. "You ready?"

Jack sends one of the controllers spiraling across the store with a well-placed kick before nodding. The scene around us flickers for a second as everything we've moved—ourselves, the toppled display rack, the crunched-up controllers—whisks back to their prefreeze positions. I blink away the momentary blur. We're standing together, Jack holding my hand, the display primly upright, and the guard advancing steadily in our direction.

". . . a couple of questions?" he says, finishing his sentence.

Jack drops my hand and hurls himself at the display stand. I leap past the falling mass and take off across the store. Earnest Guy gapes at me, helpless behind his glass-topped counter. I shoot one glance over my shoulder. The guard is disentangling himself from the heavy shelving, and his partner, who started the chase at the far end of the aisle, has just reached the debris.

I tear through the store and burst out into the mall. Jack whips ahead, faster than me, thanks to the hours he spent working out during his free time at the Center, and to the blast of pain I get from my bruised ribs every time I breathe. I dodge around mall patrons, scared that someone might try to stop me, but most people just step aside to get out of my path.

Jack darts into Fabulous Furnishings; I hurtle through the entrance seconds behind him. The front part of the store is laid out with sample room decors, and I catch a glimpse of Jack disappearing around a pair of white leather sofas perched on a carpet that's long enough to need mowing. I hurry after him and collide with someone in a green smock.

"Sorry," I say. Green Smock stumbles. She isn't much older than I am, with frizzy hair and an apologetic smile. I duck my head and slip around her. Jack is no longer in sight.

"Hey!" one of the guards shouts from behind me. "You."

I race around the white furniture set.

No Jack.

My heart bangs in my chest. To my right, a mock study advertises dark oak furniture. To the left is a girly bedroom set with a pink ruffled canopy. I choose the bedroom set and dive into the space between the bed and a dresser. A woven rug with a flower pattern skids as I drop my weight on it. I reach out for time, mentally grabbing the threads I imagine moving through the air all around me and yanking them to a halt just as my body collides with a thin-legged nightstand.

Time stops, wiping out the sounds of pursuing feet, shouting voices, and even the faint hum of the abruptly weakened fluorescent lights. Only I keep moving, right into the nightstand, which tips over and crashes down onto my back. I lie still, waiting for my ragged breathing to slow. Time hangs around me, the invisible strands firmly in my control. Things aren't just not moving, they're stopped, frozen, immobile. Even the nightstand resting on top of me seems somehow more inert. Only I can move, only I have thoughts, and for the first time all day, I feel safe.

I take a deep, calming breath, stand up, and check for my pursuers. The two guards are just rounding the white leather sofa. Neither of them is close enough to see me in my hiding spot.

I set the nightstand back into place and straighten the flowered rug. Jack is about halfway through the store, legs outstretched in his race to escape. I check the area around him. A woman is standing one row over in front of a display of sheets. Her head is twisted away from the plastic packages, probably in response to the yelling elsewhere in the store. A man stands only a few steps from the far end of Jack's aisle, one foot raised in the act of walking forward. I'll have to work fast to keep him from seeing us.

Steeling myself, I take a firm hold of Jack's wrist and let time go. The time strands slip back into their endless journey, a seamless transition without the blur of moving back to my prefreeze position. Lights brighten, the buzz of commotion fills the air, and the momentum of Jack's reinstated dash yanks both of us forward. Clinging hard to Jack's wrist, I refreeze time as fast as I can. Sound disappears again. Jack's hand tears away from mine as he hurtles forward. I collapse on the floor, smashing my knees against the hard tiles. Jack trips, too, catching himself against a shelf full of pillows, which promptly tumble into a heap.

"You could have warned me," Jack says.

"You could have waited for me," I answer. My knees hurt. I should have covered the floor with the pillows before I let time start. "Where were you going, anyway?"

"The back room." Jack tosses a pillow back on the shelf. "I figured there must be another door out of here and the guards would think that's how we got away."

I have to admit, it's a good strategy. Briefly, I consider starting time again so we can both run for the back exit but decide the back room might just bring a whole new set of complications.

Jack and I work together to put all the pillows back where they came from before making our way through the unmoving store. Even though they're frozen, I give the security guards a wide berth. We decide not to return to the original electronics store and instead take two phones from a Radio Shack upstairs. When we're done, we make our way out to the underground parking garage and hide between two cars so I can start time again without anyone seeing us.

"That went well," Jack says, standing up and stretching.

I rub the ache along my ribs. It matches the dull pain throbbing in my temple. Time work causes headaches, which get worse when you have to drag someone else along.

"You think this is fun," I accuse him.

Jack grins. "Don't you?"

"No. It's terrible—hiding, running, stealing."

"We're doing fine," Jack says. We turn and head up the parking ramp. Even though I know the guards are all the way across the mall, I still look back over my shoulder. Rows of parked cars fill the bunker-like garage, which smells vaguely of gasoline. I search the shadows between the hulking pieces of metal and find only emptiness.

"I don't know why you're so worried about everything," Jack says.

"Isn't this a thousand times better than living at the Sick? We can do whatever we want. No one gives us a schedule, there's no chores, no boring police missions. Plus, we're never leashed."

I shudder and touch my wrist. Leashes are hard and uncomfortable, and they make this buzzing noise that sounds like a thousand bees are trapped in your skull.

"We have nowhere permanent to live," I say.

"We'll find somewhere."

Jack and I step out into September sunlight so bright it makes me squint. I used to love getting out of the Center, even wearing a leash, treasuring the rare day passes that allowed me to wander around downtown, just another anonymous person in the crowd. I've lost that feeling since our escape. Now, I walk around with an uncomfortable itch at the back of my shoulders, sure someone is watching me. I shade my eyes and move closer to Jack.

We turn right and start the mile-long trek down a neighborhood commercial street back to the squat. Jack whistles as he walks. I tuck the bag of phones under my arm to make it less conspicuous. When a driver turns his head as he passes us, I flinch.

"Jesus, Alex," Jack says. "No one's going to jump us when we're just walking down the sidewalk."

"How can you be sure? We know they're searching for us."

"Listen to yourself. Next, you'll be hearing voices and wearing tinfoil hats."

We stop at a red light. There's a pet shop on our right and a line of cars idling to our left. I turn my back to the traffic so the drivers can't see my face.

"I'm not being paranoid," I tell Jack. "When Dr. Barnard found out what I can do, he said flat out that I was too dangerous to let run loose."

Jack waves a hand. "The Sick never has any money. They won't be able to do anything but pass our photo around a police station and ask them to keep an eye out. As long as we stay out of trouble, we're fine."

I must not look convinced, because he adds, "It's only for a couple more days, anyway. Once KJ perks up, we can blow town. The Portland Sick is hardly going to chase us across the country."

Is Jack right? Will the CIC give us up so easily? And what if KJ doesn't perk up? I don't voice the questions because thinking about him makes my chest squeeze so tight it hurts. I focus instead on a jumble of kittens displayed in the pet shop's front window. The smallest one, gray and striped, pounces on a knitted ball.

"What about everyone else?" I ask.

"The other spinners? What about them?"

"We can't just leave them there."

Jack gives another dismissive wave. "You don't even like half of them."

"Not all the time, but it doesn't matter. They're our family."

"I guess," Jack says, "but how is a group of twenty-four kids supposed to slip quietly out of town?"

"So you're OK with it?" The kitten, bored with the toy, starts sniffing the glass separating us. "You're OK with letting Aidan and Raul die?"

Jack faces the blinking red hand across the street.

"Look, it's great you're so altruistic and all, but I'm not going to risk getting caught again. Besides, they don't know they could live past their teens if they got off Aclisote, so they don't know what they're missing."

The light changes and Jack hops off the curb. The kitten's mouth opens in a mew. Although it's impossible for me to hear through the glass, the cry looks plaintive. I turn away and scurry after Jack.

"It just doesn't seem fair," I say. "That we're free and they're still facing a death sentence."

"Yeah, well, life isn't fair."

I chew on my thumbnail again. Jack is right. There are lots of ways life isn't fair, but that doesn't make me feel any better about abandoning the other spinners. We are the only family any of us will ever have. If we don't stick up for each other, who will?

A breeze sends a chill through the uneven weave of my sweater. I wrap my arms around myself in an effort to generate some warmth. When KJ and I talked about running away from the Center, I'd imagined escape as a one-time thing: you run, you leave, you're gone. But *gone* is turning out to be a very unstable place. It means second thoughts and hiding and always checking over your shoulder. Running away doesn't happen just once. Unless something changes, we're going to be running away for the rest of our lives.

03 ◄◄

WE STOP AT A MINI-MART FOR SOME FOOD ON THE WAY back, so by the time we near the squat, it's late afternoon. The squat is the third story of a brick building, the main floor of which houses a store called Elmer's Wonder Shoppe. The only wonder to me is that anyone makes a living out of a place that screams "tired and shabby." Curved green awnings, their tops dark with rain-induced mold, droop over ground-floor picture windows. Inside, out-of-date furniture too young to be antique shares space with bins of comic books and plastic samurai swords. Exterior bricks shed peels of white paint, and the upper stories' rusty metal windows sport cracked panes that are nearly opaque with grime. The top two floors were abandoned years ago, and Elmer's staff members never venture up there. No one does, except for us and a few hungry rats.

My feet slow as we get closer. Clouds have rolled in to cover the afternoon sun, giving the day a grayish cast, and the dreary sky matches my mood. The freeze I'd done so that we could steal food intensified my headache, which now keeps a steady beat behind my eyeballs. I hate the squat. I hate how exposed I feel hiding so close to the city center. Most of all, I hate seeing KJ lying there, an enchanted sleeper struck down by an evil spell that I have no idea how to break.

Jack gestures toward a bus shelter on the corner, half a block from Elmer's front door.

"There's Faith," he says.

My bad mood plummets even lower. Faith and Victor are street kids—brother and sister—that Jack met when he was out on a day pass while we still lived at the Center, and it's at their invitation that we're allowed to stay at the squat at all. Victor made it clear when we moved in that, because of the risk of being seen, we're not allowed to go into or out of the squat while the Elmer's staff are onsite, which most days means staying out on the street between eight in the morning and at least six at night. Jack and I have been ignoring this rule and freezing time to go in and out, a trick that will be hard to pull off with Victor's sister as witness. I glance at my watch: 5:15. The Elmer's staff won't leave for another forty-five minutes.

"Let's cross the street and double back," I mutter to Jack. "Before she sees us."

The words have barely left my mouth when Faith turns her head in our direction and nods vaguely.

"Oh." I do a poor job of sounding surprised. "Hi."

We walk toward her. The bus shelter is the kind with three plastic sides and a couple of rubber-topped benches. I've seen Faith only a few times, either in the shadowy squat or so early in the morning the sky is still mostly dark. I've been thinking of her as a thin teenager with a hygiene problem. In the clear light of afternoon, "unwashed" changes to "unhealthy." Lank hair hangs around her face like pieces of pale string. Arms verging on skeletal poke through the sleeves of her blouse. Faith's eyes are very red, and she's propped against the bus shelter as if she needs the support.

"You all right?" I ask her.

Faith studies me before answering. I used to see girls like her a lot when I did police work. Their stories were never good.

"I'm OK," she says, finally. "Just waiting for Vic."

"Where is he?" Jack asks. He sounds like a kid hoping to catch a glimpse of Santa Claus. I do not understand his fascination. To me, Victor comes off as a not-very-bright thug. Jack claims the guy is a brilliant musician. According to Jack, the two of them are great friends, but with the exception of our first day at the squat—a day I spent primarily sleeping while Jack hung out with his good buddy—Jack has been with me every day. I suspect Victor blew him off but thought it tactful not to ask. I need Jack's help too much to risk offending him.

Faith shrugs off Jack's question. The three of us stand there for a minute, watching the cars roll past, until a particularly large truck lumbers by in a gush of exhaust. Faith's frail body sways.

"Here." Jack digs through the grocery bag he's carrying and pulls out a bagel, handing it to Faith. "You hungry?"

Faith accepts the food, holding it in her cupped hands as if she isn't sure what to do with it. A palm reader would love Faith's hands. They're so dirty, I can see the lines from four feet away.

"So," I ask, "have you noticed anything going on upstairs?" Faith blinks slowly without answering. I try again. "You know, with my friends?"

"Oh." She picks a small piece of crust off the bagel and sets it on her tongue like she's conducting a science experiment. "Yeah. That is one sick dude." Faith nods to herself. "What's he on?"

"Nothing," I say. "He's just sick."

"Wow." Faith chews the speck of bagel in her mouth. "Bummer."

Jack shifts the grocery bag on his hip. "We're going to walk around for a while. See you later, OK?"

Faith stops chewing. "You better not go upstairs. It's too early."

"We know," I say.

"Cool," Faith mumbles. Her attention shifts to a poster pasted on one side of the bus shelter. It's an advertisement for a new action movie and features two tank top–wearing men with enormous muscles walking away from a bright yellow and black explosion. Both carry awkwardly large guns and sport artfully applied ash smudges. Faith watches the poster like it's the actual movie. She doesn't seem to notice when we leave.

Jack and I walk until we're sure Faith has forgotten about us, then we duck into the small parking lot on the far side of Elmer's, sliding past a dumpster to reach the rear of the building. This is the yucky part. Elmer's backs up to a freeway, which roars along at the bottom of a steep slope behind the store. A chain-link fence marking the cliff edge stands about two feet from the building, which should make for a reasonable alley, except that the fence is completely overrun by a mass of blackberry bushes. To reach the fire escape that gives us access to the third floor, we have to shove through the berry-laden sentinels, which do their best to scratch reminders that we're trespassing every time we scrape our way inside.

Jack stops walking and holds out his hand when he gets to the bottom of the fire escape. I adjust my bag of electronics so I can touch Jack's skin, then reach out to freeze time. The time strands drag in my mental grasp—less like fine threads, more like coarse ropes. It takes a huge effort to pull them to a stop, and when I do, the perfect silence allows my headache to take center stage. I rub my forehead.

"Let's be quick," I say.

Jack yanks the rusty ladder down, and moments later, we're stepping into the open space that makes up the entire top floor. I sigh, releasing time as soon as the door whines shut behind us. Something small and probably furry scuttles away from our sudden appearance. I wait for my vision to adjust to the gloom, listening to the resumed rumble of the freeway and the restless coo and shuffle of the pigeons that roost under the building's eaves. Dust floats into my nostrils, the dry scent accented with an undertone of mold.

"Shannon?" Jack calls softly. She doesn't answer, though she almost certainly heard him. All of us are primed for the slightest noise that could mean someone from Elmer's is coming up the inner staircase to investigate.

Jack shrugs and heads toward the part of the squat we all refer to as the kitchen, even though it's really just a counter with a dresser and a couple of boxes nearby. We store our food in plastic bins inside the dresser's empty drawers, and we warm liquids in our single appliance—a grimy electric coffee maker.

Carrying the bag with the cell phones, I make my way through a mess of cast-off furniture toward the corner where KJ sleeps. The squat is essentially a big open warehouse, about fifty feet by a hundred, and it houses what must be years' worth of old merchandise, mostly broken—mismatched chairs, lopsided bookcases, and teetering stacks of unmarked boxes.

As temporary residents, each of us has shifted pieces around to create relatively private "rooms" for ourselves. KJ has the section in the far right corner, under a pair of windows that face the street. Shannon sleeps beside him to be near her patient. Jack and I each carved out a room against the same street-facing wall. Victor and Faith camp out along the windowless back wall, somewhere in the dark to the left of the fire escape. Just to the right of the fire door, next to the kitchen, a tiny half-bathroom provides water, as long as we only turn on the taps (or flush the toilet) after the workers downstairs have gone home.

Shannon doesn't raise her head until I step around the armoire that marks the entrance to KJ's room. It's brighter on this side of the squat, illuminated by sunlight filtering through grimy windows. It's also a few degrees colder, since the windows don't quite shut. Our resident nurse says this is OK. Fresh air is good for the patient.

Shannon sits on the floor, slumped against a crate stamped with the word *Fragile*. In her lap, a paperback romance novel rests face down, spine cracked to show she hasn't gotten farther than about page five. KJ lies beside her, his bed nothing more than a pile of blankets and a pillow without a case.

"You're back," she says.

It's a statement, and an unenthusiastic one at that. Previously rosy-cheeked and full of smiles, Shannon's face since we left the Center has turned as pale as if she'd spent a month in a cave instead of three days in an empty building. Her tan slacks and red sweater are wrinkled and smudged with dust. A bowl holding a water-soaked rag shows the limits of Shannon's nursing options.

"How's KJ?" I ask.

Shannon shakes her head.

"The same." Her blond hair, pulled away from her face in a messy braid, sways like it's adding a second opinion.

"I can sit with him a while," I say. "If you want a break."

"It's OK." Shannon gives me a sad smile. "You're probably tired from all your errands. And it's not like I have anywhere else to be."

I stand there, feeling useless, listening to the slow rasp of KJ's breath. It sounds like even that minor activity takes enormous effort. I'm not sure which is worse—the times KJ lies so still he seems like he might be frozen, or the times he thrashes around moaning. Right now, his feet are twitching in small, uneven jerks.

Shannon wipes the edge of his blanket, cleaning off some of the dirt it picked up from trailing on the floor.

"He did open his eyes today," she says, "while I was feeding him some broth."

Hope rises in my chest, a delicate tendril reaching toward the light.

"He looked right at me." Shannon's voice catches. "But I'm not sure he actually saw me."

The tentative shoot wilts, replaced by a gush of shame at her obvious distress. I always feel guilty around Shannon. She used to be my roommate, but when she agreed to come away with me, she didn't do it because we're friends, or because she hates the Center. She did it because she cares about KJ. And as far as she knows, KJ cares for her too. She has no idea that the night before we left, KJ and I changed from being best friends to being . . . something else, and that the morning he fell sick he was planning to break up with her. I know I should tell her. I know it's wrong to use her like this, but I have no idea how to help KJ get better. I need her. KJ needs her.

Shannon kneels on the floor and wrings the cloth out in the bowl of water. The blankets over KJ's chest twitch when she places the cool cloth on his sweaty forehead.

"Did you remember to get ice?" Shannon asks.

My shame deepens. "Sorry," I mumble, "I forgot."

Shannon sighs, but doesn't say anything, which only makes me feel worse. It's as if she hasn't expected me to manage even so simple a task. All the things that filled my day—finding the right stores, stealing supplies, Jack's and my narrow escape at the mall—seem like some kind of holiday compared with Shannon's long hours in this dim corner.

I cross my arms behind my back to hide the electronic store bag I'm still carrying. "Is this . . . normal for time sickness?"

"I'm not sure." Shannon bends over KJ again, adjusting the wet cloth. "I've never tended anyone on my own at this critical point in the illness. But four days seems like an awfully long time to be this out of it, doesn't it? I heard Yolly say you were *really* sick with your first bout, and you were out for only two days." She says this accusingly, as if my recovery somehow counts against me.

"Is there anything else we can do?" I ask.

Shannon sits back on her heels. "You know what I think."

"We can't go back," I say.

"You really believe the Center is poisoning us? That *Yolly* is trying to kill us?"

Images of Yolly, the Center's matron, float in my head—her easy smile and her soft body draped in those stupid cheerful smocks. Yolly thinks we should be proud to serve our community with what she always calls "our talents." She keeps lollipops in her pockets for the Youngers and never reports a rule-breaking unless she has to. Every time she pricks our arms for the monthly blood tests, she promises that it won't hurt.

I shake my head. "I don't think Yolly knows."

"So, what, it's all some big conspiracy?"

I rub my forehead. Shannon and I have had variations of this conversation every single day since we left; today's version is doing nothing for the headache pounding in my skull.

"I told you. Only a few people know the truth. Dr. Barnard admitted everything to me when he tried to take me to the Central Office." Time has not dimmed my rage at his revelations. If anything, in the three days since we left the Sick, it's grown increasingly intense.

"He said our unrestrained skills were too dangerous for the rest of society." My mouth twitches. "I guess he thinks it's a reasonable

38

exchange that we die so Norms don't have to worry."

"Alex." Shannon hesitates, as if girding herself against the anger that must be clear on my face. "I talked to Yolly after you left with Dr. Barnard that day. She said you were raving. And when I saw you an hour later, you admitted you had a concussion. How do you know that what you remember actually happened?"

Heat flames my cheeks. "You saw how high my chronotin levels were—you were the one who did the blood test."

"But we don't know what high chronotin levels mean," Shannon says. "All we know for sure is that Aclisote suppresses them."

"We know suppressed chronotin is what makes us sick. Dr. Barnard said so. And we *do* know what high chronotin levels mean." I freeze time, take three steps and melt it again. "It means we can do that."

Shannon flinches at my abrupt shift in location. "Don't do that."

"Why not? It feels completely natural—much easier than freezing did before. You should try it."

Shannon's lips tremble. "What about side effects? Everyone says that before Aclisote, all spinners eventually went crazy. How do we know insanity isn't associated with high chronotin levels, too?"

A blast of fury races through me so fast it makes my skin itch. I want to shake Shannon until I force her to understand. The urge is so strong I clench my hands together to keep from grabbing her. How can she be so completely dense? I have explained this to her a dozen times. More.

"What we know"—only fear of getting caught by the Elmer's staff keeps me from shouting at her—"is that our natural time skills allow us to move things in frozen time and that Aclisote suppresses that power. We also know high doses of Aclisote kill us. The rest is all garbage. Horror stories to make sure we take our meds."

Shannon stands up.

"It's fine if you and Jack choose to take chances, but how can you justify risking KJ's life on a theory?" She points at the figure lying between us.

I lower my gaze, following the line of her shaking finger. Everything that gives KJ life is leached out of the body stretched before me. He's limp, expressionless. The scrub of a four-day beard stands out against his unnatural pallor like some kind of mold, an external sign of internal decay. Anger slides away from me like a passing shadow, leaving behind a quivering lake of fear. *What if KJ dies? What will I do?* KJ's lips move and he moans softly. Goose bumps ripple my arms.

"None of us knows how to treat time sickness," Shannon begs. The fading sun in the window behind her lights the strands of hair escaping her braid, making them glow like a golden halo. "The only people who do are at the Center. Help me take him back. You and Jack can stay here if you want. Yolly will know how to treat him." Shannon reaches a hand toward me. "Please, Alex. At home, no one ever died after their first attack."

Home. My goose bumps vanish. Home is supposed to be a safe place, full of people who protect you. Love you. The Crime Investigation Center is not home. I raise my head to face her.

"No."

Shannon starts to cry, an exhausted sound that only hardens my resolve.

"Just go away then," she sobs. "Leave us alone."

I turn my back on her and storm out of the room.

Jack is sitting on an overturned box in the kitchen eating a bagel spread with peanut butter. The fury that overwhelmed me while I was talking to Shannon fades, leaving me feeling a little sick. The stress of our situation has to be affecting me more than I had thought. I can't remember ever being quite that blindingly angry.

"You want to go see a show tonight?" Jack asks, voice muffled by the food stuffed in one cheek. "There's a free end-of-summer concert down by the waterfront."

"Shannon wants to go back," I tell him.

Jack licks peanut butter off his fingers. "So let her go."

The dresser where we stow our food slopes to one side, its broken leg propped up on a paint can that isn't quite the right height. Jack has dropped the empty grocery bag on the floor and spread its contents on the dresser's tilted surface: three cans of soup, bagels, yogurt, peanut butter, a bag of apples, some cookies, and a box of instant oatmeal. The bagel bag is open, and a plastic knife stands upright in the center of the peanut butter jar. I move closer, ignoring the mess, and pick out an apple.

"She'll tell them where we are. Plus, she won't leave without KJ. She wants to 'save' him." The scorn in my voice makes me cringe. Of course Shannon wants to save KJ. It's why I brought her. I should be groveling at her feet, not snapping at her like a tyrant.

"You think KJ wants to go back, too?" Jack asks. "'Cause if so, we might as well dump them both now."

I sink my teeth into the apple.

"We're not dumping anybody," I say. "Even if Shannon doesn't believe me, I'm still going to keep her from running off and getting killed." Something rattles under the dresser. I glance down and see a thick, hairless tail vanish into the deeper reaches of the squat. I step back. "Even if this place is a total pit."

"What, you don't like the accommodations I found for you?" Jack

41

waves his hand around like a game show host revealing a new car. "I think it's kinda fun. Edgy."

I drag another box over so I can sit near him. "We need to put together a plan."

"I have a plan," Jack says. "I'm going to learn how to play the guitar."

"Not a plan for *us*," I say. "For *them*. The other spinners."

Jack groans. "OK, how about this. Let's go back to the Sick and tell the other kids the truth. After that, they're on their own. They can run off, or stay, or keep taking Aclisote, or stage a revolt—their choice and not our responsibility."

Jack pops the last of his bagel into his mouth. He seems pleased with his answer, one I find totally inadequate. It's such a typical Jack solution: shortsighted, requiring little effort, and leaving the difficult decisions to someone else. KJ would never suggest a cop-out like that. We're spinners. We stick together.

"We have to do more than warn them," I say. "We have to find a way to save them."

"I thought we agreed on our next steps. We lay low until KJ's better, and then we skip town."

I fling my apple core at the empty grocery bag, which I completely miss. "That's not good enough."

Jack makes an exasperated noise. "What more do you want?"

I shake my head. I want so much: a safe place to live, money, to stop feeling like I'm seconds away from being caught. I want every spinner in the world to be free. I want KJ, alive and whole. The fear woken by KJ's wasted body returns—a depthless lake in which I could drown.

I stare at the dark corner where my apple core rolled.

"What if we could stop Barnard from raising the dose on anyone's Aclisote prescriptions?" I ask Jack. "Even if it were only temporary, it would buy us some time to figure out a way to rescue them."

"So, what, we kidnap him?" Jack laughs. I can tell he isn't taking me seriously. I lean forward.

"No. We blackmail him."

Jack stops laughing.

"With what?" he asks.

An idea builds in my head, its shaky hope offering a bridge over my lake of despair. "When you were working in Barnard's office, back at the Sick, you told KJ he was helping Sikes."

"Dr. B isn't stealing or anything," Jack says. "Sikes just pays him to delay assignments or send out a weak spinner so the rewind won't go back far enough to reveal Sikes's crimes."

I stand up and pace around the small space. "If we find proof that he was helping Sikes, we could use that to threaten Barnard."

Jack snorts. "I doubt either of those guys is stupid enough to leave a paper trail."

"Not at work, maybe, but what about at his house?" I chew on a fingernail. "Do you know Barnard's address?"

"I think so. I went there to drop something off for him once." Jack screws up his face in an effort to call up the memory: "2723 NW Upshur."

I pace faster. Ross found something incriminating when he read Sikes's emails, so why wouldn't I find something by reading Barnard's? Maybe I could even find some physical evidence—a stolen object Barnard took in payment, or a note, or a suspicious bank statement.

"If you can prove they worked together," Jack pulls the plastic knife out of the jar and starts licking off the gooey peanut butter, "then you could probably stop his experiment thing, too."

"Experiment thing?" My foot catches against the can holding

up the dresser, and I grab Jack's shoulder to keep from tipping over. "What are you talking about?"

"Didn't I tell you? A couple days before we left, I overheard him talking on the phone, asking permission to send volunteers from the Center to the Central Office to use as test subjects for some big research project he's conducting."

I clench my fingers so hard on Jack's shoulder I can feel bone through his jacket. "No, Jack, you never mentioned this before."

"Ouch!" Jack shrugs off my hand. "I guess I forgot. I mean, a lot has happened since then."

He *forgot* that Barnard wanted volunteers for a *research* project? No spinner would "volunteer" to participate in a study at the Central Office, because no one who goes there ever comes back. My fingers, loosed from Jack's shoulder, start shaking.

"Did Barnard mention when this experiment was starting?" I ask.

"Not that I heard. But it's probably soon. He referred to it as an *active project.*"

The bridge that's holding me up wobbles, a blast of vertigo threatening to tip me over the edge. We need to go to Barnard's house tomorrow. Even if it's a long shot, I have to try. Fear is weakness. Action is power. I can't bring Austin Shea back to life. There's nothing I can do to make KJ recover. But I can find a way to help my spinner friends. I have to. Otherwise, my life is not worth the price that others have already paid.

04 ◀◀

THE SOUND OF FEET RATTLING THE FIRE ESCAPE announces the arrival of our squat-mates. I check my watch: 6:09. Jack jumps off his crate, then strikes a casual pose leaning against the dresser. Too hyped up to sit still, I bend down and start searching for the missing apple core. No sense making foraging easy for the rats.

Victor stomps into the kitchen. He's holding Faith's hand, and she trails behind him like a lost puppy. He stops short when he sees us.

"You're not supposed to be here." Victor's glance sweeps past where I'm hunkered on the floor and settles on Jack. Victor always pretends I'm not around. I haven't decided if I'm more annoyed at being ignored or relieved that I don't have to deal with him.

Victor jabs a finger in Jack's direction. Victor is a stocky kid—I'm guessing eighteen or nineteen—who moves in sudden jerks that make any room he enters feel crowded. Tattoos fight for space along his beefy arms, and his hair grows in spiky thrusts all over his head.

"No coming in or out until the place downstairs closes," he says. "Rules."

I straighten, dusting the grime off my knees, and stand next to Jack.

"It's cool," Jack says. "No one saw us."

Victor's eyes narrow, distrust emanating from him along with the smell of his unwashed body. "How do you know?"

"We're here, aren't we?" Jack says. "No cops, no guy from Elmer's?"

The air around us hums, as though an electric charge is bouncing off Victor. Jack rubs a hand across his newly shorn head, and I suddenly recognize his inspiration. His haircut is exactly like Victor's.

Jack gestures toward the countertop.

"We got some food," he says. "Help yourself."

Victor glares at the pile of groceries. I rub the toe of my sneaker against the floor, wiping a small space free of dirt. Faith wanders over and perches on the edge of the dresser.

"You want an apple?" I pick one up and hold it out to her.

"Oh." Faith's skinny shoulders droop under the slight weight of her blouse. "I guess." She accepts the fruit without biting it.

Victor's hand shoots out and he grabs an apple, too, sinking his teeth into it with a sharp crunch. As if released, Faith mirrors the gesture, bringing her apple to her lips and nibbling at the red skin.

From the other side of the squat, KJ lets out a long, loud moan.

"He's worse." Victor juts his chin toward KJ's corner.

Jack shrugs. "About the same."

"He can't die here, man," Victor says. He chomps down on the apple again, ripping out a huge hunk and stuffing it in one cheek. "We can't deal with no bodies."

Hearing the word "bodies" feels like someone just pulled a chair out from under me.

"He's not going to die," I say.

Victor acts like I haven't spoken. He drops his half-eaten apple into the empty grocery bag and crosses his arms.

"Me and Faith don't like the way this deal is working out," he says to Jack. "You guys don't follow the rules. We want you out."

The room grows so still it might have frozen. I can hear my own breath, shallow and quick. We can't leave here. We have nowhere else to go.

"KJ's pretty sick," Jack says. "We can't move him."

Victor's lips draw into an ugly line. "Not our problem, man."

Faith is wrapping a strand of hair around her finger, twisting it into a slipknot and pulling it free again with an abstracted air. The apple hangs in her other hand, its red skin barely marked by one tiny bite.

"All right," Jack says. "We'll follow the rules. From now on, Alex and I won't come in until after you get here."

Victor strides across the kitchen, not stopping until he's inches away from Jack. The two guys face each other. Jack is taller than Victor, and they both have muscles, but Victor's look like he got them somewhere other than a gym. I reach out for time, brushing the strands hovering all around me. If I lunge, I could grab Jack and freeze before Victor hits him. But what then? Victor will never let us stay if he knows what we are. No Norm wants to live with a spinner.

"I could pay you." Jack shifts his weight onto his heels. "Like rent."

Victor cocks his head. "How much?"

Jack says something that sounds like "four sea notes," which makes no sense to me, but must to Victor, because he immediately turns to Faith.

"What do you think?"

Faith studies the apple in her hand.

"How about five?" she murmurs.

"Five," Victor says to Jack.

"No problem." Jack's face is all smiles again. "We get you the

47

money by Saturday, and you let us stay another week."

Victor studies Jack for a minute, then nods abruptly and juts a hand out. Jack shakes it. The tension in the room melts away so quickly my legs wobble like cooked spaghetti. Victor spins on a heel and stalks out.

"We wouldn't really kick you out," Faith says, unconvincingly. "It's just this is a really good squat and we don't want to lose it."

She sets her uneaten apple on the counter and drifts after Victor. I wait until she fades into the shadows before turning to Jack. The siblings' rooms are far enough away from the kitchen that I have to lower my voice only a little to keep them from overhearing.

"What's a sea note?"

"A hundred-dollar bill," Jack says. I blink at him. "Don't you watch any TV? It's from Latin or something."

"You just promised to get them five hundred dollars in two days?" I squeak. Jack tips his head toward Victor's room. I lower my voice again. "Where are we going to get that?"

"You said some things are necessities."

Jack is grinning like he thinks this whole mess sounds fun.

"So we're just going to start robbing people now?" I ask.

Jack's smile fades.

"Jesus, Alex. What is with you? You should be thanking me for saving our butts, not nagging me about doing the right thing. Who cares if we steal from some Norm? Victor and Faith were about to kick us out, if you didn't notice."

I bite my lip. What would happen if we had to move KJ? We can probably hoist him down the stairs the way we'd brought him up, limp and frozen. But we can't hold a freeze forever. I picture his wilted body propped up in the bus shelter, imagine a helpful passerby calling 911. I shudder.

"What if we get caught?" I ask.

"Who's going to catch us?" Jack says. "You do realize you're godlike powerful, right? You can do anything."

I start putting the groceries into one of the plastic bins. I don't feel powerful. I feel trapped.

"OK," I say, "we'll figure out a way to steal money, but let's do it Saturday. Tomorrow, I want to go to Barnard's."

"Fine by me." Jack grabs the box of cookies before I put them away and heads out of the kitchen. A few minutes later, I hear the creak of the fire door and know he's gone out.

Leaning my elbows on the dresser, I rest my head against my fists. The headache still pounds inside my skull. I should have gotten coffee when we were at the store, or at least a soda. Caffeine is the only thing that makes time headaches better. Except, if I drink coffee now, I'll never sleep. Along with my usual worries, I know tonight Victor's words will echo in my head. Is he right? Are we going to have to think about what to do with KJ's body?

"It will be all right," a breathy voice murmurs.

I spin around. Faith has appeared two feet from me, her body shadowy in the graying light.

"I'm sure he'll be back tomorrow," she says.

It takes me a minute before I understand. "You mean Jack?"

Faith nods. "Sometimes guys just need to be alone. Do guy stuff, you know? It doesn't mean anything." She comes closer and holds out a chipped blue mug.

"Jack's not my boyfriend," I say.

Faith nods again, like she understands that I mean something different.

"Want some tea?" she asks.

49

I stare at the cup. Hazy steam floats up from the top. "You have hot water?"

"I've got another coffee maker in my room." She offers the mug again.

"Thanks," I say. The ceramic warms a hand I hadn't realized was cold. I blow on the steaming liquid, releasing a waft of mint mixed with something flowery. "Where's Victor?"

"Sleeping. It's been a long day. He said the studio was crazy." She shakes her head. "Too many musicians, not enough space."

I gape at her. "Victor works at a music studio?"

"Volunteers," she says. "They let him record his stuff in return."

I sip the tea. Her words make me realize how little I know about them, about what they do all day, about what might make one day seem longer than another.

"How'd you end up here?" I ask.

"Oh, the usual." Faith gestures vaguely around the dusty space. "Couldn't get along with the 'rents."

"Yeah," I say, trying to sound knowing, though in fact, I am unable to imagine any situation involving parents that would be so bad you'd want to leave. I've never met mine. Spinners are taken from their parents at birth. "Me, too."

Faith smiles. The grin makes her face more substantial. I take another sip of tea. I've rarely talked to a Norm, rarely talked to anyone I didn't already know really, really well. I search for something to say so she won't go away.

"Do you know of other places we could stay?" I ask. Then, worried she might take offense, I add: "Not that this place isn't great—we just wouldn't want to overstay our welcome."

"I don't know." Faith sinks onto the box Jack was using and starts playing with her hair again. "We slept outside before we found this place. There's some decent spots over by the river where you can camp." She pauses. "Some of the folks there are nice."

Meaning some of them aren't.

"Would a hotel rent to us?"

"Sure," Faith says. "As long as you have ID saying you're eighteen."

ID. I trace the rim of my mug with one finger. Another item to add to the list of things we don't have.

"What about jobs?" I ask. "Anything out there we could get without, you know, a reference or anything?"

Faith twists a long strand of hair around her finger.

"Some of the restaurants will let you wash dishes when it's busy, and there's a place on Swan Island where Victor goes sometimes to off-load crates." She glances at me, presumably measuring my five-foot-six frame and finding it wanting. "You're not real big, though. And you're too cute for dock work anyway." She stares off into space for so long that I think she's forgotten my question, before adding, "Someone from the Society for Spinner Rights was looking for help the other day."

"What?" I jerk, spilling tea on my leg.

"Don't you like them?"

I mop up the fragrant tea to avoid answering.

"Yeah, spinners are pretty creepy," Faith says. "I saw one downtown once. She was waiting in a cop car while the officer got coffee. I could tell she was a spinner by the T-shirt: *Crime Investigation Center*, it said. Maroon. Not a real flattering color."

The sun has set fully now, turning the squat so dark I can barely see her. It makes her voice seems less breathy, somehow, like she's a mythical creature that gathers strength from the night.

"I don't have a problem with spinners," I say carefully.

"My aunt used to be really scared of them," Faith continues. "She said one robbed her while she was walking home. Said the guy's eyes jiggled when he talked and that he disappeared after."

"Sounds like kind of a wild story."

Faith shrugs. "I gotta admit I've wondered. My aunt never had any money. And she was usually drunk."

I decide to steer the conversation into safer territory. "What kind of job were the Society people offering?"

"They wanted someone to hand out flyers. Or maybe get people to sign a petition? I don't know. Might have been a one-time thing. They put up tables sometimes, at fairs and stuff."

"Maybe I'll check it out," I say.

"I doubt they pay much," Faith says. "Not like five hundred bucks or anything. How are you gonna get that much by Saturday?"

The heat of the tea makes my palm sweat. I shift the mug to my other hand.

"Steal it." The words are easier to say into the dark.

"Is that what you guys do?" Faith asks, as casually as if I'd said we worked in retail. "I wondered why they were looking for you."

"What?" My hand jerks again, this time splattering tea down the front of my sweater. "Who's looking for us?"

The shadow that is Faith shrugs. "Some guy. He was passing a picture of you around the youth center. You know, the one that gives free lunches?"

I have no idea what place she's talking about, but I nod anyway to make her keep talking. "What'd he say?"

"Just that you were missing and your parents were really worried. They always say that. He wanted to know if anyone had seen you."

The wet spot on my sweater sticks to my chest like a damp washcloth. "And . . . did you tell him?"

"Of course not." Faith sounds surprised.

I press the mug against my chest, a mistake since it makes the damp patch spread.

"What did the guy look like?"

"Um, I don't know. He was just a guy. Hispanic, maybe? Or white. He could have been white. Or a really pale black guy?"

Someone should put this girl in a video about the dangers of drug abuse.

"Glasses?" I suggest.

"I don't think so." Faith's voice has turned breathy again. "Maybe."

From the depths of the squat, in the opposite direction from KJ's room, comes a faint snuffling noise. Faith raises her head like a dog picking up a scent.

"I better go." She stands up. "Victor gets nightmares."

"Faith," I say, "wait."

But she's already gone. I sit in the empty kitchen, holding the lukewarm tea close against my chest, and watch the shadows deepening around me. Victor's not the only one who suffers from nightmares. I can already tell it's going to be another long night.

05 ◀◀

THE COFFEE MAKER SEEMS TO BE WORKING UP TO A BOIL
with particular sluggishness. I wiggle the cord, making sure the thing
is fully plugged in. A stingy drip of coffee splashes down into the
empty glass carafe. Jack, standing beside me, yawns.

"You're coming out with me, right?" I ask him.

"To Dr. B's house?" Jack makes a face. "I don't know. You really
think you're going to find some note from Sikes just lying around
somewhere?"

"We have to try something." I grab a mug from the counter and
sniff it to see if it's clean. Results are questionable. I rip off a paper
towel and scrub at the dingy spots. "Anyway, it seems more likely he'd
hide something there than at the Sick."

Jack makes a noncommittal grunt. I glare at the spluttering coffee.
I can already feel a headache coming from our morning errands, and
I'm counting on a pre-dose of caffeine to stave off the worst effects of
more freezes this afternoon.

"It's just so far away," Jack says.

I switch my glare from the coffee maker to him.

"It's not like you have other plans."

"Sleeping would be nice. You woke me up at freaking dawn this morning."

A second yawn swallows half his sentence. Jack was out watching his precious bands until who knows how late last night, and he was not happy when I woke him up and told him Shannon had created yet another list of things we needed to get for KJ. Fresh pajamas. Coconut water. Some kind of special sponge thing to wipe out his mouth. Jack whined the entire time, claiming nothing on Shannon's list would make any difference to KJ's recovery. The fact that he's probably right did not lessen my annoyance at his lack of enthusiasm. Like searching Barnard's house, getting supplies is at least *doing* something.

I snatch the carafe and dump the pathetic dribs of coffee into my mug.

"Fine." A fresh drop hisses as it hits the now-empty heating pad. I shove the carafe back and gulp the meager drink in a single swallow. "I'll go by myself. What's Barnard's address again?"

Jack must feel a little guilty, because he helps me decipher the TriMet map we picked up to figure out which bus will get me to Dr. Barnard's house.

"If you take the seventy-seven, you won't have to transfer." He traces the route with his finger. "Take the map with you, so you know when to get off."

I study the minimalist graphics, already regretting letting Jack off the hook. Unlike him, I haven't been out there alone, and the idea of heading into the city by myself makes me want to hide under my sleeping bag.

Jack rubs his eyes and turns toward his room.

"Have fun," he says. "Find good stuff."

Fun. Yeah, right.

I dish out a serving of applesauce and tiptoe over to KJ's corner. When I went by earlier, Shannon said he was too agitated to have visitors. I like to hold his hand, maybe feed him a little, and whisper my plans before I leave the squat. It makes me feel connected to him, even if I know he can't hear me. He's my touchstone. My lucky charm. A charm that feels particularly important given my day's plans.

Early afternoon sunbeams showcase the colonies of dust motes fogging KJ's sleeping space. I hold the applesauce in front of me like an offering. Shannon rises before I've crossed the threshold.

"He's sleeping," she whispers, hurrying forward to bar me from stepping inside. "Finally. He had a really rough morning. It's probably better not to disturb him."

"I won't wake him up." I crane my head to see over her shoulder. KJ lies in his usual stupor, eyes closed, his face weirdly expressionless. My heart clenches. "I just want to say goodbye before I leave."

"Better not," Shannon repeats. She eases the bowl of applesauce from the iron clasp of my fingers. "I'll feed him this later. Right now, sleep really is his best medicine."

"Right," I say.

Shannon pushes me out the door. "Can you remember to bring back more ice this afternoon?"

The bus ride takes forty-five minutes and is uneventful, if you call sitting on an uncomfortable seat and flinching every time someone looks at you uneventful. The bus has this narrow poster wedged in the space above the windows, advertising a TV show called *The Secret Life of Spinners*. According to the overly loud conversation between the two girls sitting in front of me, the show portrays life inside a Center as a seething nest of miscreants whose sole desire is to spy on each other and then humiliate their peers by exposing their secrets.

"Did you watch the episode where Annabelle slices Melissa up with a razor blade while they're both in a freeze?" one of them asks.

"Oh, my god!" the other one squeals. "That one was so gross. And then no one believed Melissa, but she kept, like, having all those flashbacks and stuff."

Over my head, the actor playing one of the main characters watches me, wearing the evil grin of a psychopath. By the time we reach my stop, I've chewed two more fingernails down to the quick.

Dr. Jeffrey Barnard lives in Northwest Portland, a couple of miles west of the Center. The bus drops me off four blocks away, in front of a large commercial building that, on this quiet Friday afternoon, includes a conveniently empty loading dock. I tuck myself into an unobtrusive corner and freeze time, emerging into the silence feeling only slightly less jittery.

"Twenty-seven twenty-three." I mutter the address under my breath as I jog toward my destination. "Twenty-seven twenty-three."

Dr. Barnard's home is one of six identical three-story townhouses, each painted gray with darker gray trim. Tall trees arch over the street, dappling the units with green and gold light. The townhouses have garages on the ground floor, with outdoor staircases leading up to their second-story entrances. Barnard's unit has a small Japanese maple planted at the foot of the stairs, the leaves of which are already deepening into fall red.

I stand at the bottom step and stare up at the door. It's painted an innocuous shade of plum, but something about it creeps me out. Threat radiates from the wood paneling, like there's an ax murderer waiting on the other side. I give myself a mental shake. What's the worst-case scenario? That the door conceals Barnard himself? It's possible. Barnard doesn't always work out of his office, and I know he was more banged up than I was by our car wreck, but Barnard can't do anything to me during a freeze.

The metal handrail slides under the sweat coating my palm as I force myself to mount the stairs. Logic has done nothing to ease my terror; the idea of walking inside still makes me feel like I'm about to break out into hives.

The front door's lock is a simple one. I pull on gloves and take out the set of lock picks Jack and I stole a couple days ago. Ross taught me how to use them only—what—a week ago? I kneel on the concrete landing and slip the pick into the lock. The memory of Ross guiding my fingers makes the muscles in my hand cramp so badly I have to massage them before continuing. How blind I was to not realize that a cop teaching you to pick locks doesn't say much about his moral integrity, even if he *was* right that the skill is useful. The first pin falls into place with a barely noticeable click, and I wiggle the pick to find the second one. It's hard to concentrate. My whole back is prickling like it's got a target on it.

The lock releases, the handle turning beneath my fingers. I stand, brushing hair off my damp forehead. The door continues to exude menace. I rest my hand against it and push very gingerly. I'm almost expecting the wood to react—to burn me or jump back at my touch— but nothing happens except that it glides open. I shake my head. Maybe it *is* better Jack isn't here. If he was, he'd make some smart-aleck comment about what a wuss I'm being.

It takes a massive act of will to step into Barnard's house. Being inside is worse. The place is decorated in graveyard colors—black, chrome, gray—all of it eerily spotless. The edges of the furniture look sharp. The walls are bare, making it feel like I'm being watched by featureless faces. When the front door closes, it clicks ominously. I lean my back against it, pretending the hesitation is only so my eyes can adjust to the dimmer light.

The main floor of Barnard's home is a square that's split into three rooms. A combined living/dining room takes up one whole half, stretching from the front door to the window-filled wall at the back of the house. To the right is a kitchen, and behind it, according to Jack, is Barnard's ground-floor study. On my left, more stairs lead to the upper floor. The study seems the most promising place to search, but the downstairs makes me so anxious I decide to start upstairs. Something could be hidden there, too. Right?

The guest room, as tidy and monochromatic as the living room, is unused, as is what must be a guest bath. It has nothing in it except a pristine towel and an untouched bar of soap. Barnard's master bedroom smells like him, a clinical scent like alcohol, only less antiseptic.

The drawer to his bedside table rattles when I yank it open. A quick search reveals nothing more incriminating than Barnard's chosen brand of cold medicine and the fact that he apparently likes to floss his teeth in bed. I slam the drawer shut and dig around in his dresser. It's full of clothes. This is dumb. Searching up here is a waste of time. I should be focusing on his study. I lift both pillows and find nothing underneath but smooth cotton sheets. Of course. Who hides business documents in their bedroom?

Walking back down to the main floor feels like forcing myself to enter a room full of noxious gas; my throat feels tight and it's hard to breathe. Giving the kitchen a wide berth, I cross through the living room toward the study. The door is shut, and the painted wood practically screams: *Abandon all hope, ye who enter here.*

"Come on," I mutter, rubbing the growing ache in my temple. "What are you waiting for?"

I pull the door to Barnard's office open and stare across the threshold. The room is square, with corner cabinets filled with books. There's a desk in front of me, its surface littered with papers and bulky medical texts. To my left, floor-to-ceiling windows let in streams of light that showcase the one thing I feared the most: the room is occupied.

Dr. Barnard sits stiffly behind his desk, one arm wrapped in a cast, frowning as he talks to a visitor in the chair across from him. Barnard's visitor sits with his back to me, but I still recognize him instantly. My heart starts beating extra hard.

Barnard's guest is Carson Ross.

Terror hangs like a curtain across the doorway. The empty air vibrates with warning: stay away. I grit my teeth. It's absurd to come all this way and not search Barnard's office. Narrowing my eyes as if against a strong wind, I step through the open doorway.

Pain, sharp as knives, slices my brain. I stagger. Buzzing. Like the hum that comes with wearing a leash, only ten times stronger. The office blurs. Time rips from my grasp.

"... appreciate your concern ..." Barnard's voice crashes against my ears.

I snatch at time. The strands pass through me like falling water. Panic closes my throat.

Dr. Barnard's gaze shifts in my direction. "What ... ?"

I stagger against the doorframe. My hands cling to the solid wood, desperate for something to ground me. I reach for time, grasping with every bit of strength I possess. The pressure in my head increases. Time moves relentlessly forward.

Ross spins around in his chair. I stare at him.

Barnard leaps to his feet.

I have to run. I know this, but I can't move. The world has started again, and I stand completely frozen.

Ross's face opens into a familiar smile.

"Alex," he says.

His voice releases me. Barnard shouts at Ross to grab me. I turn and run. The living room seems impossibly large. Behind me, footsteps thud, leather soles pounding against carpet.

"Alex," Ross repeats. He's close enough that I can hear his shirt rustling. I speed up. The door to the house is in front of me, the knob beneath my hand. As I fling it open, I reach out again with my mind, clutching at the invisible time strands, and miraculously, my grab holds.

But not before Ross's hand closes around my bare wrist.

Everything around us stops. In the frozen silence, the only sound I hear is my hammering heart. The living room sways around me, threat still leaching from every surface. I tilt my head so I can see around Ross's bulk. Barnard hovers, just inside his office door, mouth hanging open, midway through some shouted instruction.

Ross gazes down at me.

"Please," he says. "I just want to talk."

I try to wrench my arm free. Ross hangs on. The street through the open door mocks me, the chance of escape so close, yet so unreachable.

"I've been worried about you," he says.

"Like you care," I spit at him.

"I do care." Ross manages to sound hurt. "You know I've always valued our friendship."

"You just value what I can do for you. You value my time skills."

"That's not true." Ross's eyes are blue as the ocean and just as dangerous. "We're a team, remember? Partners."

I stand limp in his grasp. Everything about me hurts. My head. My heart.

"Living out there can't be easy," Ross croons.

"We're doing fine."

"Are you sure?" Ross watches me with an expression so caring I have to turn away—not quite fatherly, but something close. Like an uncle, maybe. It feels like he can see all the way into my soul, that he knows about everything: Shannon's crying, Victor's angry threats, Jack's recklessness, and KJ, drowning in Aclisote and lying so still in the gloomy squat. I lower my head.

"Let me help you," Ross says. "I'll rent you a house outside of town where no one will find you, just like we talked about. We can change your appearance, enroll you in school if you want. You'll be free and protected."

Ross's words float through my head like the whispers of a dream. A terrible longing fills me—to be safe, to not have to run anymore. To live without leashes or drugs and have someone take care of me. All mine if I just say yes. If I just trust Ross.

"What about my friends?"

"I can rent a place big enough for all four of you."

I study the shined surface of Ross's leather shoes.

"Why would you do that?" I say. "If anyone found out, you'd go to jail."

"So we can work together again."

"Without the Center?"

"Alex, I would never send you back to the Center. Everything I did was to get you away from them."

Tears fill my eyes, traitorous harbingers of hope. I blink them back and look up.

"Everything?" I ask. "Even killing Austin Shea?"

Ross sighs, a deep sound that fills the frozen air with invisible regret. "That night will haunt me for the rest of my life," he says. "I should have explained it all to you before we went there, but I was trying to shield you. I should have made more of an effort to help you understand." Ross shakes his head. "I know Shea's death was a hard thing for you to watch, but if it prevented even one more murder—one more killing like Sal's—wasn't it also a kind of justice?"

A headache throbs in my skull. Ross and justice. It was the reason I worked so hard for him. The one thing KJ never understood. The strain of holding time turns my vision fuzzy. Instead of one Ross standing next to me, there are two: the murderer who deceived me and the agent who always claimed he cared about me.

"I've been watching the news," I tell him. "Why hasn't Sikes been arrested yet?"

"I don't have enough evidence. Without your skills . . ." Ross shakes his head. "He's killing again, Alex. Just yesterday I rewound one of his crimes. A woman. He bashed her head against a rock and shoved her through a basement window."

A horrible feeling creeps its way across my skin, the hot flush of shame for another death I could have stopped. I study Ross's fingers where they loop my wrist. His grip has turned gentle, less of a snare and more of a handclasp.

"Forget Sikes," Ross says. "You need to worry about yourself. Barnard is under immense pressure to capture you. The regional director is screaming about consequences and lax security measures. They've even called in a team of wipers."

The prickles shift to a different kind of discomfort. I shiver.

"A team of what?"

Ross hesitates, as if he's reluctant to answer the question. He's standing so close to me I can see a vein pulsing in his right temple. I watch the beats. One. Two.

"Wipers. They're the Central Office's security force that catches spinners who've gone AWOL. They have only one mission: to stop the world from knowing what unmedicated spinners can do."

The vein on his temple wriggles, like a snake running beneath his skin. I lean away from him.

"I don't believe you."

Ross's blue gaze doesn't waver. "You think you're the only spinners who've escaped? The reason you never hear about anyone free out there is that no spinner ever lasts long. If they did, people would know the truth by now."

The logic of his statement is undeniable. Time pulls against me, and I struggle to keep from losing control.

"Come with me, Alex," Ross says. "Now. Let me take you somewhere safe. It will be just like the old days."

The old days. Something stirs in the pit of my stomach, a reptilian slither that matches the vein snaking under Ross's skin. "What, exactly, would we do together if I went with you?"

"The same work we always did," Ross says. "Find the bad guys and make them pay. You and I—between us, we have the power to make the whole world better."

The slithery feeling in my stomach spreads through the rest of my body.

"So, we'll be superheroes?" The cover of one of the comic books KJ used to read swims into my head: an absurdly muscled man standing, arms akimbo, blue cape flapping in the wind. "Simple schoolgirl by day and avenging hero by night?"

"Exactly." Ross's whole face lights up with some inner vision. "I've thought about it ever since I suspected your potential."

"What do you mean?"

Ross's teeth gleam in the room's stark light. "Justice isn't only about solving crimes; it's about laws and programs and how money gets spent."

I wriggle my arm, but Ross's grip, while seemingly benign, is quite firm.

"That's why you want to be the police chief."

"Yes, to start with, but who knows how far we could go?"

The slithery feeling gets more uncomfortable. I know how far Ross could go. With my skills under his control, he could do anything. Frame someone. Rig a vote. Eliminate his rivals. I shake my head, and once started, I can't seem to stop.

"What you're suggesting isn't justice. It's wrong."

The shining light of Ross's enthusiasm narrows into something more like a laser beam.

"And stealing isn't wrong?" His hold on my wrist tightens. "Where'd you get your new clothes, Alex? How have you been eating? You pay for all that with your allowance?"

Heat flames my face.

"It's not the same . . ." I stammer.

"Sure it is," Ross says. "We all do what we have to, to get what we need. I thought we'd been over this. Right is in results, not process."

I pull myself upright. "No."

Ross's blue eyes don't look like an ocean anymore. They look like ice.

"If you want to save yourself, you don't have any other choices."

He yanks his wallet out with his free hand and slides a business card from an inner flap with his teeth. "Take some time to think it over. When you get tired of being a rat chased around the gutters, I'll be waiting."

Ross holds out the card. I don't take it.

"If not for yourself," Ross says, "think about your friends. How long do you think they'll survive without any help? I hear KJ was pretty sick when he left the Center."

Rage stiffens all the muscles in my body. KJ never trusted Ross, and to hear Ross use his name as leverage now hits me like the ultimate betrayal. I hurl all my strength into a sudden twisting wrench, and yank my arm free. Instantly I melt time, then refreeze it just as fast. Ross remains where he is, hand still curled around the space that no longer holds my arm.

"You're a liar!" I shout. Frozen Ross just stands there, still holding out the white business card. "Stupid, lying, manipulative . . ."

And probably right, a voice in my head whispers. How long can we expect to remain undetected? Those men at the mall came within seconds of catching us. Were they really security guards? The two of them tried awfully hard to get hold of two kids who hadn't actually done anything wrong. Maybe they were wipers. I shiver.

Wipers could be anywhere. Anyone.

The pounding in my skull twists into an agonizing stab. Time tests the bounds of my control. I tighten my mental hold, forcing myself to focus, which I do—on the small white square in Ross's hand. A flag of surrender or an emblem of hope? I hesitate. Accepting it doesn't mean I'll use it. It only gives me options. The card is printed on thick paper and embossed with a raised seal. It feels smooth against my fingers when I take it. *Carson H. Ross*, it reads, *Time Agent*. Below the printed contact information of the police department, in Ross's familiar spiky handwriting, is a phone number.

I dash out the front door. Fresh air cools my cheeks but does nothing to lessen my anger. Or my fear. The card in my hand mocks my weakness. I should toss it in the gutter. I don't. Instead I slip it into my back pocket. And then I start to run.

CARSON ROSS STARES DOWN AT HIS EMPTY HAND AND then up at the even emptier space that a second ago held Alex's trembling form. A smile plays across his lips. The power, the *possibility*, in that fleeting instant of disappearance never fails to thrill him. And Alex looked so deliciously scared. She took the bait; the trap is set. Now it's only a matter of time before he gets her back.

"She's gone?" Barnard asks.

Ross arranges his features into a confused expression before turning around. Barnard stands in the shelter of his office, his broken arm in its blue-and-white sling curled protectively against his chest. The man's face is a mask of horror. Ross smothers the glee bubbling in his chest. Watching Barnard squirm is like a cherry on top of his sundae.

"I don't understand," Ross says. "Where did she go?"

"I guess she just ran really fast?" Barnard's voice is barely a squeak.

Ross makes a slow 360-degree turn to scan the room. Barnard's eyes flick from side to side in a frantic dance. What explanations is he conjuring to try to explain a girl vanishing into thin air?

"Of all the strange . . ." Ross says. "I was right on her heels and then . . ." Barnard's face turns a greenish shade of pale, like he's on the verge of passing out. Ross savors the moment for one more second before reaching down and grabbing his right leg. It's important he makes sure everyone believes he doesn't know the truth about the spinners' skills; that way, no one can suspect him of using them.

"And then my knee acted up," he says. "It does that—old training injury—and I glanced down at it, like a reflex, you know? And when I looked up again, she was gone."

"Oh." The relief in Barnard's voice is laughable. "Yeah. Well, she had a real burst of speed there right at the end. Check outside. See if you can tell where she went."

Ross makes sure to hobble as he heads over to the open door and peers up and down the street.

"No sign of her," he says, stepping back into Barnard's townhouse. "You want me to call it in to the precinct?"

"No," Barnard says, quickly. "I'll call our security force."

Barnard walks back to his desk and drops into the chair behind it. Ross reclaims the seat on the other side. When he sits, he can feel the cell phone in his pocket pressing against his leg, a present waiting to be opened. Barnard dials a preset number on his own phone and speaks sharply. Ross's hand drifts to his pocket. Does he have time for just a quick check?

"They'll be here in ten minutes," Barnard says, dropping phone on his desk.

"You really should think about getting some better door locks," Ross tells him. "She might come back."

"I will." Barnard scrubs a hand over his face, wiping away who knows what nightmarish visions. The man clearly isn't sleeping well. Bags show under the eyes behind his wire-rim glasses, and his normally immaculate clothes look rumpled.

"Why do you think she came here?" Barnard's voice holds a plaintive note.

Ross tilts his head. It's a good question. Despite Barnard's obvious fear, Ross doesn't actually see Alex as a threat—at least not a violent one. It's much more likely she came here looking for something. Keys to the Center? Information about Barnard's private research? The latter is definitely a subject worth looking into. Ross himself is fairly curious. He wonders if she found anything. He figures she must have been searching a long time if she got so tired she lost control of her freeze.

"It's probably some irrational impulse related to her Aclisote withdrawal," Ross says. "It's sad to see how quickly she's deteriorated. I hope the Center will have an opportunity to restart her treatment before it's too late."

Barnard shuffles the papers cluttering his desk, and Ross rubs his nose to hide the smile twitching his lips. Barnard knows perfectly well that Alex's actions have nothing to do with withdrawal, but he can't say that without exposing himself as a liar. The situation is almost unbearably amusing to Ross.

"Of course, you're right." Barnard checks his watch. "With the wipers on their way, I'm afraid we'll have to wrap up our meeting rather quickly. Was there anything else you wanted to discuss?"

Ross's smile vanishes. He'd achieved his first goal in coming here: getting Barnard to agree to let him know if the wipers had a line on Alex. It had taken a lot of sentimental gibberish about his worry over his former spinner, but the groveling was worth it if it meant he could keep her from getting caught. He still needed Barnard's help with a second problem, though. Ross runs the story through his head one more time, lining up his arguments against Barnard's possible protestations, before leaning forward.

"I also wanted to talk to you about Sikes."

"Sikes?"

The name has clearly caught Barnard off guard. Ross glances over his shoulder, and even though he knows no one is there, lowers his voice before speaking again.

"Yes. This is highly sensitive, and I'm trusting you to not spread it around." Steady eye contact is the trick to a good lie. Ross doesn't let himself blink. "Chief suspects someone in the force might be working with Sikes, so he's asked me to shadow the investigation."

Barnard's eyes narrow. "I thought Chief pulled you off that case after Sikes killed your partner?"

"He did. He thought Sal's death made the whole case too personal for me. Which is actually why he's asked me to help now." Ross allows himself a wry grin. "I'm pretty much the last person anyone would suspect of having anything to do with Sikes."

Barnard taps his cast. Is he confused or suspicious? Behind the cover of the desk that separates them, Ross's hands curl into fists. If Barnard checks Ross's claims with Chief, it will cause no end of trouble, as Ross was specifically told to stay clear, and a reprimand will not look good on his record. The risk is worth it, though. To be truly effective, Ross needs money, and Sikes is famous for stealing it. With Alex's help, Ross can steal some, too. One big heist should set him up, after which he will arrest Sikes, managing in one single swoop to both shift the blame for his own robbery and boost his career by being the conquering hero who finally put Sikes behind bars. Having someone else catch Sikes, while unlikely, would ruin his plans, which is why Ross wants to have some warning if the case is advancing.

"What is it Chief wants me to do?" Barnard asks.

"Given that I'm not supposed to be involved," Ross says, "Chief can't openly brief me about any new Sikes developments, so I need someone else to keep me informed. He wants you to tell me when a spinner gets called out on anything that might be Sikes related."

The finger tapping Barnard's cast increases its tempo.

"This is highly unusual," he says.

"Sikes is an unusual criminal."

There's a long pause. Ross's fists squeeze so tight his hands grow numb.

Barnard's finger slows. He nods.

"All right. I'll keep you informed."

Ross's fists relax in his lap. The rush of returning blood makes his fingers tingle.

"Thank you, doctor."

He gets to his feet. Now that he's gotten what he came for, his focus slides back to Alex and her tantalizing nearness. Ross slips his hand into his pocket and cradles his phone.

"Good luck tracking down our runaway," he says as Barnard ushers him to the door. "And if there's anything I can do to help, I'd be more than happy to."

A small shiver shakes Barnard's shoulders.

"I think it's best we leave it to the wipers," he says.

"Of course."

Barnard shuts his door with a loud clunk. Ross smiles. How will the doctor spend the rest of his day? Does he have any peers with whom he can share his true concerns? Golden afternoon sun shines on Ross as he jogs down the front stairs. Maybe Barnard will spend his time nailing his doors and windows shut, imagining that, at any moment, a vengeful Alex might reappear.

Ross's squad car is hot from sitting in the sun, but he doesn't waste time waiting for the air conditioning to kick in. Instead, he drops into the sweltering seat and opens his phone, tapping on the app he recently installed. A map opens on his screen—the city of Portland from ten thousand feet. Ross watches the antenna icon blink as it searches the airwaves for its connection.

An hour southeast of town, tucked into the forests surrounding Mount Hood, Ross has bought a house. It's small and quite secluded. Workmen are even now finishing up the modifications he's asked for: bars on the outside of all the windows, a double-doored entry with electronic locks that can't be picked, security cameras. All his plans will work more smoothly if Alex returns to him willingly, but he's not naïve enough to count on her cooperation. The renovations will be done on Monday, so he can move her in on Tuesday. Which means all he needs to do is keep track of Alex's location for three days and make sure the wipers don't get close. The map zooms down to street level. Ross brushes the screen with the gentleness of a caress. A blue dot moves fitfully down West Burnside, tracking the progress of the chip embedded in Ross's missing business card. The smile that lights his face is triumphant.

"Hello, Alex," he whispers. "Let's find out where you've been hiding."

07 ◄◄

TIME ESCAPES FROM THE LAST CRUMB OF MY CONTROL
when I enter the squat. I sag against the door, massaging my aching
temple in the murky light of our refuge. Even the faint sound of cars
passing outside makes the hair on my arms stand up. How long will it
be before the wipers find us? My body slides to the ground. My head
is pounding so much it's hard to hold it upright.

"Alex?"

Panic slams my heart against my ribs and I clutch for the time
strands, but seconds slip through my exhausted body without even
stuttering. I squint into the gloom. Jack is peering at me from the
kitchen, a frown creasing his forehead.

"What'd you do?" Jack sounds annoyed. "Get lost? It's almost dark."

"I walked most of the way back. In real time."

"You walked?" Jack comes closer. "Why? Wasn't the bus running?"

Sensory memories flash through my head: the painfully slow crawl
of the swaying bus, the smell of diesel and human sweat, the feel of
bodies bumping against mine, the tinny music leaking from too many
headphones, and the eyes. So many eyes. All watching me.

I roll my head against the door, which only tightens the knots twisting my neck.

"You should stay inside tonight," I tell him.

"What for?"

"The wipers." A voice in the back of my head can't stop screaming. I feel like I'm teetering on the edge of a cliff and the abyss is calling me to jump.

Jack bends over me, frowning. "The what?"

"Ross was there." I look up at him. "At Barnard's. He grabbed me."

"Seriously?" Jack says. "Are you OK?" I nod, which comes off more like a shudder. Jack holds out his hand.

"Come on," he says. "I made some coffee. The caffeine will make you feel better."

I let him haul me to my feet. The kitchen is filled with the bitter aroma of fresh coffee. I pour a cup and drink it greedily. Haltingly, I recount my trip to Barnard's. Jack's expression shifts between curiosity and nervousness. When I finish, he stares at me.

"The Sick has their own security?"

I hold my coffee cup close against my chest. "Ross said that's why we never hear about escaped spinners."

"Wow." Jack shakes his head. "And here I've been calling you paranoid."

There's not enough nail left on my thumb to chew, so I substitute my pointer finger. Jack frowns at the steaming coffeepot.

"How'd you lose control of time, anyway?" he asks. "Were you super tired?"

"It was more than that." I rub my head, feeling again the knife-edged slice of time tearing away from me. "My freeze just ... got broken somehow. It's like controlling time didn't work around him."

"Did he have a leash?"

"No." I shiver again. "At least I didn't see one."

"Maybe the shock of seeing Ross made you lose focus."

"Maybe."

Jack cracks his knuckles in a steady round of pops. "So, Ross thinks we could use our skills to run the city?"

"Not *us*." I drink more coffee. The caffeine is finally starting to dull the edges of my headache. "Him." I remember his card and pull it from my pocket. Here, far from Ross's deadly magnetism, the small slip of white seems far less tempting. I tear the card in half and toss it in the general direction of the trash. "I think Ross wants to be like a benevolent dictator or something."

"He could probably pull it off." Jack bends down and picks up the two pieces of the torn card. "If we worked with him, I bet . . ."

"Jack! The guy murdered Austin Shea in cold blood."

"Yeah, I know, but if we get caught, they'll murder *us*."

I stare at the card in Jack's hand. Is Jack right? Is working for Ross a reasonable price if all of us get to live?

"We're not going to get caught," I say.

"The only way we don't get caught is if we leave Portland now."

I shake my head. Outside, the sun sinks closer to the horizon. From the other end of the squat, rustling noises drift through the darkening air. It's KJ, or maybe the roosting pigeons—I can no longer tell the difference between their restless shuffles. Exhaustion settles over me with the coming night. The coffee I'm drinking only heightens the competing demands pulling me in too many directions: the other spinners hurtling toward their unnecessary deaths, KJ dwindling into the sickness, Shannon's endless errands, and the money we need to steal for Victor. I look down at my mug. In the dim light, I can barely see my hands, as if I've literally been stretched so thin I'm starting to disappear.

"We're not going to get caught," I repeat.

Even my voice sounds faint.

Jack holds out the two halves of Ross's torn business card.

"We can still hold on to this," he says. "Just in case."

I bite my lip, but I don't say no.

I dream I am back at Austin Shea's, floating through unmoving rooms, oppressive in their heavy stillness. As much as I want to go somewhere else, I find I can take only the same route I did the night I was there with Ross. When I reach the bedroom, a familiar silver moon lights the figure on the bed. Night makes the gash in his throat appear black, and I know that only time keeps the blood in his frozen veins. I can almost see it under his skin, a cresting wave of red, waiting for me to release time so it can gush into the night.

I clench my hands and realize I am holding something. It's a knife, the cutting edge jagged and dark with blood. Horror rises inside me. I drop the weapon and run to Shea, placing my hands over his wound. Dream logic tells me that if I can just put the pieces back together, I can repair the damage. I try, but it doesn't work. As soon as I get two flaps of Austin Shea's skin together, another section falls open.

"It's OK," Ross says, and I know he has always been in the room with me. He wears black pants and a shirt so crisp and white it glows like a second moon.

"Mr. Ross," I gasp. "I didn't mean to kill him. I don't know how it happened."

Ross gives me his most reassuring smile. "This is what you wanted. You said you'd do anything to help me catch Sikes."

"But he's not Sikes." The slice in Shea's neck has grown wider. Warm gore, released by my awkward fumbling, covers my hands.

"He's one of Sikes's helpers," Ross says. He sounds infinitely calm. Reasonable.

"How do you know?"

"Trust me." Ross's smile widens. His teeth shine as brightly as his shirt, though his eyes stay dark. "Remember, we're the good guys."

Shea's blood-wet flesh slips under my fingers. I try again to knit his skin together, and as I do, it starts to change. The gray beard that roughened his neck vanishes. His skin, once alabaster white, deepens to a smooth brown. Terror stills my fumbling fingers. It's no longer Austin Shea lying in this bed. The figure before me, the one whose blood soaks my hands, is KJ.

I wake with a start, my heart pounding as if I've sprinted a mile. Midnight dark fills the echoing warehouse. I blink, trying to turn the shapes around me into something familiar, but the boxes and abandoned furniture seem to have moved during the night, shifting into wavering towers that threaten to collapse over my head. The fear from my dream licks the edges of my sleeping bag, creeping over me with a draft of cold air. Holding the blankets right up against my chin, I reach out and stop time.

Safety descends with the unnatural quiet. Dust motes halt their drifting fall. The yellowish streetlight filtering through the windows dims. I loosen my grip on the sleeping bag and take deep breaths to calm my wild pulse. It was just a dream. This dank, smelly squat is the reality. I didn't kill anyone. Carson Ross used me to freeze time so he could slit Austin Shea's throat. It wasn't my fault. It wasn't my fault.

Slowly, the shapes around me settle into their benign selves. The ground, hard even with the cushion of a foam pad, presses against my spine with reassuring solidity. I release my hold on time. The air around me shifts—not a breeze, exactly, but a lightening as the molecules start moving again. I close my eyes and count the sounds in the night: the unsteady rush of cars on the freeway, the far-off clack of a train, small scrabbling noises that tell me the rodents are on the prowl. When I hear a faint rustling from KJ tossing in his makeshift bed, I finally drift back to sleep.

The next time I wake, it's because someone is shaking my arm.

"Alex!"

My eyes pop open. Jack is kneeling on the floor beside me, one hand on my bare arm. I bolt upright, holding the blankets against me as if their meager presence might offer protection.

"What happened?"

It's so early, pink leaks in through the grimy windows. And it's very quiet. Frozen quiet. I push mentally against the force that holds time at bay. Nothing moves. This isn't my freeze; I can't melt it.

"Check it out." Jack beams like the Youngers do when asked if they want more dessert. A split second later, a truck engine throbs, rattling the windows as it rumbles past. Jack hasn't returned to his pre-freeze location. Nor have I. Time is moving and I'm still awake, still sitting up and draped in blankets.

"You can do it," I say. "Change things in frozen time." The lump of dread that greets me every morning tightens my stomach with an extra twist.

"It's just like you said!" Jack leaps to his feet, nearly dancing in his excitement. "Here. Hold on." In an instant, he goes from standing at the foot of my bedroll to sitting cross-legged beside me, holding a cardboard tray with two cups of coffee. I twitch in surprise and the motion knocks over a pile of croissants newly heaped on my lap.

"Careful." Jack laughs. He picks up the fallen pastries and sets them on top of the paper bag they came in.

79

I stare at the stack of golden-crusted treats. The dread is spreading. "That's too many."

Jack plucks one of the coffees from the holder and holds it out to me. "We'll share with Shannon."

"No, I mean you took too many from the store. They'll notice that they're gone." My face feels taut, like the skin somehow shrank during the night. Jack is so irresponsible. He'll never be careful enough with this kind of power. "And how will you explain to Victor where you got those? They'd have heard you if you'd left the squat in real time."

"Who cares?" Jack's smile fades. He smacks the cup he'd offered me down on the ground. "Can't I have fun for one minute before you start hassling me?"

I pick up the cup and put my lips against the lid, steadying myself with a long swallow. When my skills first changed, I'd shared Jack's jubilation. I'd wanted to play tricks on people or sneak around at night and run free. When KJ freaked out and warned me about the risks, I, too, initially felt crushed. I sip more coffee. Jack has even remembered to add cream and sugar.

"I'm sorry." I raise the cup to toast him. "And thanks for this."

Jack settles himself on the floor, apparently too excited to hold a grudge. "I'm not a total idiot, you know. I took the croissants from the back bin instead of the counter display."

"There aren't *that* many pastries," I concede. "If Victor asks, you can say you picked them up last night."

I taste one of the croissants and discover that, even though we occasionally got baked goods at the Center, what we'd called croissants were only distantly related to the buttery, flaky deliciousness I now hold in my hands. I scoot my bedroll back so I can prop myself against the wall and savor my treat more comfortably. Jack is equally intent on his own breakfast, leaning against an old trunk and chewing happily. A full five minutes passes before either of us speaks.

"So." Jack licks the remains of his third croissant off his fingers. "I've been thinking about how we'll get the money."

"Right." The pleasure in my breakfast dims in the face of the day's unpleasant prospect. "I think it's best to take just a little bit of money from a bunch of different places. That way, it'll be less noticeable."

"Nah, that would take too long. We just have to find a place that can handle the loss."

"Like what?"

"Video poker? A drug dealer? Or what about going straight to the source and robbing a bank?"

A hundred protests crowd my mouth. I make a conscious effort to hold them back. I've already pissed off Jack once this morning, and I don't want to push him so far he goes running into the city alone with his new skills.

"If we take a bunch of money from a teller," I say, trying very hard to sound conversational, rather than like an annoying party pooper, "don't you think the teller would notice and think it was weird? It would be better if we could make it look like a normal robbery."

Jack wipes his hands on his jeans and picks up his coffee. "So let's not take it from a teller. We'll wait in the lobby of a big bank until we see someone head back to open the safe. Then we freeze time and take whatever we need."

I nibble on a bite of croissant.

"What?" Jack swirls his coffee. "Don't you think it will work?"

"No, it should work fine. I was just thinking that it's ironic. A week ago, my main goal in life was to arrest people who had broken the law, and now, I'm the one plotting crimes."

Jack laughs, apparently thinking I'm making a joke. "Wouldn't it be awesome if we could steal as much as Sikes? The guy's stolen, what—forty million dollars' worth of stuff?"

"Fifty," I say. "At least."

"Fifty million dollars." Jack repeats the words like they're holy. "And here we are sweating over a few hundred."

"It's not something to admire."

"Sure it is! Everyone wants to be rich."

"Not like that!" All the apprehension I'd felt when Jack showed me that his skills had changed comes back with a rush. "Fear that we're insane criminals is why Norms hate us. If we start stealing huge sums and someone figures out we're getting away with it because we're spinners, they'll believe they're justified in killing us off. Or at least locking us up."

Jack starts in on yet another croissant. "No one's ever caught Sikes."

"Yeah, he's a great role model." All that remains of my croissant is a pile of crumbs dusting my sleeping bag. I must have crushed the last bit without noticing. This conversation is bringing back the uncomfortable burn I felt when Ross revealed that Sikes had killed again. If I know who Sikes really is, shouldn't I report that to someone? No. I brush the crumbs away, for once not worrying about the rats. It's ridiculous to worry about Norms when they care so little about me.

"Jack, we have to be careful when we're out there."

"Duh." Jack offers me an exasperated glare from under raised eyebrows. "Except it's not really *that* risky." He stretches his arms over his head. "With skills like these . . ." Jack's arms are suddenly no longer raised. Instead, he's holding them out toward me, the final croissant resting on his palm like an offering. "We are invincible."

A sweet, buttery smell wafts into my nose. I shake my head. The three croissants I already gobbled up are making me feel a little nauseated.

"Your loss," Jack says, sinking his teeth into the pastry.

I pick up my coffee, then put it down without drinking any. Caffeine jangles my nerves. Right and wrong—concepts that used to be so clear to me—have become confused. To Jack, this is all an adventure—running away, camping out in the squat, stealing money. The other day, he called us godlike. If we really are invincible, shouldn't we be using our powers for something grander than thievery and blackmail? KJ would certainly say so. But if we quit stealing, how will we live? If we don't find a way to put pressure on Barnard, how can we protect our friends?

I shoo Jack out of my space, so I can get dressed. Searching Barnard's home was justified because it might have helped save our friends. Stealing things is necessary as long as the Norms make it impossible for us to live in the open. I pull on a short-sleeved T-shirt, then layer on a clean sweater—stolen, like everything I own. This one is wool and kind of itchy. Where will all this end, though? Will my guilt fall away once I free the other spinners? Or would that success one day turn sour, just like the too-rich breakfast that's making me feel ever so slightly sick?

08 ◀◀

THE STREETS ARE VERY QUIET. IT'S 6:30 A.M. CARS RUMBLE past only occasionally, and there's a lone woman yawning in the bus shelter. I hunch deeper into my sweater as we pass the mini-mart where we stole food yesterday. An aproned clerk stands on the sidewalk, setting out a display rack piled with fruit. Just glancing at the bananas and shiny apples makes me jumpy.

"No bank will be open before nine," I say. "I guess we can just walk around or something until then."

"Or something," Jack echoes. I open my mouth to ask him what he means when he suddenly moves from walking right next to me to walking a half step behind me.

"What are you doing?" I ask.

"Shoot, you caught me." He holds out a bunch of bananas. "I was going to surprise you."

I spin around to check the mini-mart. The clerk has gone back inside, but the piled fruit lists rather obviously to one side.

"You can't just freeze time whenever you feel like it," I say. "Someone will notice."

The bananas in Jack's hands disappear. "Pretty cool, huh? Do I look like a magician?"

"No," I lie, hoping to discourage him. "And pick those up."

Jack bends to recover the bananas he'd tipped onto the pavement in frozen time, his enthusiasm apparently undimmed by my disapproval. We've only walked a few more steps before he stops time again. This time, he does a better job of matching his prefreeze location and his body just sort of shifts.

"Jack!" A banana lies on the sidewalk right where I am about to put my foot. I manage a little hop to avoid squishing it. When I regain my balance, I see a second banana perched on a fire hydrant.

"Stop it." A third banana appears, spliced onto the top edge of a No Parking sign. A woman in a green Beetle turns her head as she drives past. She blinks at the yellow fruit, then shakes her head as if brushing off an odd fancy. A nervous flutter beats in my throat.

"Give those to me." I hold out my hand.

Jack evaporates from his position to one just beyond my reach. When he reappears, he's laughing.

"You should see your face," he chortles. "You look like Yolly does when Kimmi Yoshida mouths off."

"It's not funny, Jack." I look around, sure that someone has noticed bananas appearing and Jack teleporting around the sidewalk.

"It is too funny," Jack says. "It's hilarious." He's laughing so hard now that he manages only the feeblest protest when I snatch the remaining bananas away from him. I shove the fruit into a garbage can, scanning the traffic as I do. Cars slide by, their drivers all staring blandly forward as they thread their way through the early-morning commute.

"Jack," I lecture, "you can't let the Norms see you."

85

"I know, I know." Jack wipes away tears of laughter. "It's just so fun. How can you resist playing with it?"

I shrug, both irritated at Jack for risking exposure and jealous of the way he's enjoying his new skills. I've been able to change things for weeks, and except for about fifteen minutes when I first discovered what I could do, I've never gotten to play.

"Come on," I say sourly. "We don't have time for this. We have to focus on finding a bank to rob."

Jack dissolves into giggles again. I turn away and march down the sidewalk without waiting for him to recover.

By the time we hike the three miles into downtown, it's almost eight, and traffic has thickened to a steady flow. Streams of people hurry past us, balancing coffee cups while tapping on cell phones as they funnel into glass-fronted office buildings. We're nearing a big, fancy-looking bank when Jack nudges me with his elbow.

"Alex, check that out."

I turn. Parked against the curb by a pair of ATMs stands a big, white armored truck. A man sits behind the wheel of the idling vehicle, watching as a second man pushes some kind of trolley stacked with hard-plastic boxes over to the ATM. Both men wear blue uniforms. The one on the sidewalk has a gun prominently displayed on his right hip.

"That will be even easier than a bank," Jack says. He reaches out to take my hand.

"Wait," I say. The man across the street does something to the machine, and the face of it swings open. From what I can see around the bulk of his body, the man is taking out sealed trays and replacing them with identical ones off the trolley. "We can't get that money. It's all locked up in those boxes."

"What about the truck?"

I chew on a fingernail. If we are going to try to pull off a robbery, an armored truck does seem as good a choice as any.

"OK, but we can't freeze here. Even if we come back, we won't get our positions right and someone might notice." I scan the area. Ahead of us is a three-story parking structure. At the corner, a semi-enclosed staircase spirals its way down to the sidewalk. I pull on Jack's sleeve. "Come on."

We hurry to the parking garage and trot up two flights of stairs until we're well above the sight line for prying eyes. The steps are concrete and smell like urine. I stop at a bend and lean out the opening overlooking the street, my heart pumping much harder than the minimal exercise merits. Armored Truck Guy has finished loading the ATM and is heading toward his partner.

"Can you see the back of the truck?" Jack asks.

I shake my head. "We'll just have to guess when he opens it." Armored Truck Guy disappears between the building and the side of the idling truck.

"I'll count to five," Jack says, his voice bright with excitement. "One." I step into the corner of the stairway, pulling Jack with me so no one can see us if they happen to look up. "Two. Three." Jack links his hand with mine. "Four." I take a deep breath, focusing on a candy wrapper being pushed around by a breeze. "Five."

Jack stops time before I do. I don't realize it matters to me until it happens. This freeze feels foreign, as if I'm not quite welcome in it. I reach out with my mind and touch the unmoving strands. When I freeze time, the invisible threads feel like a sheet of fabric, taut yet pliable. In this freeze, the threads are like a solid wall.

"Let's go get ourselves some money." Jack drops my hand and bounds down the stairs. I hold my position for a second, checking to make sure no one can see us. The only thing besides me on the concrete steps is the candy wrapper, which now hangs a few inches above the ground.

Slipping between some unmoving cars, I follow Jack across the street. The security guard stands at the back of the truck, his head tipped downward as he checks the time on his watch. The truck itself is locked up tight.

"Are we too late?" I ask.

Jack points with his chin. The trolley leans against the truck's bumper. We aren't late. We're early.

"Let's go back," I say. "We'll count to five again."

"Nah, let's just hide around here somewhere. Then we can see what's going on."

I turn in a full circle, searching for a likely spot. People fill the sidewalk and cars clog the streets. No hidden corner offers shelter.

Jack drops to his hands and knees and peers under the truck. "How about under there?"

I squat down next to him. The truck offers less than a foot of space between it and the pavement. "We can't fit there."

"Sure we can." Jack starts squirming his way forward. "If you don't want to, you can go back to the stairs and wait there."

I consider Jack's offer. Going back would certainly make me less tense than crouching under an idling truck. It would also mean I was only an accessory to a robbery, rather than the thief. But going back means trusting Jack to be discreet, and as I watch his feet disappear, I realize how much I don't.

The asphalt bites into my hands. Knobby metal things attached to the bottom of the truck scrape my back as I crawl forward. There isn't really room for two. I have to scrunch myself against Jack to make sure our arms and legs are all hidden.

"Gee, Alex." Jack grins. "I never knew you liked me *that* way."

"Shut up," I say. I'm crammed so close to Jack I'm practically lying on top of him. "Let's get this over with."

With the return of time comes the chug of an engine way too close to my head. Exhaust, merely a faint whiff when frozen, turns into a heady stench now that the air is moving. The effort to not cough makes me gag.

"Can you see anything?" I whisper into Jack's neck, realizing too late that I haven't positioned myself in a way that lets me see the security guard's feet.

"A little," Jack says. A car roars past us, followed by another. The traffic light on the corner must have turned green. I try to appreciate the way the cars shield us from passersby, rather than imagining myself getting squished under each passing tire.

There's a rattle from the rear of the truck, followed by a metallic bang somewhere over our heads. My ears are still ringing when the sound abruptly stops.

"That's it," Jack says. He slides away from me and out into the frozen traffic. I wriggle myself over to the sidewalk and meet him at the back of the truck, picking gravel out of my palms as I walk.

One of the truck's back doors is wide open. The security guard is leaning forward, one hand still resting on the trolley he'd slammed down over our heads. I peer past his shoulder. Three metal racks are bolted on each side of the truck's interior. On the bottom shelves lie neat stacks of plastic trays like the ones the guard loaded into the ATM. Above them are piles of bags—big gray things with locks holding them closed at the neck, as well as slim, purse-like ones with no protection other than zippers across the top. All, presumably, hold money. Lots of money.

"Wow," I say.

"Yeah," Jack agrees. He's already stepping up on the truck's bumper, moving carefully so that he doesn't nudge the guard. I pull on the gloves I wore at Barnard's and climb up beside him.

"Let's choose the ones that are easiest to open," I say. "And don't touch anything without covering your hands. We don't want to leave any fingerprints."

"We can't take those, then." Jack points toward one of the large bags that's cinched at the top with a thick wire coil and a heavy lock.

"How about some of these?" I pick up one of the purse-like pouches. It's blue vinyl, with a zipper running the length of one side. I grab the slim metal tab and slide it open. Inside is a tidy one-inch stack of bills. I run a finger over the pile, rifling the edges to release the musty smell of dollars. For all the talking we'd done about stealing cash, I hadn't quite imagined what it would actually be like to do it. I thought I'd feel guilty or scared, but here in the perfect silence of a frozen world, all I feel is powerful. "Who do you think these belong to?"

"Some store," Jack says, covering his hands with his T-shirt so he can open a pouch. "They probably requested cash from the bank and it's safer to get it delivered than to carry all this yourself."

"Yeah," I say, "much safer." Our eyes meet, and Jack and I both start laughing. Once started, I can't stop. I laugh so hard tears fill my eyes. Jack laughs so hard he has to lean against the racks for support.

"Stop," he gasps. "I can't concentrate. This would be a terrible place to lose the freeze."

"It would," I agree, still giggling. "Here, this'll help." I take off one of my gloves and place my hand against the bare skin on his neck. Jack's shoulders straighten. It's not my freeze, so I can't feel it, but I know my own time skills are surging into him, strengthening his hold.

"Thanks," Jack says. We stand there a minute, letting our giddiness subside and Jack's power stabilize.

"How much money should we take?" I ask him.

Jack fans the cash in the pouch he's still holding. "There's probably two, three grand in this one. What if we take three of them? That should last a while."

"OK." I've never had more than twenty dollars, saved up from months of the tiny allowance the Center gives each spinner, and now I'm holding maybe five thousand? Fifty thousand? It hardly matters how much, since we can so easily get more.

Jack and I empty the money out of three pouches, shoving the bills into our pockets and then lining our shoes when we run out of space. I even tuck a few stacks in my bra.

"Next time," I say, using my T-shirt to give the pouches Jack touched a precautionary wipe before putting them back, "you should wear gloves."

"You think the police have our prints?" Jack asks.

"I'm wanted for murder, remember?" Rather than worry me, this reminder only sparks a new round of giggles. Jack starts to smile, then winces and touches a hand to his forehead. My merriment fades. Jack has frozen time a lot this morning. We need to go.

We spend the rest of the morning shopping. First, we buy two backpacks and a pair of wallets. Jack gets more coffee while I lock myself in a restroom and distribute our money among the wallets and inner pockets of the packs. We buy credit for the cell phones I'd charged last night and spend an hour trying to figure out the phones' features. Jack manages to link to the internet and find a nearby music store, where he promptly drags me so he can buy a guitar. Finally, we pick out new clothes. All the stuff we have is dirty, and buying new is easier than doing laundry. Neither of us checks the price tags. Jack buys himself a vintage leather jacket. After discovering that lots of money does not make it any easier to find a pair of jeans that fit, I pick out an absurdly overpriced cashmere coat instead. Paying for all our acquisitions with cash—even cash acquired under such dubious circumstances—makes me much happier than just taking them.

At noon, we get sandwiches, reload our already depleted phones, and grab a bus heading back to the squat. Even with Jack, I don't like taking the bus, especially since he insists on picking out chords on his new toy, which makes everyone stare at us. I shrink down in my seat and try not to think about how right now, while we're moving, I can't stop time and escape. As I proved in my car wreck, freezing time in a moving vehicle stops everything except my own forward momentum.

"Hey, Alex," Jack says, when we finally escape the bus. "Check this out. It will make you less of a spaz about freezing." Jack hands me the crumpled newspaper he'd picked up at the coffee shop.

I transfer all my shopping bags to one hand so I can open the wrinkled pages. It's the kind of paper sold near checkout counters that features pictures of three-headed alligators and rumors about which celebrities are drug addicts. Yuki used to beg Charlie for a copy whenever he brought one in for his shift.

"Is this what I'm looking for?" I point to a headline that screams: *Mideast's Spinner Population out of Control: The Real Reason We Bombed Iraq!*

Jack looks over my shoulder. "Not that one. Top of page three."

I flip the pages, folding the sheets back so they don't flutter. The headline on this page reads:

Man's Bicycle Stolen While He Was Riding It!
Sept 13 Harry Roades wasn't expecting anything unusual. He was heading home after his shift at Bagel Mania. He'd stopped for lunch with some friends, then grabbed his bike and started pedaling.

"It was a regular day," Roades said. "I was just riding up the street, listening to my music and then *wham!* Suddenly I'm sitting on the sidewalk. It was really weird. One minute I'm riding, next I'm sitting."

Eyewitness Lucas Emerson confirms the story.

"I was napping in a doorway when this guy starts screaming. I open my eyes and he's sitting there beside the wall yelling his head off. I know he wasn't there a few minutes ago 'cause I'm a real light sleeper."

Roades admits he had a beer with lunch but points out that if he'd been so drunk he'd blacked out he'd have had bruises from the fall.

"At least it was the bike that disappeared and not me," Roades said. "My friend works at the hospital and they said a girl disappeared from there around the same time. Must be some kind of time warp or something."

Emerson offered an eerier explanation.

"I think it's aliens. I've seen them around here before. They're invisible, but they have a kind of blue aura. Things were definitely bluer than normal when I woke up."

I close the paper. "I took that bike. When I ran away from the hospital. I'm also the girl who disappeared."

Jack nods. "I know."

"This story sounds ridiculous. Aliens?"

"That's the point." We cross Elmer's empty parking lot and check that no one is looking before slipping around to the back of the building. The blackberry bushes welcome us with their usual thorny embrace.

"What we can do," Jack says, "is so impossible no one believes it.

93

So if anybody sees us disappear, they'll just shake their heads and move on. It's either that or tell someone and end up in there." He points at the paper in my hand.

"I guess."

Jack picks a particularly aggressive blackberry branch off his pant leg and takes my arm. "Can you freeze? I'm tired."

I nod, still thinking about the article. Is Jack right? Are there spinner-related events happening every day that the Norms just dismiss? The world stills as I stop time. Jack puts down his guitar and reaches for the ladder at the bottom of the fire escape. Metal screeches in protest, sprinkling us with rust flakes as the ladder slides toward us.

"Even so." I hand all our stuff to Jack before climbing up after him. "If we start disappearing too obviously, they'll eventually *have* to believe it."

"Makes you wonder, though, doesn't it." Jack yanks up the ladder and wipes paint chips from his fingers. "You think all the alien abduction stories are really about spinners? Or what about the ones where people spontaneously burst into flames?"

We clatter up the stairs. "How many spinners do you think there are out there?" I ask. "Not living in Centers, I mean."

"Good question." Jack pushes the squat's door open and we walk in together.

The musty air of the squat settles around us, warm and slightly rotten. I follow Jack through the unnatural quiet toward KJ's corner, weighed down with questions and packages. We can't be the only spinners in the world who managed to escape. If there were no free spinners, the government wouldn't have passed new banking guidelines that replaced potentially rewindable PIN codes with fingerprint ID. What are they like, the free spinners? Do they hide their powers? Or have they found ways to use them without getting caught? If we find some, would they help us?

We turn the corner into KJ's room. The sight of him squeezes my heart. I've been so distracted, I forgot to melt time, so the scene before me is spread out in a gut-wrenching tableau. Sweat flattens KJ's dark hair against his forehead, and his nose stands out sharply over sunken cheeks. Shannon kneels with her usual devotion by his side. KJ's arm lies outstretched, freed from the blankets. The freeze seems to have caught Shannon in the act of washing it, or tucking it back in for warmth. It's hard to tell, since all I can see of her is her back. Her braid droops across the red cotton of her sweater like a wilted branch. A familiar wave of guilt rushes through me.

I release time with a heavy sigh. "Hey, Shannon."

She whips around. When she sees us, her face turns almost as sickly as KJ's.

"It's just us," Jack says.

"Sorry," I add, "we didn't mean to . . ." I stop. Shannon has shoved her arms behind her in an obvious effort to block our view of whatever she's holding. I slide the backpack off my shoulders and let it hit the floor with a thump. "What are you doing?"

"Nothing," Shannon says, too quickly.

I cross the space between us in three steps and yank Shannon's hands out in front of her. In one, she holds a swab of cotton, the white puff wet with the stink of alcohol. In her other hand, she holds an empty syringe.

09 ◄◄

A SURGE OF DIZZINESS DARKENS MY VISION.

"What are you doing?" I repeat.

Shannon lifts her face. All the nervousness she'd shown when we walked in has vanished, replaced by a desperate defiance. She lifts the syringe in a gesture of triumph.

"I'm saving him."

Cold settles against the back of my neck, an icy patch that inches its way along my spine. I drop to my knees beside Shannon, nearly knocking over the bottle I knew I would find. I snatch it up and stare at the black letters stamped on the label, begging them not to spell the one word I can't bear to read: *Aclisote*.

"You idiot," I say.

Shannon makes a grab for the bottle. I jump to my feet, raising the Aclisote out of her reach.

"Give it to me." Shannon lunges. I whirl away from her, leaping over KJ to get to the window. "No!" Shannon shrieks. "I need that." Her fingers close on my new coat, jerking me backward.

"Let me go!"

Jack dives across the room, and I hear Shannon grunt as he yanks her away from me. The tension on my coat abruptly loosens.

Dust billows around me as I clamber over a pile of rotting boxes to reach the window. Wrenching it open as wide as I can, I fling the bottle of Aclisote outside. Shannon screams. The clear plastic sails over a line of parked cars and hits the street below with a distant pop.

"You'll kill him," Shannon sobs. I turn around. Jack has both arms locked around her waist, although she's no longer fighting him. She hangs limply in his grasp, tears streaming down her cheeks.

"No," I say. The coldness tracing my spine sinks deeper, filling my whole body with ice. "You're the one who's killing him. How much Aclisote have you been feeding him?"

"Enough to keep him alive."

"Jesus," Jack says. "No wonder KJ's not getting better."

"Shannon." Terror makes it hard for me to form words. I'm shaking as I face her over KJ's inert body. "Tell me everything. I want dosages, frequency."

Shannon pushes herself free from Jack. Her lips are trembling, but her voice is firm.

"I told you. I've never tended anyone this sick by myself. All I know is that the staff increases your dosage. KJ was getting five and a half cc's twice a day for the last six months, so I've been giving him six."

I force my brain to calculate. I got sick after Dr. Barnard raised my dosage to five cc's, but KJ outweighs me by at least forty pounds, so he can handle more, right? Then again, I have naturally higher chronotin levels than he does. How much Aclisote does it take to kill someone? If Shannon had given him his usual dosage, would he have recovered by now? Or did the initial blast Barnard forced on him before we escaped weaken him so much that any amount after that is fatal?

"He won't be getting any more now," I say.

"Then he's going to die!" Shannon yells. "We both will."

"He won't," I say. "Look at me. Look at Jack. We're fine."

"You're not fine," Shannon says. "You're freaks. You freeze time and move things around. It's not supposed to be that way."

"Yes, it is," Jack says. "You'll see how natural it feels when it happens to you."

Shannon ignores him.

"Alex," she begs. "We have to get more Aclisote. Even if you're right, KJ's not strong enough to take a shock to his system. We need to wean him off it slowly."

I look down at the boy lying at our feet. Even all our shouting has failed to rouse him. What if KJ *is* too weak to recover? Years ago, in the Center, we all watched a video about heroin addiction, meant to teach us about the signs we might see in our police work. Former users talked about quitting, and one said withdrawal felt like the lowest circle of hell. Another said she felt like she had the flu for months after she quit, her body weak and shaky, her skin sensitive to touch. Aclisote isn't addictive, but what if the effects of stopping it are similar for someone this sick? In the state KJ is in, he'd never survive a cold, much less the flu.

"If you won't take him back," Shannon coaxes, "at least go and get more Aclisote. I won't hide what I'm doing anymore. We'll decide on a dosage together."

My hands are coated with dust from the window. I rub my palms on the thighs of my jeans, leaving behind streaks of dirt. What if weaning him slowly *is* the best way to save him? What if KJ dies because of my decisions?

A visceral memory of the night we kissed comes back to me, and for an instant, I can taste his lips against mine, hear the rumble of his voice, and feel the brush of his breath against my skin. It's like KJ himself stands beside me. Not the KJ stretched like a gray lump under dirty blankets, but the KJ who smells like spring grass and wants to know all about my day. That KJ believed in me. He'd wanted to stop taking Aclisote then. He'd still want to now, if he could choose.

I lift my chin. "No."

Tears shimmer at the edges of Shannon's eyes, eyes so dark with pain it's hard to look at her. KJ isn't the first boyfriend Shannon has lost. It was last year, after Steve's death, that Shannon devoted herself to helping at the clinic. *I won't let any spinner die alone*, she'd said.

My hands tighten against my jeans.

"This is the best way, Shannon. Really. You have to trust me."

"You wouldn't believe that if you were the one with him all day." Shannon's tears spill over onto her cheeks. "If it was you watching him fade away. You and Jack run around doing god knows what." She waves a hand to encompass our new outfits and all the bags spread out on the floor. "Shopping."

"We're not *shopping*. We're getting supplies. Things that *you* asked me to get."

Shannon's eyes drift away from mine.

I take a step toward her. "Is that why you never let me sit with him? Because you were worried I'd notice you were poisoning him?"

"It's not poison." Shannon wipes at her wet cheeks. "It's medicine."

Rage surges through me, a beast straining against the bounds of its leash.

"I should never have brought you here!" My hands are fists, knotted and trembling with the effort not to use them. "I should have left you at the Sick to die."

Shannon's eyes narrow. "If you don't want me here, then let me and KJ go home."

"Alex," Jack says. His voice holds a warning, and the idea that he might side with Shannon adds fuel to my fury.

"The Center is *not* home!" I shout at Shannon. "You're just refusing to see the truth."

"Alex!" Jack says again, louder this time.

"What?" I whirl, ready to take him on as well.

Victor is leaning against the armoire in the entrance to KJ's room.

The anger raging through me disappears as fast as it arrived, replaced by a cold fear that spreads all the way to the tips of my toes.

"So," Victor says, "you're spinners. I bet there are rewards for turning your type in."

My stomach twists.

"What are you doing here?" I ask.

Victor smirks. "I live here, remember?"

"But Elmer's . . . ?"

"Closed for the weekend. There's a sign taped to the front window. Family emergency."

I stare at him. Victor wears a greedy expression that reminds me of Ross the day I told him that my skills had changed. The memory makes the cramp in my stomach worse.

Faith steps out from behind Victor's shoulder. She wears the same washed-out blouse she had on the night we talked. A breath of hope lifts my anxiety. Faith, bringer of tea and comfort, the one who suggested I help the Society for Spinner Rights—surely she'll stick up for us now. I offer her a tentative smile.

"Is it true?" Faith's voice lacks even a hint of wispiness. My hope vanishes. Faith stamps her foot. "You're spinners?"

Shannon whimpers. She's dropped to her knees, one arm wrapped protectively around KJ's lolling head.

"Yeah," Jack says, "we're spinners. So what?"

Faith's upper lip curls as if she smells something rank. "And you didn't tell us? We let you stay here. Sleep near us." She jabs a finger at me with the force of a striking serpent. "Have you been spying on us?"

A reflexive shame, ingrained from a lifetime of Norms' taunts, flares across my cheeks.

"No, Faith, of course not."

Jack snorts. "Why would we want to spy on you? We can do much more interesting things than that." He disappears from his spot by the door, reappearing beside me at the foot of KJ's bed. In one hand, he dangles a wallet. "Like, say, this."

Victor slaps a hand against his back pocket. "What the hell?"

Jack flickers. The wallet materializes in Victor's other hand. Victor, unprepared to grasp a suddenly appearing object, drops it. Faith shrieks.

"Get out." She clutches Victor's arm. "You have to get out."

Victor bends to pick up his wallet, lips moving silently, as if he's working through a train of thought. Jack laughs. His eyes are bright. Wild. I reach for time, holding the strands just at the edge of my control.

Victor raises his head. "I thought spinners couldn't change anything in frozen time."

"So do lots of other people," Jack says. I step on his foot. Telling strangers our whole story can't be a good idea.

An ugly smile spreads across Victor's face. "So that's how you get money?"

"Yep." Jack walks over to the pile where we've dropped our stuff.

Holding one of the backpacks up over his head, he unzips a bulging pocket. Bills flutter down like confetti, drifting past his shoulders, sliding across the dirty floor. Shannon gasps. Victor laughs out loud.

"Here." I stoop down, scooping up a handful of fallen bills. "Here's five hundred dollars." I march over to Victor and thrust the wad of hastily counted cash toward him. Faith steps back at my approach. I don't look at her. "For the week. We won't stay any longer."

Victor eyes the money. "I don't think I like our deal anymore."

KJ's face floats before me, his skin so thin the veins underneath look like tiny rivers—rivers pumping poison through his body with every beat of his heart.

"You promised," I say to Victor. It takes effort to keep my voice steady.

Victor smiles. It's a wide smile showing too many teeth—like a shark's.

"So?" he says.

Shannon moans, her misery adding to the weight of responsibility threatening to crush me.

"You can't turn us in. We're too powerful," I bluff. "We can freeze time and . . ."

"I don't think our staying here is a problem, Alex," Jack says. "Not now that Victor sees how useful we can be."

A whole new set of worries climbs onto the mountain I'm already carrying.

Victor points to the bills littering the floor. "Just how much money do you have?"

Jack shrugs. "Don't know. We never counted it."

Victor's eyes gleam. "And you can get more?"

"I can get you anything you want," Jack says.

"No!" Faith and I say, in unison.

"It's too dangerous," I protest.

"I don't want them here!" Faith wails.

"Come on, Faith, think about it." Victor murmurs into her ear. The only words I catch are *everything we want* and *never go back*. Faith doesn't look happy, but eventually she nods. Victor bends down to scoop up the cash.

I grab Jack's arm.

"You can't do this," I whisper. "It's too risky."

"Oh, come on, what choice do we have?" He grins. "Besides, it'll be worth it."

"Worth it?" Every nerve in my body strains with the effort to not scream at him. "How can stealing a bunch of crap for Victor be worth it?"

The muscles in Jack's arm twitch. He pitches his voice low, an angry murmur that rattles my ear like an oncoming storm. "I don't know why *you* wanted to leave the Center, but I left so I could have a life." He pulls away from me. "If you want to spend your day panicking every five minutes, be my guest, but do it without me. I'm going to hang with Victor. With someone who can help me get where I want to go."

"And where is that?"

Jack looks at me like he's never seen me before.

"Music, Alex. If I'm going to get to have a life, I want to do something with it."

He bends down to help Victor collect the rest of the money. I watch the two of them, their matching spiky haircuts bobbing as they scoop up the scattered bits of paper. Victor laughs and punches Jack's shoulder. Jack beams.

I turn away. On the floor, KJ lies terrifyingly still. Shannon sits beside him in a crumpled heap. My anger reignites, burning through my despair. Ugly, brutal images of all the things I could do pop into my head. I can freeze time and tie Victor and Faith up so they can't report us. Beat Victor so badly he'll never threaten us again. I chew on my fingernail, picturing Victor crying, begging me for mercy.

A sighing sound makes me turn my head. Faith stands in the doorway, watching Victor and Jack with a worried expression. One hand covers her mouth; the other reaches toward her brother, as if she can see the images in my mind and wants to shield him.

My anger snuffs itself out. All my life I've resented the hateful way Norms perceive spinners. They call us treacherous, untrustworthy, crazy, and violent. *It's unfair,* I'd rant to KJ, puffed up with righteous indignation. *The Norms' doubts are based on nothing but an uneducated fear of the unknown. They have no right to make life-and-death decisions about us based on assumptions.* And now look at me. Free for a matter of days, and I'm already doing—or thinking about doing—everything that Norms accuse us of.

I wrap my arms around my chest. What is wrong with me?

Jack and Victor stroll out of the room, Jack talking animatedly about all the things they can do tomorrow, after he's had a chance to rest up. Faith drifts after them. I turn to Shannon. She's sitting cross-legged beside KJ, stroking his arm in a gentle rhythm. Regret at the way I yelled at her bows my head, and I clear my throat.

"Is there . . . anything I can get for him?"

Shannon shrugs. The misery on her face is so complete she doesn't seem to have room to still be mad at me.

"I don't know what to do," she says.

I slide down to sit on the floor on the other side of the room.

"Neither do I."

We sit together in awkward silence. Shannon's hand continues its steady caress. She's probably trying to figure out how to contact the Center. I trace an aimless pattern on the dusty floor. I'm going to have to start sleeping by KJ and Shannon. Jack and I can never leave the squat at the same time again. On top of being a robber and potential thug, I have now become my former roommate's jailer. The pigeons outside the window take up their mournful cooing. I am not the person I thought I was. When KJ wakes up—*if* KJ wakes up—will he understand the choices I've made? Will he even like the person I'm becoming? More importantly—do I?

10 ◄◄

SUNDAY DRAGS OUT SO SLOWLY IT FEELS LIKE IT'S LASTING a month. The week's bright fall sunshine sinks under a lowering blanket of clouds that alternate between dreary and wet. Moisture seeps through the squat's tired bricks. By late afternoon, the air feels dank, and the whole squat reeks of mold. KJ is still in a fever-tossed stupor, Shannon isn't speaking to me, and Jack took off with Victor around ten this morning and hasn't come back. I lie on my blankets, half watching the entrance to KJ's room to make sure Shannon doesn't sneak out, half trying to distract myself with a novel. It's not working.

I toss the book in the corner and pick up my phone. So far, all I've really paid attention to is how to call and text, but I know cell phones can do a lot more. I tap the rectangular white box in the middle of the screen and the words *search Google* pop up. I touch the box and a keyboard appears on the bottom part of the phone. Next to the flashing bar, it now says: *Search or type a URL*. I type "spinners" and hit enter.

The Secret Life of Spinners takes up all of the first few screens. It's getting good ratings, which is depressing, given that it portrays us as backstabbing torturers. The actor who looks like a psychopath is up for an award. I keep scrolling:

Spinner protest in DC turns violent

Congressional budget includes steep cuts to national CIC budget

Anti-abortion groups protest prenatal testing for chronotin

New Harvard study finds incidents of mental illness among spinner youth higher than previously reported

Northwest Division CIC set to close October 1

My thumb freezes over the final headline. I touch the screen and an article pops up.

Northwest Division CIC Set to Close October 1

Sept 16 The Northwest Region's Crime Investigation Center is set to close at the end of the month. In a statement issued to *The Oregonian*, Regional Director Virginia Chang said high levels of toxic mold have been discovered in the building, which make it unhealthy for residents and staff to continue living there. Most of the current inmates at the spinner institution will be dispersed among other Centers elsewhere in the country, though a few have opted to participate in a research project being carried out in the program's national office outside Tacoma. Police Chief Lamar Graham says the program will be "sorely missed. The partnership between the Portland Police Department and the CIC has been very successful and led to numerous arrests." There are no immediate plans to repair the Center's building, a former single room occupancy hotel in downtown Portland, which the program has occupied for the past twenty-seven years.

I read the article twice. *Closing . . . toxic mold . . . dispersed among other centers . . . research project.* Ross said Barnard was in trouble because so many spinners have escaped. Is this the consequence? The mold thing is probably just an excuse. I close my eyes and try to picture what the other Center kids are doing right now. It's Sunday afternoon, which means free time, so most of them will be in the common room. I imagine Yuki flipping through an out-of-date fashion magazine while she half-watches a rom-com on TV, Aiden and Raul arguing over a card game, Angel and Simon reading or playing a computer game . . . but that's all wrong. What I'm picturing is the past. This is a much different present, one where the five remaining fully qualified spinners are most likely huddled together, worrying about their futures, while the fifteen Youngers sit in their own common area, scared and confused.

If they all get scattered, how will I find them?

I jump to my feet and take five steps toward KJ's room before I stop. Jack isn't here. KJ can't hear my news. Shannon would only push harder to return to her friends. I go back to my blankets. Blackmailing Barnard is not going to work. I need to tell the other spinners the truth, get them to stop taking Aclisote, and help them plan a way to escape. But how do I break into the Center? And once the kids get out, where can they go? I can't bring them all to the squat. Even if Victor let them stay here, the Elmer's staff would surely notice.

Questions circle my brain so fast I can barely follow the trails of my own fears. I curl up on my blanket and try to think like KJ. He would take the problem apart logically, focusing on what he could control. I force the whirl of panic to settle. What part of this muddle can I tackle now? Center, Aclisote, shelter, warning, escape. One step. What's one step? Shelter. I let the single thought rise from the flurry.

108

We need a place to stay. It doesn't have to be perfect—it just has to be secure and hold twenty-four people.

I uncurl myself, find a pen, and start making a list.

Jack is not happy when I wake him up on Monday morning.

"What time is it?" he grumbles, squinting into the drizzle-gray light.

"Nine." I shake his shoulder again when his eyes start to drift. "I let you sleep in."

"Not when I went to bed at two thirty." He yawns. "You should have come last night. Victor picked out this amazing synthesizer he said he'd teach me to use, and then I snuck us all into this club and we heard, like, six bands. They were totally awesome."

"I'm sure they were," I say, not bothering to hide my irritation. "But we can't leave Shannon alone, remember?"

"Oh, right." Another yawn. "What are you doing today again?"

"Looking for a bigger squat." I yank the blankets off him before he gets too cozy.

"Where?"

I hold up the sheets of paper I tore out of the back of my book. Hours of Google searches have narrowed my list to motels that, based on their ratings, can't be too picky, plus some sketchy-sounding neighborhoods that might have some squat-appropriate buildings.

"I'm starting in Southeast," I tell Jack. "Tomorrow, I'll try Gresham, and then North Portland."

"Sounds like a plan." Jack stretches his arms over his head. "Good luck."

Six bus rides and five hours later, I am wet, hungry, and burdened with a thundering time headache. I'm also starting to realize that finding a place is going to take a *lot* of luck. I tried three motels, including a really divey one, and all of them refused to rent to me without ID. The woman at the third one asked me so many questions about my parents that I was certain she planned to call the cops the minute I left. After fleeing straight from her reception desk to an unlocked laundry closet, I froze time and walked a mile before letting it restart.

A replacement squat has so far proven equally elusive. Even supposedly depressed neighborhoods teem with activity, every building packed with people and surrounded by watchful neighbors. Twice, I found places that seemed possible until I froze time to check them out. One, an empty-looking house set back from a quiet road, turned out to be occupied by a very frail old man. The other, a boarded-up grocery store, had no windows or lights, which made entry nearly impossible and would have made living there even harder. It makes me understand why Victor and Faith are protective of the Elmer's warehouse. The sunlit space, with its working electricity and tiny half-bath, is starting to seem like a palace of comfort and security.

I trudge away from the boarded-up grocery store under an overcast sky. It isn't raining anymore, exactly, but the air sticks to my skin, soupy with damp. What are Shannon and KJ doing right now? Is Jack staying awake? Traffic zips past me, four lanes of drivers hunched as they squint through smeared windshields.

A block ahead, a bus stop looms out of the gray. It offers no shelter, just a metal post with the route number printed on it. I rub my arms to smooth the goose bumps popping up beneath my wet coat. The idea of climbing onto yet another bus and heading into more urban wasteland seems about as appealing as eating dirt.

Music drifts through the hum of traffic, cheerful guitar notes backed by lively drumming. Veering away from the bus stop toward the sound,

I discover a side street blocked off with a line of sawhorses. Painted signs hang from the barriers, with the words FARMERS MARKET and images of smiling vegetables dancing in a circle. People mill around on the other side, hefting canvas bags loaded with leafy sprays of greens. All around them, I see tables heaped with produce: lumpy potatoes, late-season tomatoes, carrots, and containers of fresh-picked berries.

Hunger rumbles in my stomach. I slip into the busy throng, accepting a sampling of sliced apples and a cracker topped with homemade salsa. KJ would love this place. The garden he'd kept at the Center provided us with some of our few opportunities for fresh vegetables. A smile twitches my lips as I picture him beside me, wandering through the bounty, smelling herbs, asking a vendor how she manages to grow kale so lush and green.

Suppressing images of the not-very-tasty groceries I bought for the squat, I hand over some of my stolen money in exchange for a freshly roasted sausage. It tastes even better than it smells. Taut skin bursts under my teeth, exploding savory deliciousness over my tongue. I plop onto an empty spot of curb to enjoy the sauerkraut-topped meat in comfort. The sausage is chewy, the sauerkraut a perfect tangy counterpart. I gobble another bite, lost in the pleasure of good food.

"Do you have a few minutes to save the sea lions?"

I start. A sandy-haired man stands in front of me, waving a clipboard in my direction.

"What?" I ask.

The man fixes me with an intense gaze. He's wearing loose cotton pants, woven sandals despite the chill, and a sweater someone must have knitted by hand. Or tried to knit. A smattering of holes betrays a number of dropped stitches.

"Almost a hundred sea lions a year are killed," he tells me, "simply because they are eating salmon, their natural prey."

I wipe mustard off my mouth with a squashed napkin. "Um, that's too bad."

"You can help prevent this tragedy." The man pulls a flyer from a hemp bag draped across his body and hands it to me. There are two pictures. The top one shows a sea lion sunning itself on a large rock, its mouth hanging open in a gaping smile. The bottom one shows another sea lion. This one slumps on a block of concrete, its head covered in red from a bullet hole clearly visible in its skull.

"What we're asking is that you join our organization," the man says. "The dues are only thirty dollars per year, but even more importantly, with all of our names together, we can make a statement that the legislature won't be able to ignore."

I give him back the flyer. "Sorry. I can't . . ." I start to say I can't give out my name, then switch midstream to say, "afford that."

The man's enthusiasm clicks off like a light switch. "Would you like to sign anyway?" he asks, so half-heartedly I can tell he's given up on me.

"No," I say. The bloodied sea lion gazes at me reproachfully.

I watch the man walk away with a vague sense of shame and am relieved when someone calls to him. The man hustles over to greet a woman in a long, printed skirt who is standing behind a table a few yards from me. Through the throng of people passing between us, I watch them chatting. They seem to know each other well, hugging when they meet and laughing while they talk. What would it be like to live life so lightly? To be able to blend seamlessly into a crowd. To spend your days nestled in a web of friends and acquaintances.

I take another bite of my lunch and study the pair surreptitiously while I chew. Unlike the other vendors at the market, this woman is manning one of a row of tables that offer flyers rather than food. Each person in the row promotes a different cause. I tilt my head to better read the signs attached to each table: ONLY ORGANICS; SUPPORT FREE TRADE IN GUATEMALA; STOP MANDATORY WATER FLUORIDATION; JOIN THE SOCIETY FOR SPINNER RIGHTS.

I choke on my sausage. The Society for Spinner Rights? That's the group that fought for us to have allowances, encouraged Centers to include outdoor spaces, and passed legislation requiring that newborn spinners be assigned ethnically appropriate names. Small wins, sure, but maybe they did other things, too. Like help spinners who are free. I shove the last of my sausage down without tasting it. In my head, I see KJ awake and healthy, his eyes gleaming with pride when I tell him I figured out a way to keep all the spinners safe.

Brushing bits of curb dirt from my butt, I stroll down the aisle of tables, making a show of studying the materials at each one. A flame burns in my chest, something between excitement and nerves. Life at the Center hasn't provided much opportunity to practice talking to strangers. I nod politely while a tall woman explains that drinking fluoride every day lowers children's IQ. Then I chew on a roasted coffee bean harvested from an eco-farm in the mountains of Guatemala.

I approach the Society for Spinner Rights table with feigned casualness. This table has three types of flyers, all laid out in neat stacks. I pick up each one in turn. The first is topped with the Portland Police Department seal and lists some crimes that have been solved with spinners' help. The bottom has a tagline that says: *Always report suspicious activity within three days. Call the Crime Tips Hotline.* The second flyer shows a picture of a girl standing next to a police officer with the words "CHILD LABOR" across the top. The last one has a banner headline proclaiming *Spinner Rights Are Human Rights* printed over a picture of a group of people holding signs. Memory kicks in. The picture is the same one I saw on the TV news story about the dead spinners in Puerto Rico. I'd assumed at the time that the public reaction was a protest against spinners, but looking more carefully now I see the signs indicate support: NEGLECT = MURDER. One screams: SAVE OUR CHILDREN. WHAT IF THAT KID WAS YOURS? Hope fans the flame in my chest.

"So what does your group do?" I ask the woman working at the table. She's young, with light-brown hair hanging in a frizzy mass past her shoulders. Her eyes are brown, too, and her nose is thin, with a little pinkness around the edges that gives her a rabbity look.

"We work to improve the living conditions of the spinners in our city," the woman says.

I flip the sheet over. On the back is a description of the founder of the Society next to a picture of an older man with dark-framed glasses and a goatee. The text says he's devoted his life to helping spinners. I peer at the black-and-white photo, trying to judge whether the person behind those heavy glasses knows enough to offer help.

"How do you improve conditions for them?" I ask Rabbit Lady.

"Right now, we're working on a campaign to bring entertainers into the Centers. Like the USO tours for the army, you know?"

The flame in my chest sputters. Bring *entertainment* to the Centers? How is that supposed to help us? Rabbit Lady must interpret my expression as disapproval because she launches into a prepared speech about how spinners are important members of our society and very misunderstood.

"And it's not even true that they're dangerous," she concludes, "no more than a pit bull is a naturally dangerous animal. As long as they're trained and kept medicated, they're perfectly safe."

I twist the handful of flyers I'm holding into a tight roll and jam them in my pocket. She thinks spinners are like *pit bulls?* The woman's arm is pale and lightly freckled, thin-boned and fragile. A growl tickles the back of my throat. That skin would feel soft in a dog's jaws, the blood beneath it warm and tasting of metal. Her bones would crack easily, they would . . .

Rabbit Lady holds out a clipboard, like the one the sea lion guy offered me. "Would you like to sign our petition?"

I push away the gruesome fantasy with a shake of my head. "What's the petition for?"

"When we get a thousand signatures, we're going to send it to the regional director." Rabbit Lady leans toward me, like she's sharing a secret. "It's too bad the Portland office is closing. The local CIC director is a really good guy. He's accepted lots of our suggestions."

Anger sweeps through me so violently my vision blurs. This woman—a person who claims to want to help us—thinks our murderer is *a really good guy?* At least the people who hate us extend their wrath to our institution and its leaders. This woman actually admires Barnard. I lunge for the clipboard.

Rabbit Lady looks startled. By the way her eyes are flicking around, I'm guessing she's decided that talking to me was a poor decision. I snatch the clipboard and scrawl my real name across the signature line. In the spot for an address, I write the Center's. Let Barnard see that. Let him know I'm out here—free, alive, and helping the activists, however stupid the petition's goal is.

"Thanks?" Rabbit Lady says, easing the clipboard from my rigid fingers. I glower at the innocent paper, wishing that my hate could turn the ink into poison. Then when the sheet finally lands in Barnard's hand, the poison would seep into his skin and kill him.

"What's your name?" the woman asks.

I shift my burning gaze from the clipboard to Rabbit Lady's face. She's holding the clipboard close to her nose, trying to make out my signature with a frown of concentration. As quickly as my rage flared, it is now doused.

"Why does it matter?" I edge away from the table.

Rabbit Lady studies me like she's trying to read me the same way she tried to read my signature.

"If they can't make it out," Rabbit Lady says, "the signature doesn't count."

I take another step toward the crowd.

"My name is Alice."

"Really?" Rabbit Lady peers at the signature again. "It looks more like an *x* than an *e* at the end."

"Forget it." There's sweat gathering on my upper lip. "I shouldn't have signed. Just cross it out."

"Hey," she says, her voice serious. "Wait."

I don't. Turning on my heel, I dive into the market, nearly knocking over a stack of fresh corn in my rush to get away. From behind me, I can hear Rabbit Lady calling me to come back. Through the jumble of sound, I can't make out whether she's saying "Alice" or "Alex." People are everywhere, blocking my path, no matter which way I turn. Are they doing it on purpose? I dodge in front of an immensely pregnant woman, who frowns at me.

"Sorry," I mutter. People are definitely staring at me now. I tilt my head to avoid eye contact and hustle through the crowd. Beads of sweat trickle down the back of my neck. When I reach the market's perimeter barrier, I clear it in a single giant leap and race for the bus stop.

The bus is pulling in just as I get there, and I leap, panting, through the open doors. The driver looks from me to the fare box with the eternal patience of a rock. I dig in my pocket, scattering coins onto the floor in my rush to pick out the correct fare. My back tingles with the sensation of someone watching me. I peek over my shoulder. Rabbit Lady is just down the street, struggling to get past a large family who are taking up most of the sidewalk. In one hand, she holds a cell phone pressed against her ear.

Fear makes me clumsy. I stuff money into the box, leaving the fallen change for anyone who wants it. *Come on, bus, go, go, go.* I lurch into a pair of empty seats part way down the aisle. The doors close with a tired hiss and the bus groans away from the curb.

Rabbit Lady slides past the smudged plastic windows. I slink down low in my seat, hoping against hope she didn't see where I went. How could I have been so astoundingly stupid? I've told Jack a hundred times to lay low and not make a scene, and then I go announce my real name to a spinner-related group and recklessly shove my way through crowds of people. This is exactly the kind of behavior wipers would track. I hit my forehead against the window.

What if the whole Society for Spinner Rights is set up to draw in desperate spinners? And I just walked straight into their trap? I rub the sweat on my upper lip. If Rabbit Lady called a wiper, how long would it take for one of them to track me down? I scan the people outside my window. A woman pushing a stroller glances at the bus, then pulls out a cell phone. A bicyclist zooms out of an alley so fast he almost knocks over a couple crossing the street. The door to a store pops open, and a man in a red apron hurries outside, his head turning left and right as he searches for something. Or someone.

The air in the bus grows stuffy. I feel like I'm floating between two parallel worlds, one pleasantly innocuous, the other rife with danger. Is the guy dozing under his headphones across the aisle really sleeping, or is he watching me? My fingertip is in my mouth, the nail shredding under the nervous grind of my teeth. What if the wipers have special technology that alerts them whenever someone stops time? They could follow the trail of my freezes, and it would lead them straight to the squat.

My mind brushes the time strands floating around me. The freeze waiting behind their endless drifting calls to me like a sanctuary. If I got off the bus and stopped time right now, I could race to the squat in zero real time. I dig the phone from my pocket and tap on the map feature. The squat is over four miles away, which means I'd have to hold time for at least an hour. Even if I *could* hold time that long, I'd be so exhausted when I got there, I'd be worthless if anything went wrong.

A motorcycle zooms into the lane next to the bus with an angry roar. All my failures rain down like a load of rocks: not finding a new place to live, running through a mob of people, signing that useless petition. The fingernail in my mouth tastes like mustard, adding extra vividness to the memory of the farmers market fiasco. My body tilts forward as the bus pulls up at a red light. The motorcycle squeals to a halt beside it. KJ's face floats before me, his eyes not lit with pride, but rather dark with disappointment. I bite down so hard on my nail, I draw blood.

The motorcyclist drops one leg to the ground to wait out the light. He's dressed head to foot in black leather and radiates the sinister aura of that robot guy in the Terminator movies. I watch him pull out a phone and flick through the screens. When he raises his head to scan the length of the bus, his mirrored sunglasses flash. My chest clenches. Is it my imagination, or does the man's gaze pause when it reaches my face?

The light changes and the bus grinds forward. My heart is beating so hard it clogs my throat. Did I imagine the rider's interest in me? He's still beside the window, keeping steady pace with the bus's lumbering crawl. What if this is the person Rabbit Lady phoned?

A blinker clicks, and the bus pulls to a slow stop in the middle of the block. The man on the motorcycle veers toward the curb. I stand up so I can see out the front window. The biker has shut off his engine and is hurrying toward the bus's now open doors. Terror blanks out my brain. If he gets on, I'll have nowhere to hide. He could slide a leash on me.

The man steps onto the bus. He has his helmet tucked under one arm and is obviously scanning the occupants, stopping instantly when he sees me, still standing smack in the middle of the bus. Our eyes lock.

"Alex," the man says.

Instinct overwhelms thought. I bolt for the bus's back door. Harsh diesel fumes envelop me as I shove my way outside. I sprint across the sidewalk and plunge into the thick leaves of a hedge. Branches catch at my hair, tear my skin. I struggle through them, scrambling until I reach a spot between the hedge's green shelter and a parked car on the other side. My brain is spinning so fast I can barely concentrate enough to grab time.

Blessed silence takes over the world. I huddle in the frozen quiet, listening to the ragged gasps of my breath. Leaves tangle my hair. My cheek stings where a branch must have scratched it. I stand up on shaky legs.

The motorcyclist has left the bus. He's standing on the sidewalk just outside the door, head turned in the direction of my panicked flight. A wave of nausea threatens the sausage in my belly. I try to memorize what he looks like, but with my fear and the distance between us, I can't absorb more than the most superficial impressions: Hispanic male, slim build, straight brown hair long enough to brush his collar. Remembering the inexplicable break in my freeze when I was at Barnard's, I tiptoe around the hedge, making a huge detour to avoid the bus and the biker.

I run down the middle of the road in frozen time. When my head starts hurting so badly I can barely focus, I duck into someone's garage, melt time, and pull out my phone so I can navigate side streets. Two blocks later, a truck driver slows to ask me directions, and I fail to stifle a small scream, startling an old lady out power walking.

All through my stumbling trek back to the squat, only one thought runs over and over through my head: the wipers are here, and they're after us.

The crumbling masonry of the squat no longer promises security. The dark windows hide any hint of what is happening behind those silent walls. Have KJ and Shannon already been discovered? Is someone lurking there in the dim light, waiting to grab me the second I step inside?

I wrangle the last shreds of my energy so I can stop time. It wavers under my control, the threads so fine I know I have only minutes before they slide away. I climb the ladder as quickly as my exhausted legs will carry me. No obvious clues offer either solace or confirmation of an intruder—no trace of running footprints in the dust, no obviously askew object betraying a struggle. I creep forward a few steps. Jack is sitting in the kitchen, the picture of relaxed boredom—one hand sunk in a bag of potato chips and his head bent over the screen of his phone. Time wriggles away from me.

"We need to leave the squat right away," I announce, before Jack has a chance to do anything except start at my sudden appearance.

"What?" Jack says, so loudly my head throbs. "Why?"

"I think I've been followed."

He jumps to his feet, his head whipping around to search the room's duskier corners. "And you led them *here*?"

"Not on purpose! But what if they can trace us?"

Jack frowns. "Who could have traced you?"

It takes a supreme effort to not scream at him.

"There was this man. He followed me onto a bus. He knew my *name*." The man's voice echoes in my ears, insistent, eager. I swallow. "I know he's a wiper, and I was thinking—what if wipers know when we freeze time? They could follow the freezes and trace me back here."

"Alex." Jack sits down again. "Think it through. If the wipers could sense when we froze time they would have caught us days ago."

The logic of Jack's words refuses to penetrate my brain. How can he sit there talking when we should be evacuating right this very instant?

"Well, what if the wipers use spinners? They could rewind my whole day and find us that way."

Jack makes a dismissive gesture. "What happened after you saw this guy?"

"I froze time," I say. "And ran."

"Then he couldn't have followed you. Even if he called a spinner and they waited until now to do a rewind, all they'd see was you disappearing. They'd have no idea where to look to pick up your trail again."

The words take a second to sink in, and when they do, a little of the terror wrapping my body eases. I froze a lot today, enough that anyone rewinding it would lose my trail multiple times.

Jack cracks his knuckles. "Did you find another place for us to stay?"

I shake my head. My legs are shuddering visibly now, the uncontrollable trembling of released adrenaline. I sink to the floor, massaging the quivering muscles.

"We need to warn the other spinners right away. We have to get out of here. We'll look for a place somewhere . . ." I raise my head.

"What is it?"

"Did you hear that?" I whisper.

"That's just Victor walking around."

"No—listen—someone is talking."

Jack's mouth opens, then closes. We both hold very still. I hear the sound again, and this time I can tell it's coming from KJ's corner. I'm on my feet again, even though my legs are shaking so badly I'm not certain they'll hold me. There are two voices, one male and one female. I can't hear what they're saying, but I am absolutely sure it's not Faith and Victor.

"Were you watching Shannon?" I whisper to Jack. "The whole time I was gone?"

"Yeah." Jack shoots a guilty look at the chips. "Pretty much."

Prickles crawl over my skin. I underestimated Shannon, and overestimated Jack. She must have managed to sneak out. Who's over there? Ross? Barnard? Wipers? I tiptoe forward, Jack at my heels. Time barely trembles when I brush it. I still haven't recovered. If I can even stop time, I won't be able to control it for long. The male voice speaks again. Shannon laughs.

Jack and I creep up to the armoire and peer around it. There *are* two people in the room. One is Shannon, kneeling in her usual spot beside the bed. The other is KJ. I take a gulp of air. KJ is not sleeping. He isn't tossing and turning, either. KJ is sitting, propped against a pile of pillows, his face shining at me as I burst into the room.

11 ◀◀

JOY SHOOTS THROUGH ME WITH THE FORCE OF AN exploding firework.

"KJ!"

My best friend gives me a wobbly smile.

"Alex?" he croaks. No wonder I didn't recognize his voice.

I sink to the floor on the opposite side of the bed from Shannon. I want to throw my arms around his neck, kiss him, and tell him how much I missed him. But I can't, not with Shannon sitting a few feet from me, beaming at KJ with her whole heart in her eyes. My smile trembles. I realize I wanted KJ to recover so desperately that I'd never allowed myself to picture anything past the moment when he gained consciousness. Now that it's happening, I feel like I'm stepping into a brand-new world, one where I'm not really sure of the rules.

I pick up KJ's warm fingers and squeeze them between my cold ones.

"How do you feel?" I ask. A stupid question—mundane and meaningless.

"OK," KJ answers. "Tired."

"He just woke up five minutes ago." Shannon smooths the covers over KJ's chest possessively. "It's like a miracle."

I swallow the *I-told-you-so* that dances onto my tongue.

KJ's eyes roam around the room, taking in the stacks of boxes and piles of furniture. They stop at the figure hovering in the doorway.

"Jack?"

Jack grins. "Hey, buddy."

KJ's head swivels back toward me. "Who else is here?"

"Just us four," I say.

"Where are we?"

Shannon purses her lips. "They call it the *squat*."

"It's a warehouse," Jack explains. "I knew these street kids from before. They've been letting us stay with them."

"Victor and Faith," I say. "They live here, too. They know about us."

KJ's hand hangs limply within my own. I remember how I'd felt when I first woke up from the sickness: confused, exhausted, and very weak.

"You hungry?" I ask him.

KJ nods gratefully. "Starving."

Shannon takes KJ's other hand.

"He should eat something light," she says. "Maybe some chicken broth or Jell-O."

KJ looks down at their linked fingers, then back at me. A frown forms between his brows. I wonder how much KJ remembers about the time before he'd fallen sick, and I'm not sure what makes me more nervous—that KJ will think he and Shannon are still an item, or that he'll blurt out that they aren't.

"There's some food in the kitchen," I say. "I can make you something."

KJ opens his mouth, clearly full of questions. Shannon puts a finger against his lips.

"Shhh," she says, "no more talking. What you have to do right now is rest. I'll fill you in on everything later."

I squeeze KJ's hand and stand up. KJ slumps back against the pillows, the frown still wrinkling his brow. Shannon's hand slides from his lips to caress his cheek. Her face is shimmering with a happiness I can't bear to witness. I watch her moving fingers, so pale against the newly healthy dark of KJ's skin. Something ugly rears its head inside me. Running away together was *our* plan—mine and KJ's. *We* are the ones who figured out the Center was rotten. *We* are the ones who deserve a cozy reunion.

I force myself to swallow my jealousy. I used Shannon's affection to get her here; it's not fair to resent her for it now. At some point, she'll find out he prefers me and . . . a twist of discomfort dims my happiness. And we'll all have to deal with that later. Cradling the blissful fact of KJ's recovery close inside my chest, I slip out of the room to get him some food.

The four of us eat dinner on the floor around KJ's bed. By Shannon's decree, we keep the conversation light, which, surprisingly, works. Jack makes macabre jokes about how horrible KJ looked when he was sick. Shannon laughs and never once mentions the Center. I read an article out loud from the newspaper about a kid who rescued a herd of wild horses. KJ listens to everyone with a half-focused gaze, leaning back against the pillows and yawning a lot. By the time Jack pulls out his guitar to plunk out the few cords he's learned, KJ is fast asleep.

"In the morning we should wash his sheets," Shannon says, as we carry our dinner mess back to the kitchen.

"It's easier to just get new ones." Jack glances at his watch. It's full-on dark now, the only illumination coming from the glow of the streetlights outside the window.

Shannon drops some trash into a garbage bag and picks up the coffee maker. Dried residue from KJ's broth crusts the sides.

"I'll wash up," she offers.

"Thanks," I say, and then with a rush of answering generosity, add, "I'll go out early in the morning and pick up a real breakfast."

Shannon nods and carries the dishes off to the bathroom. Jack checks his watch again.

"I'm heading out," he says. "Victor has studio time tonight, and we're going to try the new synthesizer."

I fish a cookie out of the bag and nibble on it. Jack heading out into the night ignites a litany of worries, but the fear feels muted under the glow of KJ's resurrection, so I offer only a few mild cautions. Jack promises to be careful to cover his tracks, and he vanishes.

I put away the rest of the food. It's not that late, but the whiplash emotions of this long day have worn me out, so I head over to my sleeping space. *KJ's awake.* I take off my sweater and pull on the T-shirt I've been sleeping in. Without the numbing dread of KJ's possible death, my mind feels free in a way it hasn't since we left the Center. I know most of our problems haven't changed, but for the first time it feels like things are actually turning in our favor.

I wriggle out of my jeans and drape them over a broken lamp, freeing a roll of paper that flops to the floor—the flyers I picked up at the farmers market. I unfold the pages and flip through the crumpled sheets. Coffee beans, organic apples, fluoride. I smooth out the last one. The Portland Police logo is smeared from rain and rough treatment, but the tagline at the bottom is readable, even with the limited glow from the streetlights: *Call the Crime Tips Hotline.*

It was just over a week ago that Ross and I broke into a place called

Tom's Bar and found evidence that proved its owner was the elusive Sikes. At the time, I believed Ross and I were a team and that we were on the verge of arresting Portland's most notorious criminal. An echo of my euphoria in that moment washes over me. Arresting Sikes was vital to me then—an undeniable achievement that would give my restricted life meaning. I study the paper in my hand. Ross and I aren't a team, and my life is no longer counted out in months, but that doesn't mean I can't finish the job I started.

My phone is charging next to my bedroll. I unplug it and dial the hotline.

"Hello?" I say, after a recorded voice invites me to leave any information I have to offer about an active crime. "I'm calling about Sikes?" My voice sounds squeaky and way too young. I clear my throat. "I work at a place called Tom's Bar, and I was in the owner's office putting something back in his safe, and there was this envelope labeled like receipts or something, but it didn't have receipts in it." I'm talking too fast. I lick my lips, visualizing exactly what I saw so that I can describe it accurately. "There was a painting in there. Sunflowers. I'm certain it was one of the ones Sikes stole. Matt—that's the owner's name, Matt Thompson—he doesn't know I found out, and I thought, well, I thought I should report it. So you can follow up." I add the combination to the safe, a number that is still burned in my memory. "Thanks."

I hang up. The phone rests in my hand. It's shaking a little bit, and for a split second, I think it's on vibrate and the hotline is calling me back, until I realize it's my hand that's quivering. I did it. I turned in Sikes.

I plug the phone back into its charger and climb into bed. Dark settles around me. It's not pitch black, but merely soft gray, which is somehow comforting, just like the rustling of the birds outside my window, and the gentle sigh of KJ's even breath. I close my eyes. Soon, the cops will know who the terrible Sikes really is. It might take a couple days, but they are sure to follow up, and when they do, they'll find what they need to put Sikes in jail for a really long time. This is justice—real justice—not Ross's twisted imitation. I smile to myself as I drift off to sleep. KJ is recovering, and I have finally done something that is unequivocally good.

12 ◀◀ *CARSON ROSS*

ROSS DOESN'T NOTICE THE MESSAGE ON HIS PHONE until he's pulled into the precinct's underground garage. From the time stamp, he guesses Barnard must have called while he was in the shower. Ross skips the elevator and hurries up the steps that lead into the building from the garage while he replays the voicemail. Tuesday's eight a.m. briefing is in three minutes, and he's already been late twice this month.

"Hi, Carson. I checked the call sheet this morning, and there's a mission on it related to Sikes. It's to a place called"—Barnard's computer keys click in the background—"Tom's Bar over on SE Oak. Seems an employee called in an anonymous tip. Claims she saw a stolen painting in his office safe. Probably a crank, but you asked me to pass along whatever I heard. They assigned the case to Agent Marquez. He'll be here to pick up Raul at eleven."

Ross stops dead on the second-floor landing. An employee saw the Van Gogh? That's impossible. Sikes would never have been that careless. But then who . . . ? Ross puts his hand out and steadies himself against the bannister. Alex! It has to be. The two of them are the only people besides Matt Thompson who know about the contents of the safe. A tiredness that has nothing to do with lack of sleep settles on Ross's shoulders. How could Alex do this to him? She knows that unmasking Sikes is a career-making arrest for him. Calling it in anonymously won't even get her any credit for it. Ross leans against the metal railing. The renovations to his hideaway are now complete. He'd planned to nab Alex after the briefing; now, he'll have to find a way to stop Marquez's mission from succeeding first. But how? If he goes to Tom's Bar now, he'll be seen in Raul's rewind.

"You OK there, Carson?"

Ross's head jerks up. Police Chief Lamar Graham is walking down the stairs toward him, one hand clasping the sheaf of notes he uses to lay out the day's assignments.

"Staff meeting is this way," Chief says.

"Sorry." Ross forces himself to smile. "I was just going to run back and get my jacket out of my car. It's supposed to pour all day."

"You can get it after the meeting." Chief holds up his stack of papers. "There's a lot going on in the city this morning."

Ross's smile stiffens. He should have claimed he was sick. He sneaks a glance at his watch. The briefing will last at least an hour, which doesn't leave much time to figure a way out of this mess.

Chief pushes open the door to the hall, giving Ross no choice but to follow.

"How's that last rewound murder case coming?" Chief asks. "You identify the guy who shoved that woman into the basement?"

"Almost." Frustration makes it hard for Ross to act naturally. He wants to slam his fist into a wall. "I'm checking out the suspect's alibi, to make sure the case is rock-solid before turning it over to the DA."

"Well, pick up the pace, because the mayor is pushing me for results. She wants the spinner program to go out on a high note." Chief shakes his head. "No idea why. That Center has been a pain in the city's butt since it opened. I am not going to miss the protests and crazy rumors. Who you got pegged for the murder?"

"The rewind wasn't very clear," Ross says, "but it's looking like Joseph Sully."

"Sully? Never took him for a violent type." Chief claps Ross on the shoulder. "Guess you never know about people, do you?"

Ross, unable to think up an appropriately pleasant expression, hides his face by stepping back to open the door for his boss.

The briefing room is crowded, and as usual, the building's HVAC system fails to compensate for the mass of humanity warming the space. Ross can already feel his shirt sticking to his back by the time he takes a seat at an almost-empty table at the rear of the room. He doesn't realize until after he chooses it that he's sharing space with Jim Cannon. Officer Cannon, who has butted heads with Ross on more than one occasion, makes a pointed effort to move his chair away when Ross sits down. Jerk. After Ross becomes Chief of Police, Cannon will definitely be on the list of folks to weed out.

Chief Graham brings the meeting to order and starts droning out the latest crises: a drive-by shooting that made a splash in the press, a council member's demand that they roust more of the homeless people who sleep along the waterfront, updated protocols for their final time missions. Ross listens with half an ear while his mind worries about his more personal problem. He can't stop the rewind, but he can get rid of the physical evidence, which should at least slow down the investigation. With Alex nearly in his grasp, all he needs is a couple of days. Who can he send to empty the safe? It has to be someone he has leverage over. Someone who could toss the office and make it look like a burglary. Someone like . . . Joseph Sully.

Laughter ripples through the overheated room, presumably at some joke Chief made. Ross joins in with an extra hearty chuckle. Joseph Sully meets every criterion—he's a shifty character with a history of breaking and entering. The guy even has a day job loading boxes at a warehouse, so it won't be hard to track him down. Just like it won't be hard to convince him to help, not when Ross can offer him a deal that he can't afford to refuse. He'll tell Sully he's been pegged for murder but that if he follows a few simple instructions, Ross will see to it that he only goes down for criminal mischief.

Chief moves on to the day's assignments. Ross relaxes into his chair, rocking it onto its back legs. The rewind will put Sully in Tom's Bar, but even if they track him back to a conversation with Ross, it won't matter. Ross has a legitimate reason for talking to him. He'll tell Chief that Sully's alibi worked out and peg the murder on Fred Watson instead. He's never liked that guy much either. And if anything goes sideways, he can clean it up later on. He'll have Alex back, and a short freeze can add or delete any evidence Ross needs to make his accusations stick.

Ross brings his chair back down on all four legs and slides his phone out of his pocket, opening the tracking app under the shelter of the table. The ruse with the business card has worked even better than he'd hoped. Not only did he discover the kids' hiding place, but Alex has kept his business card with her this whole time, allowing him to track her wanderings around the city. It seems she freezes fairly often, too, which is good, because it means she's getting worn down.

"Agent Ross?" Chief's voice cuts through Ross's musings. He tilts the phone against his leg to cover any telltale glare.

"Yes, sir?"

"Agent Mullins is out on vacation the rest of the week, so I'll need you to cover her beat in Old Town."

"Beat work?" Ross hates beat work. Especially in Old Town. All the crazy people hang out there. "I'm a detective, sir."

"A time detective," Chief says, "for a program that is ending. I'm going to be looking at reassignments for all of you in the next couple of weeks."

The phone in Ross's hand buzzes, the signal that the app has connected with the tracker. Ross presses the screen against his leg to muffle it.

"I've got some active cases that need my attention."

"Understood," Chief says. "I don't expect you to be in Old Town all day; just stop by a few times so the locals see a presence, all right?"

"Yes, sir."

Jim Cannon smirks. Ross waits until Chief is occupied with an officer on the other side of the room before he lifts his hand and studies the small screen. The blue dot tells him Alex is tucked away in her hideout. Ross clicks off the phone. The Old Town assignment is an insult. He'll do the minimum, but no more. As soon as he gets the Sully thing sorted out, he'll go and find Alex. She's likely to try to evade him, but she can't run forever. He'll just keep showing up until she's too exhausted to freeze. By early afternoon, Alex will be his, and after that, his real future will start—a future that does not involve the Old Town beat or Officer Cannon or being told what to do by soon-to-be-ex–Police Chief Lamar Graham.

13 ◀◀

I WAKE TO THE SOUND OF RAIN, A STEADY DOWNPOUR turning the windows into gray blurs. I rub my eyes, trying to scrub away the dream that woke me—a dream filled with endless visions of faceless pursuers. "KJ's awake," I whisper. The words, so magical last night, fail to entirely remove the dread filling every cell of my body. I roll out of bed. Food will help. A real breakfast shared with my best friend, who will use his logical brain to help smooth out the tangles blocking our future.

I'm smiling when I walk into the kitchen. At least I am until I see Shannon standing at the counter and humming to herself as she measures out fresh coffee.

"Good morning, sleepyhead." Her smile is blinding. "We were hoping you'd be up soon. Weren't you going to go out and get us something to eat? KJ and I are starving."

Last night's bliss shrivels a little bit more.

"I'll go ask KJ what he wants to eat," I say.

"Eggs." Shannon states with annoying certainty. "And you can't go in there right now. He's getting dressed." She pours water into the coffee maker and presses the Brew button. "Hey, while you're out, do you mind picking up a few other things we need?"

The words *do your own stupid errands* dance on my tongue, and I press my lips together to keep from blurting them out.

"Sure," I say.

Shannon hands me a list and goes back to her happy song, either totally oblivious to my irritation or else choosing to take my gruffness for sleepiness. I put on my coat and head down into the spiked arms of the blackberries.

The checkout guy at the mini-mart looks up when I step inside. I hurry down the nearest aisle, not sure if his attention is friendly welcome or mistrustful scrutiny. Luckily, Shannon's list is short: ibuprofen, a loaf of bread, cream cheese, toilet paper, half-and-half, and a bag of oranges. At the counter, I add candy bars and a newspaper. KJ likes doing crossword puzzles.

The bell over the door jangles as I'm collecting my change. I duck my head instinctively before recognizing the people standing in the doorway.

"Jack!"

Jack's body shifts, only slightly, but enough that I realize I've startled him so much he froze time. I glance at the clerk. He's sliding the drawer shut on the register and doesn't seem to have noticed anything unusual.

"Alex." Jack rubs his forehead. "You're up early."

I pick up my grocery bag and hurry over. "Have you been out all night?"

Jack nods. Victor shakes himself, scattering raindrops all over the floor.

"I'm getting a soda," he announces, wandering toward the

refrigerator section. Jack glances over my shoulder and I follow his gaze. The clerk is watching us.

"Grab me a soda, too, OK?" Jack calls to Victor. He rubs his head again. "Something with caffeine in it."

I study Jack's face more carefully. Tension pinches the corners of his mouth downward, and his eyes are skipping around the room as if he's checking the perimeter. I take his arm and usher him to a spot deeper in the store, stopping next to a rack of postcards.

"How'd it go last night?" I ask.

"OK. The studio was great, but then Victor wanted to get some stuff and . . ." Jack spins the rack of postcards. Pictures of mountains and city skylines twirl in a fuzzy whirl. "Tell me again what Ross said about the wipers?"

A weight settles in my stomach, heavy, cold, and depressingly familiar. "Was someone following you?"

"I don't know." Jack scans the store again. "Mostly I just felt weird. Victor would want me to freeze time, and I'd try to find a place we could hide and nothing seemed safe enough. And there was this one guy." Jack shivers. The cold in my stomach spreads up to fill my chest.

"What did he look like?" I ask.

"I don't know. I didn't really get a good look at him." Jack waves his hands like he's brushing away flies. "It was probably nothing."

The cooler door in the back of the store slams and I hear the clump of Victor's boots as he stomps back toward us. I bend my head close to Jack's.

"Where's Faith?"

He shrugs. "She refuses to be in a freeze, so Victor gave her some money and she went off on her own. Buying drugs, I assume."

Victor's footsteps come closer.

"What if she tells someone about us?"

"Victor promised she wouldn't."

My chewed-up fingernail is back in my mouth, not at all comforted by a secondhand promise. Victor clomps up beside me. He smells like grimy clothes overlaid with expensive aftershave. On his back, the pack we'd bought the other day bulges.

"You buying?" he grunts, holding up two giant bottles of soda. I want to tell him to pay for it himself since he took most of our money, but I'm afraid he'll whip out a stack of hundreds or spill stolen loot on the counter when he opens the pack. I pull a crumpled five-dollar bill from my pocket and carry the two sodas over to the clerk. When I bring them back, Victor twists the top off his drink and takes a deep gulp. He doesn't thank me.

Outside, the rain still gushes. I peer through the downpour, searching through the cascade of wet for any sign of someone out there watching us.

"This sucks," Victor mumbles.

"You should have picked up an umbrella while you were out," I say.

"I'm not wasting this shit on umbrellas." Victor adjusts the sleeve of his jacket and I catch a glimpse of a heavy gold watch. The glittering metal looks suspiciously out of place against Victor's tatted-up arm.

"Can't you just, like, freeze time and then sweep all the frozen raindrops out of your way?" Victor asks.

"No." I step out into the rain. The two boys follow me, Jack plodding at my heels, Victor bouncing along with his loaded pack.

"There's Faith," Victor says. He sounds relieved. Faith is huddled in the plastic bus shelter. She isn't wearing a jacket and her T-shirt clings to her skin.

"Hey, Faith," Victor calls, "I got you a present."

Faith lifts her head, eyes softening when they land on Victor. She reaches out a hand toward him, and Victor grabs it.

"Dang, sis, you're freezing." Victor rubs his meaty hands over her fingers. Jack and I squash ourselves into the shelter behind Victor. Faith's gaze slides toward us, and her welcoming expression fades.

"Come on." Victor doesn't seem to notice her change of mood. "Let's go up to the squat and get you warm."

Faith shakes her head. "It's eight o'clock. One of the Elmer's staff just opened the shop."

"So?" Victor jerks a head in our direction. "These guys can get us in any time we want."

Faith's attention settles on me. I'm pretty sure she's high, because her pupils are so wide her irises appear black. Goose bumps dot her bare arms. She looks like a cat that got dunked in a bath—a pissed-off cat oozing contempt.

"No," Faith says. "I can't."

"Sure you can," Victor coaxes. "You don't have to *do* anything. Just take Alex's hand for a second and then . . ."

"No!" Faith repeats more sharply. She's shivering, though whether it's from cold or fear or just distaste, I can't tell.

"I don't want her to touch me," Faith says. "They're . . . unnatural."

Water drips down the neck of my shirt. The rain is cold. My head hurts. The grocery bag is straining against my arms.

"I know they're weird," Victor says. "But they won't hurt you. I won't let them."

"They're cursed." Faith's voice grows hysterical. "I don't want to be part of their . . . mutation." She pulls her hand out of Victor's. "How can you trust them?"

I squeeze the wet bag of groceries against my chest. Faith's face is twisted into an ugly scowl, any prettiness wiped away by her disgust. Her words hang in the air between us—familiar words that have been flung at me my whole life—mutation, unnatural, cursed.

"Take these up," I say, shoving my bag into Jack's arms. "I'm going to get Shannon and KJ some breakfast."

I hear the whispers as soon as I melt time. Standing alone in the squat's morning light, I pause, the bag of take-out breakfast balanced awkwardly in my arms. The words are soft, but this time I recognize the voices at once.

"... so you don't think we should go back?"

Shannon, of course. She's the only person I know who can nail wounded innocence quite so perfectly.

"No way," KJ says. "This is a dream come true. Think of all the things we can do now that we're on our own."

I grip the bag in my arms so hard I hear the Styrofoam containers inside it squeak. Of course, KJ has always dreamed of leaving the Sick, but I thought his dream included being with me.

Shannon gives a pathetic sniff. "But how can you be *sure* that Aclisote is bad?"

"I guess we won't be completely sure until none of us gets sick again," KJ says.

An edge of Styrofoam jabs the inside of my elbow. Is KJ not convinced that Aclisote is killing us? With a sinking feeling, I wonder again how much KJ remembers about the days before he got sick.

"Spinners help people," Shannon says. "We solve crimes. Why would the Center want to kill us?"

"Because we're powerful," KJ says. "Our time skills scare them."

Shannon drops her voice. "They scare *me*, too." There's a rustling sound like blankets being shifted. I picture KJ holding Shannon's hand, or worse, the two of them snuggled up together under a blanket. I massage my temple. I've been stopping time so much lately, even a short hold ignites a headache.

"Have you tried freezing since you stopped taking Aclisote?" KJ asks.

"Once," Shannon says, "nothing changed, though. It was like freezing always is for me. The way it's *supposed* to work."

KJ says something else, too softly for me to hear. I hold my breath, straining to catch what they're saying, before I realize I'm blatantly eavesdropping. I rattle the bag in my hand and take a step forward, a loud one that makes the floors creak.

"Hello?" I call out, pretending I've just arrived. "You guys up?"

"Over here," KJ answers.

I walk around the armoire. Streaks of watery sunlight filter through the opaque windows, casting soft bars across KJ's blankets. Shannon is scooting over, but a dent by KJ's side makes clear where she's been sitting. She's washed up since I left this morning and wears one of the clean shirts I brought her. Instead of a bedraggled braid, her hair falls in damp waves down to her waist. She's practically shining with prettiness.

I push a stray bit of my own hair in the general direction of my ponytail. Unlike Shannon's becoming locks, my wet strands cling to my neck like seaweed.

"Breakfast," I announce.

KJ smiles up at me, a wide grin that crinkles the top of his nose and makes me feel suddenly out of breath. He does remember. I'm sure of it.

"Thanks," he says.

Shannon straightens the blankets over KJ's legs. I sit down on the floor across from her, passing around Styrofoam boxes filled with scrambled eggs, muffins, and sausage, along with to-go cups of chocolate milkshake. I figure KJ can use the extra calories.

"Where's Jack?" KJ asks.

"Didn't you see him when he came in?" I ask. They both shake their heads. "Must have gone straight to sleep then. He and Victor were out all night."

KJ attacks his food with enthusiasm. For a while, the only sounds are the scrape of plastic forks and the coos from the pigeons outside.

"So." KJ swallows a bite of muffin. "Sounds like I missed out on a lot while I was sick." He uses the back of his hand as the napkin I forgot to get. The gesture removes some crumbs but doesn't erase the grease smearing his lower lip. "Want to fill me in?"

The shimmery spot on KJ's lip makes it hard to keep my eyes off his mouth. For the first time, I understand why girls wear lip gloss. I focus on my eggs while telling KJ how we'd gotten out of the Center and into the squat. KJ listens attentively, and even though I leave out the more graphic details, he still expresses comforting dismay when I talk about the car accident and the unpleasantness of Victor and Faith. Shannon adds nothing, eating her food in small, neat bites.

"Wow," KJ says, when I'm done. "That's amazing."

KJ's words warm me more than the hot food resting on my lap. I pick up my milkshake to give my hands something to do.

"I don't know if everything she's done is amazing." Shannon's eyes flick between me and KJ, her mouth pinched so tight the edges could be stapled. "What about all the stuff you and Jack have been stealing?"

KJ raises his eyebrows. "What'd you guys steal?"

"Everything—food, clothes." I gesture at his bedding. "It's not like we had any money."

"You do now." Shannon shifts her position, so she's sitting shoulder to shoulder with KJ. "A whole backpack full. I saw it."

"You have a backpack full of cash?" KJ asks. "Where'd you get that?"

"We took it." I glare at Shannon. "From an armored truck, in frozen time."

KJ nearly drops his plate.

"We needed cash to pay off Victor and Faith," I explain. "They were threatening to throw us out."

Shannon sniffs. "I think you and Jack caved in to Victor's demands way too easily. I doubt they really would have turned you in. They're not exactly the deal-with-authority type."

"You think we should have *negotiated* with them?" I stab my fork into the bottom of the Styrofoam tray, snapping two of the tines. "Have you talked to Victor?"

KJ starts at the venom in my voice. "Whoa, Alex. Chill."

My head whips in his direction. "She has no right to criticize our choices. Jack and I were doing everything we could to survive. All she did was sit here and whine about missing the Center."

Shannon's cheeks flush pink. "I took care of KJ. You were hardly ever here."

The unfairness of her accusation momentarily stills my tongue. I pick up my cup, squeezing the paper container so roughly that chocolate shake oozes out over my hand.

"No one has to worry about me being sick anymore," KJ says, scooping up more eggs. "Now we're all free and safe. Everything from here on will be easy."

A blast of wind rattles the windows over our heads. I know KJ well enough to understand that the lightness of his comment is an effort to heal this obvious rift, but the words still rankle. I put the shake down on the ground.

"Actually," I say. "We're not safe."

KJ looks up.

"Alex." Shannon's voice holds warning. "There's no need to share *all* your theories right now."

The battering wind has forced rain through the cracks of the ill-fitting glass. Water slides through the opening, fingers of wet encroaching into the room.

"They aren't theories," I say. "We need to leave Portland as soon as possible. All the spinners do. If we don't . . ."

What am I doing? KJ looks so happy right now, and the things I have to tell him will turn that joy into the anxious gnawing that keeps my stomach feeling like it's filled with battery acid.

KJ's fork hovers over his plate, a forgotten hunk of egg impaled on its tip. "If we don't, then what?"

My eyes meet his across the empty space between us. All the worries from the last few days swarm around my lips, begging to be let out, but he looks so frail, the fork hanging from his hand in a way that suggests even holding such a slight weight takes effort. Do I want to tell him everything because he needs to understand the truth? Or do I want to tell him because the burden is too much for me to carry alone?

"Alex," KJ says, "what aren't you telling me?"

I take a very deep breath. KJ *does* need to know. He just doesn't need to know everything yet.

"The Center is going to be closed at the end of the month. All the kids will be relocated, and some are going to the Central Office."

Shannon inhales sharply. KJ's fork slips from his fingers.

"It's not true," Shannon says.

"It *is* true." I keep my eyes fixed on KJ. "It was in the news. According to them, the Center is closing because of toxic mold, but that's just a cover story. Ross told me the regional directors are cracking down because the four of us escaped."

KJ frowns.

"You talked to Ross?"

He sounds so disappointed. I rub my thumb against the spilled milkshake coating my palm, scrubbing it so hard my hand burns.

"Yes." I can hear the defensiveness in my voice. "I saw him when I broke into Barnard's house."

"You did *what*?" Shannon sounds horrified.

"I wanted to prove he worked for Sikes," I say. "To help the spinners."

The frown on KJ's face deepens. It's not an angry expression. He looks confused, like he's working through a particularly complicated math problem.

"After all this." He motions around the room, managing to encompass both the dirty surroundings and his own wasted self. "You're still working with Ross to track down Sikes?"

"No! I mean, yes, I do want Sikes caught, but I'm not working with Ross. I called Sikes's real identity into the hotline by myself."

KJ sets his plate down on the floor, abandoning his half-eaten food altogether.

"Same old Alex." He sighs. "Always trying to save the world."

A gust of wind sends a cold blast into the rapidly cooling room. The resignation on KJ's face is worse than anger. How many times has KJ asked me to forget Sikes and spend more time with him? How many times have I pushed him away because my ego wanted to make a difference?

Shannon looks at me as if she'd like to throw me out the window the way I chucked the Aclisote. She reaches over and strokes KJ's arm.

"Oh, sweetie," she says. "You are a million times more important than some anonymous thief."

KJ studies Shannon's hand as it caresses the dark hair on his forearm. When he lifts his head, his whole face is one big question mark.

"I wonder." He picks up his milkshake. "If I'm well enough to freeze time."

"Not yet," Shannon says. "You're still weak."

"I'll be quick." KJ presses her hand before extracting his arm from hers. "I want to see if my skills have changed."

Shannon shakes her head. "It's too soon."

KJ sucks down a final gulp of shake and hands me the empty container. Two weeks ago, I would have made a joke about him treating me like a waitress. Two days ago, I would have been ecstatic that he was able to move his arm at all. Today, all I do is reach for the piece of trash. KJ doesn't let go.

Shannon continues lecturing: "You know people are more likely to get sick when they're overtired, and in your condition . . ."

KJ's hand slides down the side of the cup. When his fingers touch mine, I understand. My heart contracts in my chest. I can almost feel the thought as it slides through his mind: *freeze time.*

Shannon's tirade cuts off mid-sentence. Stillness settles around us, a slice of time outside of time. My heart starts beating faster. KJ and I haven't been alone together since the night we kissed. Memories come back to me. KJ's face so close to my own, the unexpected softness of his lips. He'd called me brave then and promised we'd face everything together.

KJ lets go of the cup.

"I guess it worked," he says.

"Think it will stick?" My hand still feels gummy from the shake. "Try melting and see if things go back."

"Not yet." KJ twists around so he's facing me. He's sitting close enough that our knees touch, and the point of contact tingles, as if my blood had been replaced by champagne.

"We need to talk," he says.

Shannon's frozen body fills the space behind KJ's shoulder.

"I couldn't tell her," I say. The words pour out in a rush. "I needed both her and Jack to save you. Shannon knows how to take care of sick people. I was pretty beat up at that point, and besides, I had to go out to get food and stuff. No one else could freeze time like me. Not at first."

"I didn't say you had to take care of me," KJ says. "I'm just saying that Shannon risked a lot, and she doesn't deserve to get hurt."

The unspoken criticism ricochets through the squat like a muted scream. I curl my hands in my lap, twisting my fingers together, so they look like a ball of pink and white worms.

"There never seemed to be a good moment to tell her," I say.

The excuse sounds lame, even to me. KJ shifts his body, a restless movement that moves his knee away from mine.

"I get it," he says. "I mean, it's not like I can expect you to break up with my girlfriend for me."

Girlfriend. The champagne in my veins goes flat. Is that how he still thinks of her?

KJ flops back on his pillows. "What am I supposed say to her? Oh, hey, Shannon, thanks for saving my life and all, but I wanted to tell you that the night before you left the only home you've ever known, in order to take care of me, I was busy kissing someone else."

His words replay in my head—once, twice, three times. In none of those do I hear him saying that kissing me was anything but a mistake. Behind him, Shannon remains in her frozen crouch. When time stopped, it caught her staring at him with an expression of heartfelt anxiety. Clearly, *she's* not the kind of person who would run off to chase criminals while her boyfriend lay deathly ill.

"Shannon really loves the Center, you know," KJ goes on. "She told me once that she thinks of Yolly as an aunt. Yolly doesn't have a lot of family outside of us, so I think she encouraged her. The Center was home to Shannon in a way it never was for you and me. That's the reason she has such a hard time accepting the truth."

I study my hands again. The worms that are my fingers are starting to strangle each other. Somewhere in the back of my mind, I register that they hurt.

"Shannon gave you Aclisote for four days after we got here," I say. "She almost killed you."

"I know." KJ scratches his cheek. The stubble that had built up over the past few days is gone. His hair is clean too, and wet, just like Shannon's. I know from experience that it's hard to wash your own hair in that small bathroom sink. Were they in there together while I filled Shannon's latest order? Giggling under the cold spray. Running their hands through each other's hair to rinse out the suds.

"Can't you see this from her perspective?" KJ asks. "If you really believed that Aclisote was the only thing that might save me, wouldn't you have done what she did?"

I stretch my fingers, soothing the cramped muscles one by one. KJ's shoulders droop under the burden of the position I have put him in. They are such thin shoulders, the bones starkly visible from so many days of sickness.

"So, what do we do?" I ask. "You keep being Shannon's boyfriend, and you and I go back to being friends?"

"I don't know." KJ's shoulders sink even further. "Maybe I should just tell her what happened."

He sounds like he's offering to drink poison. I indulge in a brief fantasy of Shannon being miraculously out of the way, before succumbing to the bewilderment on KJ's face. That and hard reality.

"The only reason Shannon stays here is because of you," I say. "If you break up with her, she'll run back to Yolly." I flick a muffin crumb off my leg. "She'll tell them where we are because she thinks the Center will help us."

"She's not a bad person, Alex."

I nod. I know Shannon isn't a bad person. I know KJ is right that Shannon only did what I would have done in her situation. These facts don't make me feel any better. I study my ruined nails. Once again, in my efforts to help people, I've only managed to create a situation where everyone involved is going to end up getting hurt.

KJ puts a hand to his forehead. The gesture is familiar, and a new layer of guilt piles onto the growing mass. How long have we been sitting here in the frozen stillness?

"You're tired." I sound like a weak imitation of Shannon—weak because she wouldn't have let KJ hold time for this long. She wouldn't have made him feel bad, either. She would have put his health first. "You should melt time. We don't have to figure out any of this right away. That's the whole point, isn't it? That we have a future now?"

KJ starts to say something, then seems to reconsider. Time stirs the still air. The transition isn't smooth—the old giddy swing of things being put back into their prefreeze positions whirls around us. It doesn't make me feel dizzy like it did when the freeze was mine; it's more like a second of disorientation, and then I'm back, sitting up next to KJ, his empty cup in my hand.

" . . . freezing time is too dangerous." Shannon finishes the rant she started before the freeze. "You should definitely wait longer before trying it."

KJ's fingers once again rest against mine. This time, I am the one who pulls away, taking the cup and placing it onto my dirty plate.

"You're right." KJ sinks back onto his pillow and allows Shannon to fuss over him.

"So." I stand up. "I guess I'll . . ." I gesture vaguely around the cluttered space. What can I say? Leave the room, so I don't have to be around you two? "Clean up our dishes."

Neither of them stops me.

I take as long as I can squashing our plates into the trash, then move just as deliberately as I put away the groceries Jack dumped on the counter. KJ's freeze may be over, but the conversation within it is harder to forget. I wish I didn't know how much KJ admires Shannon. I wish I didn't know how much he still cares.

14 ◀◀

KJ WALKS INTO THE KITCHEN AS I'M PUTTING AWAY THE last of the groceries, Shannon following him so closely it's as if she's afraid he's about to tip over.

"Is there still coffee?" KJ says, heading for the pot Shannon made earlier this morning.

"Help yourself." I hand over a clean mug with exaggerated cheerfulness. "I even got us some creamer."

KJ fills the mug, then pours a second one for Shannon.

"What do you say we get out of here for a while," he says. "I haven't breathed fresh air in a week."

Shannon shakes her head. "It's raining, and you need to rest."

"The rain stopped," KJ says, reaching for the half-and-half I left on the counter. "And I'm rested."

I step back to give him room, which allows me the opportunity to study him upright for the first time. The sight makes Shannon's worries about him tipping over more legitimate. KJ, a thin guy to begin with, now brings to mind a scarecrow come to life. His sweatpants hang from his bony hips. His T-shirt floats over a concave stomach. I busy myself wiping the dresser down with a damp rag to hide my dismay.

"Is there anywhere nice out there we can go to?" Shannon asks me.

I picture the neighborhood outside, the street of endless cars filled with quizzical drivers, the houses with their carefully shielded windows, behind which anyone could lurk. What's the safer choice? An isolated area where we'd be easy to spot or a city street crowded with a million eyes? I clench the rag so hard that dirty water puddles in the spot I'd just cleaned.

"There's a park nearby," I offer. KJ's grin only sort of eases my anxiety.

Just after nine-thirty—after they finish their coffee and Shannon cuts a length of twine off an old box to hold up KJ's pants—we head for the door. I take Shannon's wrist, then brush my fingers across KJ's just long enough to connect us while I stop time. The trip down the fire escape takes much longer than usual. KJ's presence makes me newly aware of the steepness of the steps, the short leap needed to reach the ground, the irritating scratches from the blackberries. KJ is breathing heavily by the time we reach the bottom, and Shannon and I exchange worried looks behind his back. One day of rest isn't nearly enough to compensate for five of near unconsciousness.

I lead them to a spot between two parked cars where we can hide and wait for KJ to recover before melting time. The light brightens, the whirr of cars floats through moving air, and the scent of dirty pavement intensifies.

KJ inhales the weak fall sun.

"This is great," he says. He sounds so pleased that for a minute I relax into an answering beat of happiness. We are here, out of the Center, KJ healthy against all odds. But then, a car backfires, and my stomach rolls into a too-familiar knot.

"Come on." I stand up. Scattered clouds flit across the sky, giving the day an unsettled feel. "Let's get off the busy street."

KJ glances at me, clearly surprised by the urgency in my voice. I chew a fingernail and motion for them to hurry. The two of them stand up and we all head for the crosswalk on the corner.

"I can't believe that we're outside like this," KJ says. "Totally free."

Shannon tilts her face up into the sun. "It is pretty nice."

"Yeah." I jab the walk button, scanning the drivers' faces to check if anyone is watching us. "Sort of."

KJ shoots me a sidelong glance. "Only sort of?"

"I guess I'm not used to appreciating it." The little white crosswalk guy lights up and we step into the street. "What with you being sick and everything."

"I'm fine now."

We finish crossing. A man waits on the corner, head bent as he lights a cigarette. His eyes follow us as we pass by. The weird feeling I had yesterday, of floating between two versions of the world, one benign and one not, returns. Like a flickering shadow, the man's expression alternates between curious and menacing.

"Let's keep moving." I grab KJ's elbow and hurry him up the sidewalk, with Shannon trotting at our heels.

"What's the matter?" KJ asks.

"That guy." I glance back the way we came. Smoking Man stands at the corner, still watching us. He's not the man on the motorcycle—this guy has darker skin and short kinky hair—but does that matter? There can't be only one wiper in the city.

"The Center has signs up at the runaway centers," I say, "with our photos on them. The cops probably have them, too."

KJ twists around. "And you think that guy might be a cop?"

"He could be." I drag KJ forward so he'll stop gawking. "That's why we have to get out of Portland."

"Where would we go?" Shannon asks.

We turn the corner and enter a residential neighborhood that lies a few blocks north of the squat. The street is quiet, with neat houses tucked behind tidy lawns. I slow my pace. Shannon takes KJ's hand, and I realize I'm still holding onto his arm and release it.

"I don't know yet," I say. "Wherever it is, I think we should take local transit and avoid major bus lines and train stations as long as we can. In case they're watching them."

"Do you really think Dr. Barnard has time to stake out the train stations?" Shannon asks.

"The cops could be," I say.

The sidewalk is narrow for three people, forcing us to walk close together. Every few minutes, my fingers brush KJ's. Is he noticing the contact, too? Is he purposely swinging his arm so his knuckles touch mine?

"What if we rented a house to stay in?" KJ says. "Out near the coast or something—you know, like those vacation rentals they advertise on TV."

Or maybe he's completely oblivious. I shove my hands in my pockets.

"How would we pay for it?" I ask.

"You have all that cash. We could load some on a prepaid credit card, then do the whole transaction online."

"That might work," I say. "Do you think they have any big enough to hold twenty-four people?"

"*Twenty*-four people?" KJ says. "There's only four of us."

We're nearing the park. A woman walking two dogs turns the

corner ahead of us, moving in our direction. I nudge KJ to get his attention, and cross the street.

"Don't tell me you're worried about *her* reporting us," Shannon says.

"You never know."

"Seriously, Alex? When did you get so paranoid?"

The lingering headache I woke up with reignites with a small pulse.

"I'm not paranoid," I say. Jack called me paranoid a few days ago, but he isn't saying that anymore. Jack understands now. "You have no idea what it's been like out here."

A school bus rumbles past us. Through an open window comes the chatter of small children. A girl wearing a knitted hat waves to us.

"I can see what you mean," Shannon says, waving back. "It's real scary out here."

When we were Youngers, Yolly used to tell us to take the high road when we'd get in arguments with other kids. *If you don't react,* she'd say, *they won't have reason to tease you.* I channel my better self, ignoring Shannon and focusing my attention on KJ.

"I've been thinking a lot about how we can get back into the Sick," I say, "and I finally have an idea. What if we follow Mariko in?"

"What if we what?" KJ asks.

"Mariko. The mail lady." Talking this through with KJ gives my step an extra bounce. It's what I've been dreaming about ever since we escaped. "I was thinking first about following the staff in, but they mostly go through the garage, and it's got that gate on the outside and a locked door on the inside, so we'd have to wait around in real time for a second person to leave after the gate opened, and I'm pretty sure there are cameras down there. Mariko always makes her deliveries right around noon, so we won't have to hang around the front door for ages looking suspicious."

I'm talking too fast and with an animation that is wildly inappropriate for this topic of conversation, but I can't help it. The relief of having someone to work this through with is so great I feel as giddy as a Younger on a field trip.

"Alex," KJ says. "I know who Mariko is. I'm asking why you would want to go back to the Center."

The clouds drift back over the sun.

"To talk to the other spinners," I say. "If we tell them the truth about Aclisote, they can stop taking it and then they'll be able to escape."

"You want to sneak out of Portland, on public transit, with twenty-four kids?"

KJ's doubts fall over me like a second shadow.

"We can't just leave them behind."

Shannon, who has remained quiet the last few minutes, chooses this moment to join the conversation.

"Have you considered that some of the kids might not want to leave the Center?"

"Have you considered," I snap, "that they are all going to die?"

"Whoa, whoa, calm down." KJ waves his hand. "It's not that I don't want to help our friends, but there's no point surviving the sickness just to turn around and get caught again. Our plan was always to get ourselves out of town and settled somewhere before we even think about helping anyone else."

"Yeah, but that was before we knew the Center was closing!"

"Not for another two weeks."

A silver sedan cruises past us, moving more slowly than seems natural. I watch it glide by from the corner of my eye. A similar car passed us earlier—or could it be the same one?

"You sound like Jack," I say.

"Then Jack is being reasonable."

Is Jack reasonable or is he heartless? I veer left, guiding our path away from the sidewalk and into the park. Except for the distant barking of dogs, the place is empty.

"To rent a place for a couple weeks, we'll definitely need more money," KJ says. "How did you and Jack knock over an armored truck, anyway?"

His tone is conciliatory, but I'm not feeling appeased. The grass we're walking over is speckled with dandelions. I kick at one of the overblown blooms. A cloud of white seeds floats into the air like an entire corps of twirling ballerinas.

"We just froze time when the truck's door was open," I say, "and took whatever we wanted."

I kick another flower and release another puff of white. Once, when I still lived in a Children's Home, one of the matrons told me that if I blew all the seeds off a dandelion, my wish would come true. I wish no one was chasing us. Kick. I wish we were safe. Kick. I wish the KJ I imagined when he was sick was the same person I'm walking with now. Kick.

"Talk about the perfect crime," KJ says. "No witnesses or video evidence. The only way to make it better would be to rob some place that's closed for a few days so no one can rewind it."

Cold washes over me, like I walked through an icy waterfall. A hundred news reports flash though my brain, the words overlapping in a chorus of proof: *I locked the safe, and when I came back the money was gone. No one entered the building while we were out. Video surveillance showed no one in the area at the time the crime occurred.* The air in the wide open park seems to grow thin. How could I not have thought of this?

"KJ?" I step on some delicate white puffs, tramping over the seeds I so recently released. "What if Matt Thompson . . . what if *Sikes* . . . is a spinner?"

KJ stops walking. We stare at each other.

"Oh, my god," he says.

Sikes is a spinner. A grown-up, adult spinner. It seems so obvious. Jack called Sikes a criminal genius, but it wouldn't take that much intellect if he was one of us. All he'd have to do was wait until a door was almost shut, then stop time and take what he wanted. Sikes's only brilliance was timing his crimes so they couldn't be rewound.

"That's terrible," Shannon says. "If he's a spinner, he's never going to get caught."

Dots dance in front of my eyes. The green park fades, replaced by the memory of me in the squat, my hand wrapped around my phone as I spill Matt Thompson's secrets. A spinner's secrets.

"Yes, he will," I say. "I turned him in."

My face must be doing something weird, because KJ and Shannon are both staring at me with worried expressions.

"They're going to arrest him." I clutch KJ's arm. "Matt Thompson is a spinner and he's going to spend his life in jail because of what I did."

"Isn't that a good thing?" Shannon asks. "I thought you always wanted him arrested?"

"He's a *spinner.*"

"He's a thief, Alex," KJ says. "And a killer."

But is it his fault? Sikes and Shea worked together. What if Matt Thompson was merely a tool in Shea's hand, just like Ross used me as a tool in his?

"I have to warn him."

There's a bench a few feet away, tucked behind the shelter of a large hedge. I stumble over and plop down on the seat. How can I judge Matt when I've done the same things? If he goes to jail, it will be because my actions have hurt yet another spinner. I can't do that again. I *can't*. We spinners have to stick together. I grab my phone and pull up the search engine.

KJ and Shannon come join me on the bench. They both move warily, like I'm a bomb they're afraid might explode if they touch the wrong wire.

"What are you doing?" KJ asks.

I type a question into the waiting box.

"I'm going to tell Matt Thompson the cops know he's Sikes."

"He's a really dangerous man, Alex."

Is he? My finger hovers over the phone's keyboard. I shake my head. He's a spinner.

"I won't do it in person," I say. "I'll just leave him a note. I'll put it in his office."

"That's a crazy idea. Going to Sikes's office is ridiculously risky."

"He won't be there." I hold up my phone. Tom's Bar has a downloadable menu and a basic website with a few photos that make it appear nicer than it is. Across the bottom, its address and business hours are prominently displayed. "They don't open until four in the afternoon, and they stay open until two a.m. If I go now, no one will be there."

Shannon's mouth drops open. "You're really considering breaking into a bar to warn the guy you've always wanted to arrest?"

"I'm not considering it," I say. "I'm doing it. Today. Now."

"Alex," KJ says. "I admire your principles, I really do, but we have

159

to stay focused. Forget Sikes. Let's work on finding a safe place to live."

Echoes of all the other times KJ asked me to stop worrying about Sikes reverberate in my brain. Am I making a mistake? I stare down at the image on the phone. *Portland's Friendliest Bar* shouts a tagline near a photo of wholesome-looking people laughing around a sun-dappled table. When KJ and I planned to leave the Center together, everything seemed so simple. We'd been given a chance for a new life, and I was going to make sure I did things right this time. But what does "right" mean? Does it mean making sure the friends I rescued stay safe? Or risking even more to make sure other spinners have a chance to survive, too? Is it stopping a criminal, or warning one of our own? The picture on the phone dims as the screen heads toward sleep mode. When I was in that bar, it seemed dingy, and the floors were sticky. Which version of Tom's Bar is the real one? The phone winks out, the flashy pictures replaced by a reflection of a girl with eyes so haunted I barely recognize them as my own.

"Come on," KJ says. "Let's see if we can find something on that house rental site."

He reaches for the phone, and I let him slide it out from my limp fingers. The screen lights up again, and KJ starts typing.

"What do you think?" he asks. "The coast or the mountains? I bet Mount Hood's pretty quiet this time of year."

Out on the street, on the far side of the sheltering hedge, brakes squeal. I flinch, primed to grab for time even before I jerk my head around.

Shannon leans against KJ's shoulder. "I've never been to the beach."

I peer through dark leaves, one piece of my mind on the verge of stopping time. A police car is cruising down the street, slowly, like it's trolling for something. My throat tightens. The windows are tinted, and I can't tell if the driver is looking this way.

"How about that one," Shannon says. "It's got a hot tub!"

The car rolls down the street and turns the corner. I rub my arm. I'm wearing another wool sweater, and the fibers bite like little pinpricks against my skin.

"I think we should freeze time and move somewhere else," I say.

KJ looks up.

"I don't get why you're so worried about getting caught all the time." He's speaking carefully, like he knows he's going to piss me off. "It's not like we're sitting ducks. If anyone comes near you, you can just freeze time and run away."

The ache in my head twitches. "You make it sound easy."

KJ frowns. It's a concerned frown, but I can tell he's not concerned about us getting caught. He's concerned about me. I take a deep breath, making an effort to sound calm and rational, even though my chest feels like someone stuffed it with frantic butterflies.

"Everywhere I go," I say, "I can feel people watching me. Like the other day, I was at this farmers market, and there was this woman who wanted me to sign her petition. When I did, she started asking questions. And then later, this guy followed me onto the bus. I'm pretty sure she called him."

KJ's frown deepens. My words falter. I can tell I've failed the rationality test.

"And you think this man was after you?" KJ prods.

"He knew my name!"

The look on Shannon's face is hard to read—worry? Amusement? Does she *pity* me?

KJ puts a hand on my knee. "I understand that you're freaked out. You've been through so much in the past couple weeks, it's a miracle you're functioning at all. But I'm worried about you." He gestures to my fingers, at the nails, scabbed and chewed to the quick. "You're all over the place. Shannon says you get really mad at the drop of a hat, and you're twitchy and scared of everything. Why don't we spend a quiet day in the squat? Let's look through these listings and find a place we can stay for a while, away from all this. Like a vacation."

I stare down at the hand resting on my jeans-covered knee. KJ, my best friend and the guy I thought would always be there for me, believes I'm crazy.

Shannon tilts her head, peering over at me from KJ's other side.

"Alex, I know we don't completely agree about the Center, but have you considered that maybe some of your reactions have to do with the fact that you're not taking Aclisote anymore?"

"What? Like some kind of withdrawal?"

"It's possible," KJ says. "We don't know anyone who's been off it as long as you have."

Suspicion tingles the back of my neck. KJ and Shannon are holding hands. What if one of them froze time while we were sitting here? Neither of them can change anything. They could stop time for ages, and I'd have no way to tell. I imagine their heads bent close together, the two of them discussing how to deal with me, while my own inert body sits beside them, nothing but a silent statue in their private conference. I search their faces for signs of guilt. Strain pinches the skin on KJ's cheeks. Is he tired from our outing? Or is it the beginning of a headache?

I stand up, letting KJ's hand fall from my leg. I no longer think there are two versions of the world. There is only one, and it's not benign. The world is a terrifying place, full of people who want me dead, and friends I can't be sure of. If KJ doesn't understand that, then how can he judge if what I'm doing is right?

"Take my hands," I say, holding one palm out to each of them.

KJ curls his free hand against his chest. "Why?"

I scan the park. There's no one in sight. Leaning forward, I brush two fingers against each of their cheeks and stop time.

"So you can get back without being seen," I say. "In fifteen minutes, I'll find somewhere to melt time. You can get to the squat by then, can't you?"

"Where are you going?" KJ asks.

I step away from them. "Tom's Bar."

Shannon's mouth drops open in a silent *oh*.

"Are you serious?" she asks.

I nod. The security of a frozen world fills me with strength. I snatch the cell phone back from KJ and start walking away.

"I'll see you at the squat in a couple hours."

"Wait." KJ's attempt to stand is thwarted by Shannon, who hangs onto his arm like an anchor.

"Don't do this," he says. "It's a huge risk and for what? To save a murderer?"

My foot catches on an exposed root, and I stumble. A small voice in the back of my head whispers that KJ is right and I'm being stupid and reckless. I shush it. KJ and Shannon both think the world is bright and sunny; they don't see the shadows hiding just beneath the surface. I regain my balance and walk away. A restful "vacation" can wait. I'm going to make sure my actions don't destroy another spinner's life.

15 ◄◄

IT TAKES ME OVER AN HOUR TO PICK UP SUPPLIES AND get across town, even with three freezes when I suspect someone is watching me, which means it's well after eleven by the time I'm cruising the sidewalk outside Tom's Bar. The place takes up part of the ground floor of a low-rise brick apartment building, next to a secondhand clothing store. The inside is dark, with a CLOSED sign hanging crookedly behind the window on the front door. Dusty, unlit neon decorates the windows above taped-up flyers announcing that a band called The Hungry Carnivores is playing at the Crystal Ballroom Thursday night.

Cars parked along the curb offer little in the way of shelter to hide in while freezing time. I shove my hands into my pockets and keep walking. The neighborhood is a few blocks east of the river that splits Portland in half, and leans toward light industrial, which means that while there are lots of blank-faced warehouses, there aren't a lot of quiet corners to duck into. I end up walking five blocks before I find a sufficiently sheltered hiding place. Time skids to a halt. I jog all the way back to Tom's.

The door to the bar is, as I expected, locked. I press my face against the window and peer into the darkened interior, which looks completely unchanged from when Ross and I visited a couple weeks ago. Colorful liquor bottles line the mirror-backed shelves behind a long wooden bar. The space in front is filled with chairs that are stacked, legs up, on a dozen different small tables. The memory of being here with Ross is so strong I almost expect to see him reflected by my side in the glass.

With the aid of my supplies—a thin pair of gloves and a set of lock picks—it takes only a few minutes before I'm inside. The stink of spilled beer and deep-fry oil hovers in the bar's stuffy interior, mixed with a rancid burnt smell that makes me wonder about the chef's cooking skills. I relock the deadbolt and head toward the short hall leading to Sikes's office. The burnt smell grows stronger the closer I get. It's not really a food smell, more like the sharp bite of singed plastic. I reach the hall. To my left, the kitchen echoes with emptiness, and to my right...I skid to a halt. The door to Matt's office is ajar, emitting wafts of the bitter stench, along with the glow of turned-on lights. My glove-covered palms grow damp. Is someone here? Very carefully, I push the office door the rest of the way open and step inside.

The room is empty. My breath whooshes through my nose as I release it. I shut the door, lean back against it, and survey the space.

The first time I came here, I was impressed by how pristine the office was, especially in contrast to the casual grime of the bar. The room is square, with a second door in the back that Ross said led to additional storage. Sleek, Scandinavian-style furniture hints at the occupant's access to money.

Today, however, the office is in shambles. Piles of paper litter the desk's glossy surface. Books list sideways on half-emptied shelves. A knee-high paper shredder sits beside the desk, encircled by tiny bits of fragmented documents. The safe, the one that held the incriminating painting, hangs open, its interior black with smoke and the charred remains of Matt Thompson's secrets.

I put my finger in my mouth before remembering that my nails are covered with gloves. Does Sikes know the cops are after him, or is he just closing shop now that his partner is dead? I spit out a snippet of glove-thread. I need to warn him—make sure he gets out of town fast and never returns. But how? Given the state of his office, he may not be coming back here, so he would never see a note. I scan the room, seeking inspiration, and my eyes land on the computer. Perfect. I'll send him an email from his own account telling him what I know. The oddness of the sender will surely make him read it.

I pull up the leather office chair and release time so I can use the computer. It's in sleep mode, but Ross and I found the password during our original break-in, and I type it into the sign-in box from memory—*Impervious*, spelled backward and mangled with symbols: $-U-O-!-V-R-E-p-m-1. The empty blue screen is replaced by an image of a tropical beach. I study it. The Center didn't allow us much computer access. Where do I find emails?

The bottom of the screen has a row of little icons. I click on five before I find the right one. Messages populate the screen, some in bold font and others not. I click on one and read what looks like a confirmation for a food order, which is neither interesting nor helpful, as the message doesn't show an obvious place for the sender's address. I kick the underside of the desk. How do you send an email to yourself?

Something in the wall at my back rattles. My heart slams in my chest like I just mainlined six cups of coffee. The computer mouse skids onto the floor as I spin the chair around, stopping time before I've even circled halfway. The only thing behind me is the storage room. Hesitantly, I try the handle. It's locked. My heart slows from an all-out sprint to a fast gallop. The noise was probably rats, a sound I should recognize without freaking out, after so many days of living at the squat.

I let time loose as I kneel to retrieve the computer mouse. The underside of the desk is as dark as a cave, and it takes three tries before my shaking fingers manage to close around the hunk of plastic. Maybe his email address is in a sent-mail file. Aren't there sent files? I'm sure I've heard someone talk about those. Crawling out from under the desk requires an uncomfortable, backward squirm. The carpet scratches my palms. It must be new, because it has a weird chemical smell that even the burnt stink can't completely cover up.

Heat brushes my skin, a flash of warning I recognize at the same instant that a hand closes on the back of my neck. I scream. The grip on my neck tightens.

"What the hell do you think you're doing?"

The voice—male and very angry—rings through the empty office. My mind lunges for time, then hesitates on its brink. The man's hand is flat against the skin of my neck. If I freeze, he'll come with me.

Sweat traces a path down the side of my rib cage. I twist my head. Just past my shoulder stand a pair of large black running shoes.

The man shakes my neck, knocking my head against the hard wood of the desk.

"I asked you a question," he says.

The space under the desk turns claustrophobic, the sides pressing closer together.

"Please," I squeak. "Don't."

The shaking stops, which doesn't make the space I'm jammed in feel any less threatening, nor my brain any more focused. Why didn't I ask Jack to come with me? The man drags me to my feet, slowly, without letting go of my neck. I stand on wobbly legs, blinking in the harsh office light. The closed office door, the only thing I can see in front of me, undulates beneath the press of my fear.

Think. I need to *think*. The man's grip is inescapably tight. I can feel each separate finger digging into my flesh. Time—my only weapon is time. If I can shock him with its sudden absence, even for a split second, it might be enough to break his hold. I yank the world to a stop, and at the same moment, twist my body away from his.

The man's hand remains soldered to my neck. His body follows my movement, leaning over me as I rotate forward so that he ends up curled over my back. I squeeze my eyes shut. *Let go. Please. Just. Let. Go.*

The man laughs.

"I guess that explains how you appeared here so suddenly."

My heart, galloping a second ago, stops in my chest. I know that voice. I've talked to him before. My captor is Matt Thompson, which means my captor is Sikes.

My legs turn liquid. All my theoretical heroism about warning a fellow spinner pales under the grip of this very real man. KJ's warnings strangle my tongue. Sikes is dangerous. A murderer.

Sikes grabs my bare wrist and straightens up. He takes his other hand off my neck and wraps that arm around me, pressing my back against his stomach and pinning my arms to my sides. I squirm. He's taller than I am and much stronger. My efforts are useless.

"Hold still," he mutters. Adjusting his hold so he has one hand free, while still maintaining contact with my skin, he opens one of the desk's drawers. I crane my neck. The drawer is deep. Sikes's arm is partially buried as he digs around the bottom. What's in there? A knife? A gun? Only Sikes's rough grip keeps me from melting onto the floor.

Sikes's arm slides out of the drawer holding a metal band, hinged in the middle, so it hangs like an open jaw. It isn't a gun, or a knife. Sikes is smarter than that. A leash won't hurt me, only render me powerless.

The cool metal touches my skin, instantly sending a low-level buzzing into my brain. Time wrenches away from me, leaping back into its recently abandoned groove. Sikes lets go of my arm. Even knowing it's impossible, I try to take time back. The effort is as useless as trying to find a handhold on an infinite glass wall.

"Sit," Sikes orders.

I turn around. The man facing me is average height, white, and clean shaven, with dark hair clipped tidily short. He points to the desk chair, and I sink into it. There's no point in trying to run. Sikes could overpower me before I so much as tensed a muscle. Or *he* could stop time and I would freeze like everyone else. When time resumed, I could be anywhere, most likely bleeding my life out in some deserted hiding place where no one would find my body for days.

Sikes perches on the desk in front of me and places one foot on each arm of the chair, creating a sort of cage with his body and the chair.

"I've seen you before," he says.

I nod. Fear mingled with the buzz of the leash has turned my thoughts into mush. Sikes's eyes narrow.

"You said you were a high school kid who wanted an interview," he says, referring to the cover story I made up so Ross had time to finish searching his office. "I knew there was something sketchy about you."

My tongue feels like it's glued to the roof of my mouth. It takes all my effort to force it to shape words.

"I came here to warn you," I say. "The police are coming to arrest you. They know you're Sikes."

The man's expression barely flickers. "Don't lie to me. You think I can't figure out who you are? You're Alexandra Manning, Carson Ross's tame spinner."

I shake my head. "I don't work for Ross anymore."

"Come on." Sikes gives a disgusted snort. "Jeffrey Barnard might be naïve enough to believe Ross when he says he had nothing to do with your disappearance, but you and I both know you couldn't have gotten out of the Center without help."

I shake my head harder. It's stupid and pointless, but for some reason, I can't stand to have anyone, even my probable killer, think that I am being controlled by Ross.

"I left the Center to get away from Ross. And from Barnard. He was going to put me back on Aclisote."

"You're not taking *any* Aclisote?"

I pull at the leash. If only the buzzing would stop, so I could think clearly. "Of course not."

Sikes's eyebrows rise. "That's not good."

Why is he playing this game when we both know he knows everything? He's obviously a spinner; the office door didn't open before he appeared behind me. Anger shoots through my fear, and I straighten in the leather chair.

"Why have you never done anything to stop the CIC?"

"Me?" Sikes sounds genuinely surprised. "Why would *I* stop them?"

"Because you're one of us!"

"One of . . . ?" Sikes blinks. "*I'm* not a spinner."

My head throbs. "Yes, you are. You couldn't have done all those robberies without stopping time."

"I'm not a spinner," Sikes repeats. He holds out a hand to me. "You can feel when someone has it, right? Try me."

I stare at the proffered hand. It's pale and large, each finger as thick as two of my own. Sikes waggles his hand impatiently. I grasp it, then reach out for time. The solid wall of the leash's resistance meets my searching mind, but there is no answering pull coming from the hand resting in my own. Sikes is telling the truth.

"If you're not a spinner," I ask, "how did you get into the office just now?"

Sikes frowns. "I've been in the office the whole time."

"You . . ." I turn my head, searching for the hiding place I must have missed. The door to the bar is still closed, the bookcases are flush against the walls, the storage room . . . my search ends. The inner door is wide open, revealing a gleaming executive bathroom.

All the facts I thought I knew scatter like so many piles of debris. I reach for time and once more fail to detect any answering pulse from Sikes's limp hand.

"You have to be a spinner," I say. "It's the only way your crimes make sense."

"Aren't you the clever one." Sikes drops my hand and stands up, no longer bothering to guard me in my chair. "Did you figure that out yourself, or did your pal Ross clue you in?"

"I did."

"Huh." Sikes picks up one of the stacks of paper scattered across his desk and fans the sheets in his hand. "Well, it was a good gig, but now it's over. Time for me to move on to new adventures somewhere far, far away."

The papers scatter as Sikes tosses them into one of the boxes on the floor, the pages an unintelligible riot of words and numbers. I stare down into the mess. Just beyond the leash's smothering buzz, understanding whispers a terrible truth.

"You're not a spinner." The next question takes effort. "But you know one, don't you?"

"I used to."

"Who?"

Sikes straightens. The eyes that meet mine burn. "His name was Austin Shea."

The room tilts. All the fancy furniture lists to one side, as if the whole building has been caught on the swell of a giant wave. I clutch the arms of the leather chair to keep from falling over.

"Austin Shea was a spinner?"

"That's right." Sikes picks up another stack from his desk and starts flipping through it. "I might not be out there helping every pathetic kid locked up in the Center, but I did save one spinner. He was homeless and semi-crazy when I found him, with no idea how to control his skills. I helped him."

"You used him."

"I gave the guy a nice life." Sikes puts down the paper. "He might not have loved the work, but he was grateful. We were a team."

A team. Sikes and Shea. I had my facts right—I just had their roles reversed. Ross knew. He'd told me that Shea was vital to Sikes's operation. I just hadn't understood what he meant.

"We killed him," I say. The words come out softly, the air barely able to squeeze past the lump in my throat. "I killed a spinner."

Something flashes in Sikes's eyes, a spark of anger—or maybe hurt—so deep I have to look away. Sikes squats down by the paper

172

shredder and starts shoving handfuls of files into its vicious maw. The engine hums as the sheets dissolve into tatters.

"Not exactly doing your part to save your fellow spinners, either, are you?" he says.

I killed a spinner. The memory of Austin Shea lying in his moonlit bedroom returns to me, as clear as the night it happened. He'd been sleeping so peacefully. I picture his silken sheets. His gaping throat. All those pints of blood frozen in his veins, waiting for the release of a single heartbeat.

Sikes shoves more papers into the shredder. The buzzing in my head sharpens into pain.

"Why did you come here?" Sikes asks.

"I told you." I see no reason to lie. "Ross and I searched your office, and so I called in a tip to the hotline telling them who you were. But then I thought you must be a spinner, so I decided to warn you."

"How noble of you." Sikes points to the scorched safe. "Too bad someone already did me that favor."

"That wasn't you?" I ask.

"Not me." Sikes's laugh is hollow. "There were things in there I wanted to keep."

The stolen painting—priceless sunflowers daubed on a piece of canvas—dances in front of my eyes. It's completely destroyed. Who would have done that? I claw at the leash's immobile clasp.

"Let me go," I say.

Sikes looks up. "Why should I?"

"You owe us!" My voice sounds shrill, and I struggle to control it. "Everything you stole—the money, the painting, all of it—you got because of a spinner. It's only fair that you do something for us in return."

The shredder's noisy hum stops. "I owe *you*?" Sikes rocks back on his heels, his expression cold. "You're the person who not only killed my spinner but also just admitted to turning me in to the cops. I'd say, if anything, you owe me."

Tears burn in my eyes. "I was just trying to do the right thing."

"You can tell that to Dr. Barnard when he comes here to get you after *my* anonymous call."

I twist my arm inside the confines of the leash.

"Please," I beg.

A loud banging sound interrupts my appeal. Sikes's head swivels toward the noise.

"Police!" a voice shouts. Another bang. "Open up!"

Sikes is on his feet in an instant, his face so close to mine I can feel his breath against my cheek.

"What did you tell them?" he hisses.

My mouth goes dry. "The safe," I whisper. "I told them about the painting. That's all."

"Do not attempt to leave the premises," the voice at the door shouts. "I have a time search warrant."

Sikes grabs my arm. His head whips toward the empty safe, then at his computer. The hand circling my wrist tightens. He yanks me out of the chair and holds my body against himself like a shield. I can tell he's weighing his options. Desperate options. None of which will end well for me.

"Let me go," I squeak. "The evidence is gone. They can't arrest you."

"There's more evidence to find if they get suspicious and start digging," he mutters. "And once they see I'm packing, they'll think the same thing you did—that I'm the one that burnt the safe, or ordered someone to."

From the front of the bar comes the unmistakable crash of breaking glass. Sikes hooks his arm around my neck, the inside of his elbow crushing my windpipe.

"Here is what is going to happen." His voice rumbles in my ear like the growl of a cornered beast. "I am going to take off your leash, and then you are going to freeze time." The pressure on my windpipe increases. My face feels like it's expanding with the blood that can no longer pass through my neck. "Do you understand?" Sikes asks.

Tiny stars dazzle my eyes. Wheezes scratch at my throat. The light in the office is fading. I claw at Sikes's arm. "Yes," I mouth. "Yes."

Footsteps crunch over broken glass. Sikes's grip loosens. The leash falls from my arm. I draw in a life-affirming lungful of air and reach out for the time strands.

The steps outside stop. The pressure on my neck releases. I lean over, sucking in deep gasping breaths. Sikes's other hand clenches my arm more tightly than any leash.

"Let's go," he says.

I stumble beside him as he drags me from the office. Two frozen police officers are striding across the bar toward us. Both have their guns out. Sikes leads us in a wide circle around them. Glass glints on the beer-soaked floor. Outside, three cop cars block the street.

"Don't do anything stupid," Sikes says. "You'll be in as much trouble as I will if they see you now. We need to get at least ten blocks away before you let time go."

We head to the right, toward the river and downtown. The police cars hunker on the street beside us, their blue-and-white shapes somehow both familiar and terrifying. Two are empty. The third . . . my steps falter. In the driver's seat of the third car sits a time agent, Tito Marquez, and in the back, where normally a prisoner would be, is Raul.

175

My feet seem to have grown roots. I remember Raul at eleven, telling the teacher in our Youngers classroom that he would only read books about dinosaurs because extinct animals deserve to be remembered. Raul announcing to Yolly that he was a vegan because Jack convinced him VEGAN was an acronym for *Very Expensive Groceries and Nutrition.* Raul nailing his signature twisting basketball dunk, the one I could never block even when I saw it coming.

Sikes yanks on my arm. "Come on, hurry up."

I lunge for the cop car. Sikes stumbles after me, presumably too surprised by my sudden change in direction to resist.

"Where are you going?" he demands.

I grab the handle of the police car. It's locked. "I have to help him."

"This is not the time for a rescue." Sikes's voice is sharp.

The front door is also locked. I bang my fist against the window. Raul's head is turned to watch the police as they force their way inside Tom's Bar, his expression mildly curious. How can I be so close yet still unable to reach him?

"You're not going to get him out," Sikes says.

"I have to." The tears are back, blurring my vision.

"You're not. Look." He points inside the car. I lean forward to follow his finger, pressing my face against the glass to see through the reflection. It takes me a second to understand what Sikes means. One of Raul's arms rests on a bar that runs along the partition separating him from Agent Marquez. Above the expected leash banding his wrist is a second, thinner band—handcuffs. I catch my breath. Raul is handcuffed to a rail in the back of the car.

"Why would they do that?" I ask.

"Because Barnard knows what you can do, and he knows that you're out here. They're taking precautions."

I bang the glass again. "We'll hide somewhere and wait until they let him out."

"Why would they let him out?" Sikes pulls on my arm again. "You don't have to be in the room to do a rewind."

I strain away from Sikes and smack the glass until my hand stings. I raise my foot and kick it as hard as I can against the car's door. I don't even dent it.

"That's enough." Sikes grabs my other arm above the elbow and pulls me away from the car. "Save your energy for the freeze."

I struggle against him, even though I know it's hopeless. He's too strong, and Raul is too trapped. Agent Marquez holds the keys to both the car and the handcuffs, and I am quite sure Barnard's new "precautions" will require the agent to stay locked in the car until time stops. Sobs choke me. Sikes frog-marches me down the sidewalk, and after a few minutes, I give up fighting. I let him lead, trailing behind him like a reluctant child. Gray pavement passes under my feet, block after block.

Branches brush my face. We've walked all the way to the river, near the esplanade that follows the east bank, and Sikes is dragging me deep into some bushes that grow between the pedestrian walkway and a partially filled parking lot.

"We're far enough," he says. "You can let time go."

Air moves, but the day doesn't feel any brighter. Sikes releases me.

"Wait here a few minutes," he says. "We don't want to leave together."

My knees go slack, and I drop to the ground. There's space between the bushes, and it's clear someone has hidden here before. Cigarette butts and empty beer cans litter the dirt. Sikes peers through the branches.

"It was interesting to meet you, Alex," he says.

I touch my throat. It's tender, which probably means it's bruised. Sun flashes over me for a second as the branches part. I pull my legs up against my chest and rest my head on my knees. An ache from so much freezing squeezes like a vise across my skull. I am so tired. I can't rest for long, though. Sometime in the next few minutes, Raul is going to freeze time. He's going to rewind everything that happened in Sikes's office. Agent Marquez will see Sikes attack me. He'll see whoever burned up the safe.

He'll also see a spinner appear out of nowhere and then see me and Matt Thompson just as instantaneously disappear. Agent Marquez is going to learn that we can change things in froze time.

The spinners' most dangerous secret is about to be exposed.

16 ◀◀

MY POCKET IS VIBRATING. I PUT MY HAND AGAINST IT before remembering it's my phone.

"Jack?"

"Where are you?" The tension in Jack's voice makes the temperature in my leafy hideout drop by ten degrees.

"Near the river. What happened?"

"Nothing." He clears his throat. "I think someone is following me."

My fingertips feel like they've been dunked in ice water. I lick my lips and pitch my voice barely above a whisper.

"A wiper?"

"I don't know," Jack says.

Out on the esplanade, two women power walk past my hiding place, talking loudly about someone named Chris. I pull my knees in tighter.

"Where are *you*?" I ask Jack. "I thought you were at the squat."

"Downtown. I couldn't sleep."

The *whoop-whoop* of a siren leaks through the phone. Jack swears, and for a moment, all I can hear are rustling noises. I grab hold of a branch, not sure if I want to push it aside and run, or rip it off to use as a weapon.

"We need to get out of the city." Jack sounds out of breath.

"You're OK?"

"Yeah, yeah. I froze and went somewhere else."

I release the bush. A smear of sap marks my palm. I rub my hand against my leg, but the goop doesn't come off.

"Before we go, we have to warn the other spinners."

Jack makes an exasperated sound. "Alex, give it up already. We have to get away from the wipers."

"They know."

"Who knows what?"

"The police know what we can do." There's a stick digging into my back. I shift sideways and bang my tailbone into a rock. "Or they will soon. I had to freeze time, and Raul is going to rewind it, which means his agent will see me disappear."

Jack swears. "All the more reason to go now."

"No! Don't you get it?" Branches press against me on every side, leaves tickle my skin, and the smell of trash invades my nostrils. I roll onto my knees and crawl out onto the esplanade. "Barnard will try and cover it up, but it won't work. Not for long. And then all the Norms will panic, and the only way to calm them down will be to get rid of spinners."

Visions flash before my eyes: Raul's body stretched, unmoving, on a steel table; Yuki crumpled on a bed, her arm wired with multiple IVs; a long row of white sheets draped over still, human forms. All the spinners dead because of me. Just like Austin Shea.

"Come with me to the Sick." I brush dirt from my knees and start walking. "Please, Jack. We can talk to more of them if there are two

180

of us. Then, I promise, we'll get out of town. KJ has an idea of where we can go."

Even through the phone I feel him hesitating.

"How would we get in?"

"We'll follow the mail lady, Mariko. She always gets there at noon."

Silence stretches between us, the eternal pause between the ticks of a clock. I clutch the phone like a lifeline. Confronting Sikes by myself was a mistake, and I don't want to make it again.

"All right," Jack says. "I'll head there now."

I reach the Center at 11:40. Jack isn't there yet, so I wait in the alcove of a shuttered building. The Sick is across the street and half a block to my left, which means I have to poke my head out into the open whenever I look for him. I tilt my head down so my hair covers my face. I should have gotten a hat. Or a head scarf. A motorcycle cruises by, its deep roar bringing flashbacks of the one I saw from the bus. I check my watch: 11:47. The motorcyclist passes me without turning in my direction.

Jack shows up at 11:56.

"Thanks for coming," I say.

Jack grunts and squeezes in beside me. He watches the traffic passing along the street. I chew on a shred of fingernail and do my own surveillance. The Sick is located in the low-rent part of downtown, squashed in with a few by-the-week hotels, a soup kitchen, and some shady bars. Not many pedestrians bother with this area, and the few that do tend to talk to themselves. The only people out today are some painters who have two tall ladders set up to work on a building further up the block. I watch as a man in a paint-splattered jumpsuit climbs down one of the ladders, shifts it a couple yards to the left, then climbs slowly back up. The fingernail crunches beneath my teeth. This doesn't seem like a very efficient painting strategy. Maybe they're not real painters. Maybe they've been hired to watch for us.

"Will Victor be pissed when he wakes up and finds out that you ditched him?" I ask Jack, more to distract myself than because I care.

"Probably."

I glance at him. Jack's jaw is set in a hard line. "You guys not getting along?"

Jack keeps his eyes fixed on a man at the far end of the street. "Victor's careless. He never wants to hide when I freeze or melt time. He thinks it's funny if things just disappear."

I check my watch instead of pointing out to Jack that he recently thought the same thing. 11:58. Mariko should be here soon with the mail. The thought has barely cleared my consciousness when Jack nudges me.

"There she is."

Mariko is across the street, pushing a wheeled cart in front of her like a stroller. Despite the warm day, she wears long pants. Her hair, pulled back in a ponytail, swings to the rhythm of her gait. Jack and I watch her disappear into the building next to the Sick, then reappear and proceed down the block. Jack drops one hand over mine.

"You want to do the honors?"

I nod, a nervous jerk that's more like a muscle spasm. We both stick our heads out and watch Mariko clomp her way up the ramp that curves along the side of the Center's front stairs. In my mind's eye, I picture the shadowed lobby on the other side. Charlie will be on duty again, or maybe that other guy. What's his name? The one with the red beard. Mariko stops at the front door and starts to rummage through her bag. Sam. That's it. Samuel Kelly.

"What's she doing?" Jack asks.

"Ringing the doorbell," I say.

"No, she isn't. The doorbell is on the other side."

Jack's right. I lean forward, squinting to better see what's going on. Mariko pulls a stack of mail from her bag and starts fiddling with something on the left side of the front door. Seconds later, she steps away and starts back down the ramp. The door hasn't opened. I peer at the spot where she was standing. To the left of the front door, waist high in the rough gray of the Center's stone walls, I can just make out a darker gray rectangle.

"What is that?" Jack asks.

"A mail slot." I slump against the alcove's wall. "Is that new?"

"Probably," Jack says, as we watch Mariko stride purposely down the street toward an office building. "They did let four spinners escape. They'd have to do something to improve security."

My eyes flick from the suspiciously oblivious painters to the Center's roofline, which I know hides security cameras. What if they've tilted them so they point not at the front door, but outward, so they can see people lurking across the street?

"We should leave," I say.

"Leave Portland?"

The cameras are too far away to see, but I can sense their red recording lights, pointing like lasers in my direction: Here she is. Come and get her.

"We can't." I abandon our meager hiding spot and emerge onto the sidewalk. "Not until we think of some other way of getting into the Sick."

Jack doesn't move. "What about FedEx?"

The Center's windows stare at us, dark and menacing in their blankness.

"What about it?" I ask.

"A package would be too big to fit in the mail slot."

"So?" I turn to face Jack. If anyone *is* watching us from the Center, all they'll be able to see is my back. "We're not FedEx."

"Let's send a package. Then when the delivery guy shows up, we can follow him in."

"We wouldn't know what time they'd deliver it."

Jack twists his fingers, his knuckles cracking in stuttering unison.

"We can pretend to be FedEx ourselves."

The imaginary lasers are burning into my scalp. It's all I can do to keep from sprinting down the street.

"Come *on*, Jack."

Jack steps out of the alcove and starts walking. "All we have to do is get a uniform."

I put a hand against the pulse throbbing in my neck. Shannon once told me about a guru who could control his own heartbeat through meditation. I press my fingers against the fluttering beat. Deep breathing, I tell myself. Calm thoughts.

A flash of blue and white in the corner of my eye shatters my attempt at inner peace. A block ahead, a police car waits at a red light, facing our direction. My hands clench.

"Look!" Jack seizes my arm.

"Where?" I swing around, sure I'm going to see yet another cop.

"That clothing store." Jack points down the street. "If I got those slacks and a top in matching navy, I'd look like a delivery guy."

I glance at the police car. The traffic light is still red.

"What if they recognize you?"

"I'll wear a hat." Jack glares at me. "What's wrong with you? I thought you were desperate to get inside."

"I am."

The light changes. The cop car's engine revs with an ominous rumble as it accelerates in our direction. Glare turns the windshield into a mirror, and then, abruptly, it clears. A scream bursts in my chest, my effort to strangle it resulting in an ugly choking noise.

"What?" Jack asks.

Ross's face appears behind the glass, and his eyes lock onto mine.

"We have to freeze." I grab Jack's hand and drag him into the closest storefront. "Now."

A bell tinkles as we step inside. I'm moving so fast, I barely take in the shelves crammed with paint, art books, brushes, crayons, and custom paper that crowd the store's narrow aisles. A woman with a purple streak in her hair and a silver nose ring glances up as we dart past. I flash her what I hope is an innocent smile and dive into a section lined with large pieces of poster board. The towering sheets create a tunnel effect. Neither the clerk nor the people passing outside the store windows can see us.

Jack yanks time to a stop.

"What happened?" he asks. "Did you see something?"

"Ross," I gasp.

Jack's face pales.

"He's out there," I say. "He saw us."

"Let's get out of here."

Ross has pulled his car over to the sidewalk. I can't tell if the engine is still running, but his head is turned in the direction of the art store.

"Do you still want to do this?" Jack asks.

I draw a ragged breath.

"Yes."

We walk down the street to the clothing store and pick out

a relatively uniform-like outfit. In a back room, I find an empty cardboard box, which I stuff with Jack's regular clothes and a note that says *Donations*, then reseal with tape. On the top, in black marker, I write out the Sick's address.

Walking the three blocks back to the Center, we hammer out the rest of our plan: Jack will ring the bell while I wait nearby. If the door opens, I'll freeze time, come over and touch Jack, then melt and refreeze as fast as I can so the two of us will be in the freeze together. If, on the other hand, the Center does have some way of accepting deliveries without opening the door, he will hand over the package, and we will both just walk away.

Time hovers around me, a still blanket to steady myself against. We duck into an underground parking garage a block from our goal, start time again, and then peek out toward the place where we last saw Ross. The taillights of his blue-and-white car are just visible, parked in front of a fire hydrant around the next block. I'm straining for the sound of his door opening when the car peels away from the curb.

"He's leaving," I say.

"Great," Jack says, "maybe he didn't see us after all."

The image of Ross's eyes locking with mine through the windshield burns in my memory. Did I imagine it? Dread coils inside me, a lion waiting to spring.

"Maybe."

We slide out of our shelter, and head to the Center. The building seems just as menacing as it did when we'd left it ten minutes ago. I wait on the opposite sidewalk, pretending to adjust the laces on my sneakers, while Jack marches up the Center steps. Through my bangs, I watch as he pushes the bell beside the heavy front door. Someone must have responded, because I see him lean toward the speaker panel to announce himself.

At the end of the block, a police car turns the corner.

My mouth goes dry. It can't be Ross, can it? How could he know which direction we went? Time's endless strands quiver at the edge of my control. On the Center's front step, Jack waits, oblivious. I stand up. The car cruises closer.

Jack shifts the box he's carrying from one hand to the other. The gesture is the sign we've agreed upon if everything is going as planned. But it's not going as planned—not at all. The car slows in front of me. I take in a gulp of air that doesn't reach my lungs. Time shimmers around me. The car's window opens with a whisper.

"Alex?" Ross asks. "Is everything all right?"

A silent scream fills my throat. Ross unlatches his seat belt. The door to the Center cracks open. I snatch time to a stop so hard my whole body clenches.

The freeze does not bring comfort. Ross sits before me, radiating menace; the Center looms above me, rife with danger. I force my feet to move. Crossing the road feels like wading through rushing water, every step an effort to overcome invisible resistance. One foot forward. Another. I reach the stairs leading up to the doorway. They are painfully familiar. Here is the chip from the time some protesters threw rocks, there the mold stain that looks like a bald man wearing glasses. Memories lay themselves before me like pictures in a photo album: racing up the stairs with KJ to avoid being late after an outing; skipping down them beside Ross as we head out on a mission; stumbling up them just weeks before, my arm bleeding from the attack by one of Sikes's men, naively believing I was heading to safety.

Now I know better. Now I know I am entering a building run by someone who wants me dead. The narrow strip of black at the edge of the Center's front door gapes like a bottomless abyss oozing with some unnamed threat. I start climbing the stairs. It's just the

Center—my home for the past seven years. Time is frozen, so there's no reason to panic. The danger is behind me. The danger is Ross. It still takes every ounce of my will to climb the final step.

Jack stands in perfect stillness, one hand clasping the Center's front door. He's tilted the cap so it covers his eyes. I touch his wrist. His hand is warm and solid. Mine is cold and quivering. I let time move forward for the briefest possible instant before snatching it back under my control. Jack's hand twitches.

"Let's go," he says, pulling the door open another few inches.

"Wait." The gap at the edge of the door shimmers with evil.

Jack frowns at me. "What for?"

He sounds suspicious. The horror whispering to me from the other side of the door saturates my mind, and I suddenly wonder what Jack plans to do once we get inside. Why is he being so helpful when he initially thought my plan was foolish? Does he really want to warn the other spinners, or does he have his own reasons for heading into the Center? A tremor shivers my shoulders. How does anyone ever really know what someone else is thinking? I thought I knew Ross, but I was wrong. I don't even seem to know KJ.

"I'll go first." Swallowing my terror, I yank the door open wide and plunge across the threshold.

Buzzing explodes in my head, a bomb sending bits of shrapnel flying around my skull. I clamp my hands over my ears. Pain knocks me to my knees. Knives are slicing through my brain, tearing my control, ripping the time strands into fluttering wisps.

Something clangs. Not inside my head, but outside, in the world, the moving, unfrozen world. I stagger to my feet. Vertical lines cross my vision, making it hard to see across the lobby. I turn. Jack stands on the front step, door caught in his hand, face blank with shock.

I shake my head. The buzzing fades to a dull roar, and the scene around me grows clearer. These are not hallucinatory lines blocking my vision. They're bars. Someone has erected metal bars just inside the Center's front door, as if they were framing in a new, much smaller entrance hall. Except this is no entrance. It's a cage, and the opening between it and the front door has just clanged shut.

Panic wells up in my chest. I launch myself against the bars, wrenching at the unyielding metal. Someone behind me shouts. Footsteps clatter on the tiled floor.

"It's a trap!" I scream at Jack.

Jack's mouth opens wordlessly. For a brief second, we stare at each other. Then his gaze moves past me and focuses on something behind my shoulder. His pupils widen. The next instant, Jack disappears, and I'm left in the cage, alone.

17 ◀◀

A BREEZE BLOWS ACROSS THE CENTER'S EMPTY FRONT steps, lifting a stray leaf into the air. I watch the tiny piece of green float into the open sky before the Center's heavy oak door swings shut and seals out the sun. Behind it, very faintly, I hear the sound of Ross's car as it drives away. All my fears focus into a kind of surreal clarity. I rest my forehead against the bars of my prison. The hard metal drills the relentless buzzing deeper into my brain, but I don't move. These bars are the only thing still separating me from the place I've fought so hard to escape.

The familiar smells from the Center's industrial cleaning solutions sink in through my pores. I tighten my grip on the bars, waiting for the voice I know will come.

"Hello, Alexandra." Dr. Barnard sounds out of breath. He probably ran all the way from his office in his eagerness to greet his captive. "I was hoping you'd come by for a visit."

I study the Center's front door. Bits of dirt darken the corners of the inset panels, ancient grime from decades past. The oak is scratched, heavy, and completely solid.

"Let me go," I say, even though I know the plea is hopeless.

"I can't do that." A metallic click tells me he's unlocked the other side of the cage. I make a feeble effort to stop time, barely even disappointed when the expected block keeps me from grabbing hold. The cage snaps shut behind Barnard. "You're a very sick girl."

"Liar." I speak the words without heat.

Barnard pries one of my arms away from the bars.

"In your condition," he says, "you're a danger to both yourself and society."

The leash fits snugly around my wrist, its buzz barely adding to the hum already burning my brain.

"Go to hell," I say.

"You know we don't allow rudeness like that here," Barnard says. He searches my pockets, removing my phone, gloves, and lock picks. "I expect your behavior to improve once we get you back on your medication."

I make a belated effort to pull away from him, but even with his arm in a cast, my struggles earn me nothing more than a sore shoulder.

"Let's go." Barnard uses his good arm to twist my hand around to the middle of my back, forcing me to turn and face the lobby. Except for the cage, it hasn't changed. The same worn tile I've crossed a thousand times, the same dusty photographs, and the same grainy security feed playing in Charlie's guard station. Charlie himself is the only person standing outside the metal bars, an expression of dull surprise crimping his round cheeks.

"Open the door," Barnard barks. Charlie starts, fumbling with the cage's door before managing to swing it open.

"Charlie," I beg, "don't let him do this. It will kill me to go back on

191

Aclisote. It's all a lie, what they've been telling you. Didn't you see me just appear on the monitor? Everything's a lie . . ."

Barnard wrenches my arm higher up my back until the pain cuts off my words.

"She's raving," Barnard says. Unlike me, he sounds calm, even clinical. "She's been off Aclisote so long she's starting to go mad."

The endlessly repeated lies work their magic. Charlie backs away, probably expecting me to attack him at any minute. I know anything I say will only add to Barnard's argument that I'm insane. I wonder how Barnard will explain my appearing in the Center and Jack disappearing off the doorstep. He'll probably just delete the video footage and claim Charlie was imagining things. The front desk guard is a nice enough guy, but he'll never be mistaken for smart.

Barnard muscles me away from the entrance. The disorienting buzz in my head lessens as we get farther from the cage. I reach out with my mind and give the blocking wall a tentative push. Time flows on. Even out of the cage, the leash on my arm keeps my skills firmly in check.

"Alex!" Yolly barrels down the stairs, her soft-soled shoes thudding on the steps in her hurry to reach me. She wears a cotton smock printed with kittens chasing balls of colorful yarn. Brown hair perches on her head in stiff curls that even her headlong rush doesn't muss.

"Oh, thank goodness." Yolly throws her arms around me, forcing Barnard to halt. She pulls me close, patting my back and murmuring words of reassurance as she presses my face against her well-padded chest. We always rolled our eyes about Yolly, the Center's frumpy matron, with her kindergarten-teacher voice and misguided conviction that the Center was just a slightly unusual but happy family. Now, her vanilla perfume wafts over me and fills my eyes with unwanted tears.

"We've been so worried," Yolly croons. "Are you feeling sick? Is that why you came home? Where are the others?"

"I'm not sick." My voice is muffled by her chest and by the tears coursing down my cheeks.

"It's OK, dear," Yolly says, still patting me. "We can talk once you get settled." She pulls a tissue from her pocket and dabs at my face. "Amy is off duty today," she tells Barnard, referring to the Center's nurse. "I can take her up to the clinic."

Barnard's grip on my arm does not relax.

"I'll take her." He pushes me forward, shoving me out of Yolly's embrace.

"Surely there's no need for that," Yolly protests.

"She's been raving," Barnard says. "If we don't treat her soon, she might get violent."

Yolly starts up the stairs in our wake. "The poor girl must be terribly ill."

"I'm not sick," I say again. "I'm better than I've ever been. I can change things in frozen time."

Yolly winces, and I see her exchange a knowing look with Barnard.

"It's true," I say. Frustration makes my voice come out so high I know Yolly will mistake it for hysteria, but I can't help myself. "Take off the leash and I'll show you."

We've reached the top of the stairs. Yolly pushes open the door to the clinic and watches me pass inside with a sorrowful expression. Empty chairs haunt the small waiting area next to the nurse's desk. The sight of this space reawakens the panic that despair momentarily dimmed. I already know exactly how the fake leather seats feel against the backs of my legs, know the contents of the well-thumbed magazines littering the lone table. I remember the smell of alcohol and the taste of Aclisote, chemical sweet, as it hits the back of my throat.

"No," I say, struggling to back out the door. Barnard twists my arm upward again, sending fresh jolts of pain all the way to my shoulder.

"Now, dear," Yolly says to me. "You know we have to get you back on your meds."

"No!" I shake my head. My struggling feet slip on the smooth tile. Behind me, Barnard blocks me like a living wall. I can no more move him than cut through the buzzing haze that blocks me from time. "He'll kill me."

"Come on." Barnard pushes me forward, his greater weight moving us deeper into the room.

"Please." I'm babbling. "Let me just show you. I won't do anything bad, I promise."

"Should I call Charlie?" Yolly asks.

"Get me something to put her under," Barnard snaps.

The idea of Barnard making me unconscious horrifies me even more than taking Aclisote. He might never let me gain consciousness again. I stop flailing.

"I'll cooperate."

"We'll see," Barnard says, only slightly reducing the tension on my arm.

I force my feet to move me across the waiting area and into one of the sick rooms, then wait meekly while Barnard orders Yolly to lock us in and prepare a syringe with Aclisote. He probably doesn't trust me to keep it down if he gives me the more typical oral dose. The dosage he orders is low, which is mildly surprising but not reassuring. He can always up the dose later on. He's the only doctor on site. The expert.

Before she leaves, Yolly asks if he'd prefer she make up an IV drip, and Barnard says a syringe is safer. I might pull out an IV. I collapse onto the edge of the bed and wonder where Jack is and if he's already back at the squat. I try not to picture Jack telling KJ and Shannon what happened. Poor KJ. He's been awake for only a couple days and I've already ruined everything.

Barnard paces the room, twisting open the horizontal blinds and snapping them shut again before he could have done more than glimpse the street outside. Every few seconds, he checks his watch. The gold band glints in the overhead light.

"Where are the others?" Barnard asks.

I shake my head.

"Tell me where they are," he says, abandoning all pretense now that we're alone, "and I'll let you live longer."

"No."

"That's OK." Barnard taps the hard surface of his cast. "One of them will probably come looking for you pretty soon."

The rap of his restless finger blends into the buzz of the leash. I rub my forehead.

"They won't come."

"Why not? You kids have a fight?"

"No, they're just . . ." I am about to say they aren't stupid enough to duplicate my mistake when I realize that Barnard might not know Jack was with me. He probably thought I'd followed a real delivery guy in. By the time Barnard reached me, the door had shut, so he wouldn't have seen Jack disappear.

"What was in the lobby?" I ask instead. "The thing that broke my freeze?"

Barnard's face brightens. "Pretty effective, isn't it?"

"What is it?"

Barnard studies me for a moment, then shrugs, presumably deciding that now that I'm in his clutches, bragging about his new toy hardly counts as a risk.

"It's called a chromoelectronegator. It emits an electronic pulse that interferes with specific brain patterns—in this case, the ones you use to freeze time."

"Like a leash."

"Sort of." He chuckles, as if I might find something funny about this vile technology. "Except the chromoelectronegator offers a kind of bubble of protection. If you're anywhere within its range, the pulse keeps you from being able to freeze time."

"So if time is already frozen . . . ?"

Barnard says nothing, which doesn't really matter. I already know what happens if you walk into a chromo-whatever.

Barnard checks his watch again. "Why did you come back, anyway?"

I say the first thing that comes into my head. "I wanted to get my stuff."

Barnard nods as if this is reasonable, as if I might really want the hand-me-down crap they dole out to us. A coil of hatred twists through me. The fact that he can be so calm when he has every intention of killing me makes me want to dive across the room and strangle him. The only thing stopping me is the knowledge that he would sedate me. I try instead to focus my hatred like they do in movies, blasting it through my eyes in a laser point to roast the flesh off his bones. It doesn't work.

"How long do I have?" I ask him.

"I'm afraid you're no longer a viable research candidate." Barnard tilts his head, considering. "So it won't be long."

Research? I shudder.

"You didn't give me very much Aclisote. At least not enough to kill me."

"An article in a recent science journal showed that extreme swings in Aclisote dosages can cause a bad reaction."

"You don't care."

He shrugs again. "I don't. Unfortunately, Yolanda read the article too, so I have to at least pretend to be cautious. It's just for a couple days. Your time skills should normalize over the next forty-eight hours. By Thursday, I can transfer you to the Central Office."

Sweat tickles the edges of my hairline. I picture a sterile room with spinners locked in cages like rats in a lab. The sweat drips along the edge of my cheek. Days. I will probably only live a few more days.

A rattling at the door announces Yolly's return. She carries a tray lined with a clean paper towel in one hand. Neatly, in the center, beside a packet holding an alcohol swab, lies a syringe.

The sight of the needle sucks all the moisture from my mouth. I slide up higher on the bed, pushing myself as far away from the gleaming needle as I can.

"Do you want me to do the injection, doctor?" Yolly asks.

"Please."

Barnard steps to one side of my bed, ready to hold me down if I protest. Yolly sets the tray on the bedside table and pulls on a pair of blue latex gloves.

"You'll feel much better after this, Alex," Yolly says. "Everything will go back to being just the way it was." Her voice holds a pleading note, and I realize that despite her optimistic words, Yolly doubts I'll ever regain what she considers my sanity.

"He's sending me to the Central Office," I say.

Yolly pauses in the act of rolling up my sleeve.

"I said we *might* have to," Barnard lies smoothly, "if the treatment here doesn't go well."

Yolly finishes my sleeve and turns back to the tray. When she rips open the swab, I see her hands are shaking. The sharp tang of alcohol leaches into the room. I flinch when Barnard places a hand on my shoulder. Yolly might delude herself that his gesture is meant to be reassuring; I recognize the weight of a jailer's touch.

The alcohol swab leaves my arm cold.

"Yolly," I say, keeping my voice as calm and rational as I can manage, "I know I've been a pain sometimes, but I do appreciate how you always do your best to care for us. You were the one person I missed while I was gone."

Yolly's lip trembles just a tiny bit. "Thank you, Alex. That means a lot to me."

She picks up the syringe.

"Shannon misses you, too," I say.

The syringe wavers.

"How is she doing?" Yolly asks. "Is she sick yet?"

"She's fine. We were hoping you'd do us a favor." I feel only slightly guilty lying about the "we" part.

"Of course, dear."

Yolly prods the inside of my elbow for a vein. When the needle pricks my skin, it's so quick it barely hurts.

"Pull all our medical files," I say.

"Alex." Barnard's voice holds warning.

Yolly depresses the plunger. I keep talking, quickly now, racing the liquid that's flooding into my bloodstream. Counting down the seconds until Barnard can make Yolly leave.

"Look carefully at the dates and dosages. People with low dosages of Aclisote never get sick, and everyone who dies is getting high dosages. Aclisote doesn't treat the sickness; Aclisote *causes* it. Dr. Barnard knows this. Check his private correspondence, there has to be something..."

"That's enough, Alex." Barnard's fingers dig into my shoulder bones. "Aclisote dosages are based on chronotin readings, not on whether someone is sick or not. Yolanda knows that as well as you do."

Yolly removes the spent syringe and dabs my arm with a cotton swab. She has her lips squashed together like she's trying not to cry. My flare of hope dwindles. Yolly doesn't believe me.

"I think it's best if we leave you alone," Barnard says. "Your talk has upset Yolanda."

Yolly nods her thanks at this false show of concern. I watch as the two of them leave the room, Barnard murmuring reassuring lies as he pats Yolly's broad back. The lock clicks when they shut the door.

I lie back on the bed. Beams of sunlight leak through the almost-closed blinds of the room's two windows, casting narrow bands along the ceiling. No one comes into the clinic. The clock on the wall across from me says it's only a little past noon, which means most kids will be downstairs eating lunch, though some of the Youngers might be running around in the gym. I picture Simon and Aidan arguing over their favorite football team, Yuki flicking back her long dark hair before she picks the tomatoes out of her sandwich, Calvin barely glancing up from his book as he ... I shake my head. No, not Calvin. Calvin won't be there. Calvin died from Aclisote poisoning a week before I left the Center.

The wail of a siren screams below my barred windows. I roll onto my stomach and hang my head over the edge of the bed. Hair falls across my face, chopping my view of the floor into alternating lines of light and dark. Do the others talk about us, the four missing spinners?

Probably not. We never talk about kids once they're gone. Four is a lot to lose at once, though. Wouldn't there be rumors? Aidan was in the room when I took Jack the day we escaped. He might have seen me appear for a second, and he certainly saw Jack disappear. Wouldn't he have told someone? Or has Barnard wiped out that possibility by making him sick?

Prickles slither over my skin. Maybe Aidan is gone, another victim of the supposed "time sickness." And it's all my fault.

Seconds tick forward, the dwindling moments of my life irretrievably slipping away. I study the muted swirls on the floor tiles. I've been gone from the Center just a week. What did I accomplish with my brief freedom? The empty room mocks me. I should have warned the other spinners right away, before the Center had time to set up new traps. I should never have gotten sidetracked by trying to blackmail Barnard and warning Sikes and worrying about every random bump in the night.

A dust mote whispers across the floor tiles, carried by an invisible puff of wind. I watch the insubstantial speck until it melts into the surrounding air. Now that the worst has happened, the terrors that have kept me in knots are fading, and the path I should have taken is painfully clear. Life is what matters. Friends matter.

An image of KJ's face swims into my mind, his black hair and happy grin as clear as if he stood before me. I reach out a hand. Air washes between my fingers, leaving them as empty as the hole opening inside my chest. I will never see KJ again. I'll never get to apologize for my anger and jealousy. I'll never get to tell him how much I love him.

I curl up into a ball in the center of the bed. My head aches from the buzzing of the leash. Or maybe it's the Aclisote. Maybe even that small dose is enough to bring back the sickness. Hot tears burn my eyes, then drip down my face as my breaths turn into sobs. Aclisote is back in my veins, and this time, the poison is here to stay.

18 ◀◀

IT'S DARK WHEN I WAKE UP. THERE'D BEEN A NOISE, some sound that pulled me into consciousness, but now that I'm awake, I can't hear it. I open one eye and peer out into the room. The dim light only accentuates its bleakness, sparse furniture colored by the mustard glare of a streetlight coming through the windows. I bury my face in my pillow, seeking the escape of sleep.

"Alex!"

The hiss shoots me into full consciousness. I bolt upright. The blind that covers one of the windows hangs crookedly, the top edge barely clinging to its frame. On the floor in front of it, jagged pieces of glass litter the linoleum. I rub my eyes, afraid what I am seeing is part of a dream. Through the smashed pane, KJ's face beams at me like a giddy jack-o-lantern.

"KJ?" I stammer. "What . . . ?"

"No time." He rips away the dangling blind and thrusts a hand through two of the window's four vertical security bars.

"Quick," he orders, holding out a long skinny orange thing that, for a confused second, I think is a snake. "Take this and plug it in."

I leap from the bed and grab the heavy-duty extension cord,

stretching it across the room until I find a socket. As soon as the plug hits home, a screaming whine fills the room, coupled with the smell of burning metal. Sparks cascade like Fourth-of-July sparklers. KJ is cutting through the first of the four window bars with a handheld electric saw.

I scramble for my shoes and cram them onto my feet. KJ, perched on the upper rungs of what must be a very tall ladder, reaches up to press the saw against the top edge of the now partially detached bar. As I watch, the metal falls away, dropping to the ground below.

"How'd you get here?" I shout, but my question is drowned out by the whine of the saw. I race over to the room's other window. The broken glass will have triggered the Center's silent alarm system. I peer down the street, searching for a flash of red and blue lights.

KJ's saw bites into the top of the second bar, and another chunk of metal falls away. KJ starts on the third bar. Four more cuts to go. I lean my forehead against the cold glass. Slanting out from the Center's stone walls, KJ's ladder gleams pale silver in the midnight dark. At its foot, I can make out Shannon, craning her head to watch KJ work. Splotches of white splatter the ladder's rungs; they must have borrowed it from the painters down the street.

The outer door to the main room of the clinic bangs. Someone is coming. KJ pulls the saw free and slams the spinning blade against the third bar's upper edge. There is no way he'll be done before they get inside.

"Hurry!" I yell at KJ. He must read my lips because he nods.

I whirl around and survey my limited options—bed, dresser, chair. I dash for the bed. Shoving as hard as I can, I heave it toward the door. It slides about a foot and stops. Voices invade the clinic, coupled with the patter of running feet. Sweat makes my palms slip against the bed's frame. I wipe them on my pants and hurl myself against the metal edge. It slides forward, and this time I plunge after it, keeping the momentum going until the bed smashes against the door. I glance back at the window. Three bars are now gone; a blast of sparks shows KJ working on the fourth. I pick up the room's lone chair and heave it on top of the bed.

The voices are right outside the door. I recognize Barnard's angry growl, Charlie's confused patter, and Yolly's anxious squeak. Keys rattle in the lock. I lean against the bed, adding my own weight to the meager blockade. The door thumps.

"She's blocked it!" Charlie shouts.

"Together." Barnard this time. "On three."

I brace myself against the bed, but the impact of their combined weight shudders my pile of obstacles. A second heave and my feet skid out from under me, knocking me to the floor.

"Again," Barnard orders.

I scramble upright. The door is open about a foot, still partially blocked by the bed. Through the gap I can see my hunters. Barnard's face is red with effort, his glasses slipping down the ridge of his thin nose. Charlie looks excited by the commotion. Yolly hovers behind the two men, her mouth puckered with anxiety. Barnard and Charlie both take a step back in preparation for their next attack.

"Alex!" KJ calls over the saw's whine.

The two men lunge. I leap for the window, barely outrunning the bed as it skids away from the door. KJ shoves one hand through the gap, the other still holding the moving blade against metal.

"Grab her!" Barnard yells.

Outside, a siren wails. Yolly screams. Glass crunches under my shoes as KJ's hand closes around mine. The saw bites deep into the final bar.

Time stops.

Silence. KJ and I stand, hands clasped, a foot apart, both panting. Behind him, police lights tint the unmoving air lurid blue. I turn my head. Barnard was running so fast the freeze caught him floating in midair. His teeth are clenched, his unbroken arm stretched out, fingers inches from my shoulder.

"That was close." KJ wriggles his own fingers, still clamped inside mine. "You're kinda hurting my hand, though."

The tendons on the back of my hand are standing out like wires.

"Sorry." I relax my grip. "Your freeze. Has it . . . ?"

"Changed?" KJ says. "Yeah. This will stick."

I look around the trampled room—the smashed chair and frantic people, the metal dust and snaking cord.

"That was . . ." I try to think of an adjective big enough to capture my stunned relief.

"Amazing?" KJ offers. "Impressive? Heroic?"

"Yeah." I smile at him. "All those things."

KJ smiles back. Something warm spreads through my insides, mixing with the reprieve I am only beginning to accept. I put a hand against the window frame.

"Let's get out of here," I say.

KJ wriggles the saw, pulling it out of the nearly severed bar. Together, we force the bar back and forth, until we can bend it far enough to unblock the window. KJ starts down the ladder. I make to follow, when an idea stops me. Turning back, I weave my way past the frozen people and scattered furniture, out into the main clinic. In the desk, I find a pencil and scrap of paper.

Yolly, I write, *now you have to believe I was telling you the truth when I said my skills have changed. Barnard has been lying to you about a lot of things.*

Aclisote is poison. Please, believe me. I add my cell phone number. Barnard took my phone, but Earnest Guy at the store said I could reprogram the number into a new one. I fold the paper into a square and slip it into Yolly's pocket before climbing out the open window. I know it's a long shot, but if she believes me, there's a chance she will help the other spinners.

KJ is waiting on the sidewalk, next to frozen Shannon. In the amber light from the streetlamp, KJ's face shines like gold. I drink in the familiar lines of his cheek, admiring the proud arch of his nose and the full lips I kissed so briefly.

KJ wraps me up in a tight hug. "When Jack told us they'd caught you . . ."

He buries his face in my hair. I squeeze my eyes shut so I can't see Shannon. KJ smells like fresh air, and he's so warm and solid I never want to let him go.

"What happened?" KJ murmurs. His breath lifts the strands of my hair so they tickle the back of my neck. "Jack said your freeze broke as soon as you stepped inside."

"It was a chromo . . ." The word tangles my tongue. "A zapper."

KJ pulls back, enough to see my face, but not enough to let me go. "A what?"

"A zapper. Barnard has one." I describe it the way Barnard did, though I'm not sure I'm making much sense. I've been this close to KJ a million times— squashed up with three others on a sofa watching a movie, crashing into him while playing basketball in the gym, leaning over his shoulder as he coached me on how to use a computer. But now his closeness is as noticeable as a third person standing between us. I can't concentrate on my words because I'm distracted by KJ's arm wrapped around my waist, and the heat of our bodies where they press together. We are so close that when I breathe in, I take in the warmth of his exhale. It tastes sweet, tinged with an intimate scent that turns my knees to jelly.

KJ's brow wrinkles. He pulls one of his hands free and presses it against his temple. When he leans back, Shannon's worried face zooms into view again. I slide out of his embrace.

"Are you OK?" I ask.

"Yeah." He grimaces. "I don't know how much longer I can hold this freeze, though. Do you think you could take over after we get that leash off?"

"I'm not sure. They gave me Aclisote in there. I don't know if it was enough to block my skills again, but I wouldn't want to risk finding out here."

"I was afraid of that."

I gesture toward Shannon's still form. "What about her?"

"As of this afternoon, she still couldn't change anything."

I think of all the things I want to tell him, quickly followed by all the reasons why this is not a good time.

"We should go," I say.

KJ picks up a backpack that's lying on the ground behind the ladder. After rummaging a minute, he pulls out a pair of bolt cutters. I hold out my arm. One snip and the leash falls away, taking with it the low buzz rattling my brain.

"Thanks," I say, rubbing my wrist.

KJ puts the cutters away so he can take both my hand and Shannon's before he melts and refreezes time. A brief blast of external sound, and then it's just the three of us.

"You're here!" Shannon starts to cry. "I thought the ladder was going to tip over and . . ." The rest of her sentence is lost in sobs.

"It's OK." KJ pats her shoulder, but his eyes are on me. "What happened to your neck?"

"My neck?" My hand touches the memento Sikes left behind. "Oh, yeah, I forgot about that. Let's just say you were right that going to Tom's Bar was a bad idea."

"Sikes did this to you?" KJ touches my chin, raising my head so he can better see whatever the bruises look like. "What happened?"

"It's a long story." I shake my head. "I'll tell you later."

KJ runs two fingers across the place where Sikes tried to choke me. My breath catches. Shannon sniffs.

"We told you not to go there," she says.

"I know." I step back and KJ's hand falls away. "And rescuing me put both of you at risk. I'm sorry."

Shannon looks up at the broken window with a wistful expression.

"At least you got to see everybody," she says.

Barnard's confessed intentions leap into my mouth, but I swallow them. The furious anger she's triggered in me over the last few days feels distant right now. She's suffered too, and convincing her of the truth can wait. A moment of awkward silence settles between us, which KJ breaks by digging into his backpack again.

"Here." He pulls out a light-blue rain jacket decorated with small yellow ducks and holds it out to me. "I brought you this."

"Um, it's cute?" I say.

KJ tosses it at me with a grin. "It's to keep anyone from following us too easily. I can't keep time frozen all the way back to the squat. If we're wearing different clothes, they're less likely to spot us."

He hands Shannon a second jacket, then unzips his black sweatshirt to reveal a colorful rugby-style shirt underneath. From his back pocket, he pulls a stretchy hat, and slides it over his hair.

"Clever," I say, with genuine admiration.

"Thanks." KJ rubs his temple again. "But it won't count for much if we're not far away from here when time starts."

"I'll help." I take hold of his hand. Shannon immediately grabs the other. Some of the tension in KJ's face eases as both our skills sync with his.

The three of us head east toward the river. Cool night air fills my lungs as I swallow deep gulps of freedom. City streets welcome my footsteps, lights twinkle with celebratory glitter, even the icy blue from a pair of cop cars feels festive. I want to dance my way along the sidewalk. I'm alive. I'm free. I've been given another chance. This time, I won't blow it. KJ's hand is warm and solid where it's cradled inside my own.

We walk long enough to cross the river before KJ says he can't hold time anymore, then keep walking for another hour, since we're all too nervous to wait for a bus this late at night. By the time we make it back to the squat, it's somewhere after two a.m. KJ is so exhausted, Shannon and I half-push him up the ladder. Shannon leads him off to bed, and KJ, stumbling with fatigue, follows her without protest. I watch their retreat into the darkened interior with only the smallest pang of jealousy. The two of them just saved my life; anything but gratitude seems inexcusably petty.

I wake feeling tired, but calmer than I have in weeks. Voices drift toward me from the direction of the kitchen—Victor, judging from the collected mumbles, talking to Faith and Jack. I stare up at the brightening windows, appreciating the warmth of my sleeping bag and even the grungy familiarity of the squat. The clarity that came to me at the clinic still holds my former fears at bay. The four of us need to leave town, secure a home base, and come up with a strategy to get the other spinners out of the Center. Challenging, but we have ten days before the Center closes, and these are not insurmountable obstacles. Not for us. Not if we all work together.

The volume from the kitchen inches higher, intruding on my tranquil musings. I sit up. This is not a friendly conversation. Someone is very angry. Rolling out of bed, I rummage through the clothes piled on my floor, pulling on my rather dusty jeans and a moderately clean sweater. The argument, now even louder, is starting to make sense.

"One more day! You promised another day!"

Victor's voice is ugly with threat. I don't waste time finding shoes and jog, barefoot, in the direction of the yelling.

"So?" Jack's undisguised disgust makes it clear his infatuation with Victor is over. "We've got more important things to do now."

"We had a deal, man."

I turn the corner toward the kitchen, and the peaceful feeling I woke up with dissolves. Victor and Jack stand in identical poses— shoulders back, chests arched. Victor's face burns with an angry flush. I can see only the back of Jack's head, but from the rigid set of his neck and shoulders, I imagine their expressions match too.

"Guys," I say.

Faith, squashed in the corner between the crooked dresser and the wall, is the only one who seems to hear me. She's holding a bag of coffee grounds in one hand while the other pulls on the strands of her lank hair. When she sees me, her eyes grow wide.

"The deal," Jack leans his face a few millimeters closer to Victor's, "was that I help you steal recording equipment, and you let us stay. Well, we don't need to stay in this nasty hole anymore, so now the deal is off."

"The squat's not a nasty hole," Faith whispers. Jack flicks his closed fist in her general direction, and Faith cringes back into her corner, hugging the coffee against her chest like it might protect her.

"You touch her and you die," Victor hisses.

Jack laughs. "I would never touch your pathetic druggie of a sister."

The flush on Victor's face deepens into a shade closer to purple. He swings an arm toward Jack, who disappears, instantly reappearing on a stack of boxes three feet away. A grim smile stretches his lips. Victor stumbles, the momentum from his foiled punch nearly knocking him to his knees.

"Jerk," Victor pants. Blotchy, red patches darken his neck and cheeks. He lunges for Jack, and the next moment, he's lying on the floor and Jack is sitting on a different box. Blood trickles from Victor's nose, and a horrible sound slides from his lips, somewhere between a gag and a moan.

Shock holds me in place. Faith screams. She jumps up, hovering a foot from Victor's prone body, clearly torn between a desire to protect him and terror at the thought of getting in Jack's way. Victor's body shifts. Now his arms are splayed out, head tipped back, a red spot blossoming beneath one eye. Jack has regained his perch. The exposed underside of Victor's chin shines in the dull kitchen light, pale and vulnerable.

"Jack!" I yell. "Stop it!"

Jack's head whips in my direction. For an instant, I hardly know him. The careless amusement that usually stamps his features is gone, replaced by a boiling rage that makes me instinctively back away. His eyes, unfocused holes of fury, stare blankly at me. It's as if he's been transformed into some lethal beast, a charging rhino or threatened tiger. Then Jack shakes his head, and his eyes slide back into focus. His face blanches as pale as Faith's.

"Alex." Jack slides down off his box throne. "You're back! How did you get out?"

He comes toward me, reaching out a hand stained by Victor's blood. I back further away.

"KJ and Shannon rescued me."

"They did?" Jack massages his knuckles with the other hand. "I thought you were gone for good." He looks down at his fingers and seems startled to see they're bloody.

KJ bursts into the kitchen, wearing nothing but boxer shorts. Even in the midst of the disaster around me, my pulse leaps at the sight of his barely dressed body: dark skin stretched smoothly over muscles and ribs, the valleys lightly sprinkled with curling black hair.

"What the hell . . . ?" KJ says.

I wrench my gaze away from his chest and follow the direction of his accusing finger. Victor lies in a heap on the kitchen floor. Faith, presumably having decided it's safe, kneels beside him.

"Vic," she croons, stroking her brother's bruised cheek. "You OK? Talk to me."

KJ turns from crumpled Victor to unhurt Jack. "You did this while he was frozen, didn't you?"

Jack's expression turns mutinous. "He deserved it."

"No one deserves that," I say. "He never had a chance."

Victor moans.

"He has more of a chance than we do," Jack snaps. "We're the ones the wipers are after." His glance jumps between me and KJ, a jittery flick so fast he couldn't possibly have focused on either of us. "They're getting closer. That's why I came back, to warn you."

For once, the talk of wipers doesn't send me into a tailspin of panic. I study Jack more closely. His collared shirt is crumpled into a network of wrinkles. Veins redden the whites of his eyes.

"Where did you see wipers?" I ask.

"They're everywhere." Jack twists his hands together, popping one knuckle after the other. "We have to get out here. Now, or they'll catch us all."

"Maybe someone *should* catch you if that's what you do with your skills." KJ motions again toward the boy on the floor. Victor is sitting up now, holding his stomach like he might be sick. Faith rubs his shoulders.

"Who cares about him?" Jack says. "He's a jerk."

"What's wrong with you?" KJ asks. "You're acting like the kind of paranoid monster Norms think we are."

"Whose side are you on?" The rage leaps back to light Jack's face with shining intensity. He faces KJ in the same position he'd stared down Victor. "How'd you get Alex out of the Center, anyway? Who helped you?"

KJ squares up in front of Jack. His hands are clenched, and his back is so tense it's nearly vibrating.

"Stop it!" I shout. "Both of you."

Neither one moves. Something in the distance shatters. It sounds like an echo of everything that's breaking between us.

"Come on." I place a tentative hand on KJ's shoulder. "Let's all just leave. If we . . ."

Shannon pushes her way past me and flings herself against KJ's bare chest. Unlike KJ, she took the time to dress, choosing a pale cardigan that makes her look like a schoolteacher at a particularly conservative elementary school. Or would have if her face wasn't taut with terror.

"Someone's coming!" she gasps.

Jack whirls around. "What?"

Shannon buries her head in KJ's chest. His hands move automatically to stroke her blond hair.

"Can't you hear them?" Shannon whispers. "Someone is coming upstairs."

All six of us hold completely still, listening. I strain my ears and hear nothing. A second passes. Then, from the depths of the warehouse, the floor squeaks.

I grab for time, snatching at the infinite strands and locking them into place. Silence descends. Skirting the others, I race toward the back of the squat. In its dusky recesses, two men stand a few feet from the door that leads down into Elmer's. One holds a flashlight. Both are creeping toward what must be the unmistakable sound of people shouting. Just behind them, a vase lies in pieces on the floor, toppled from a pile of junk Victor used to block the door.

All the fears that had abandoned me come flooding back. What if Jack is right? What if the wipers have finally found us?

I sprint back to the others, letting time go as I enter the kitchen. The transition melts seamlessly. Thank god. One dose of Aclisote hasn't been enough to change my skills.

"Shannon's right," I whisper. "Two people by the back stairs. We've gotta go."

"Wipers." Jack's face turns ashen.

"I'll take Shannon," KJ says, grabbing her bare hand in his own. "Where do we meet?"

"The parking lot by the mini-mart," I whisper. "There's an alley behind the dumpster."

KJ nods. Faith whimpers.

"Victor." She shakes him. "Get up."

Jack turns to me. "Alex."

"What?" I snap.

He recoils like I've slapped him. "Never mind." He disappears.

Victor hauls himself to his feet and leans against the wobbly dresser. Blood still leaks from his nose, bright streaks of scarlet against the pallor of his chin.

"Come on, hurry," Faith begs. I can hear the tears in her voice.

Shannon wraps both her hands around KJ's. "Let's go," she says, pulling him away from me. The sound of people moving through the squat is now unmistakable.

"What about them?" KJ asks me, nodding toward the two Norms.

"I'll deal with them," I say. "You guys go. Quick." KJ nods, and he and Shannon vanish.

I cross to Victor and Faith and put a hand on each of theirs. Faith flinches. I don't let go. Victor has been nothing but rude since the day we stepped foot in the squat. He's threatened us, blackmailed us, and taken advantage of Jack's admiration. Faith openly despises me. Even so, I know I can't leave them to the mercy of whoever is heading this way. The two of them allowed us shelter, however dirty and grim it might be, and neither one turned us in. In our world, this might be the closest to friendship with a Norm we ever get.

"Trust me," I say, and stop time.

Faith gapes around the silent kitchen, taking in the filtered light and the dust motes hanging in the air.

"Everything's frozen?" She touches her ear, as if unsure it still works.

"Yeah." I step away from them. "Go get your stuff together. I can't hold this for long."

"Sit here," Faith tells Victor, settling him down on one of the boxes Jack recently deserted. "I'll be right back."

Victor nods. I hurry to my own corner and find my shoes, then shove some clothes into a backpack. The sleeping bag I leave where it is. It will take too long to erase all evidence of our stay, and it's a useless effort, anyway. The free ride at the squat is over.

Faith is waiting in the kitchen when I return. She's folded their blankets into a neat roll and strapped them to the top of a large backpack. Given the speed with which she got all their stuff together, I'm guessing this isn't the first time they've had to leave in a rush.

"You guys have somewhere to go?" I ask.

Faith nods, draping a patched duffle bag over Victor's shoulders. "Our cousin can usually put us up for a while." Her drifting gaze focuses on me. "Where are you going?"

I shrug.

Faith fiddles with a ring weighing down her thumb. "Try the Pegasus Motel. Out on Eighty-Second. They take cash and don't ask questions."

I adjust the strap on my pack. "Thanks, but we're leaving town."

Victor mutters something under his breath that includes the words *deal* and *filthy spinners*. Faith takes his arm and helps him to his feet.

Victor manages the fire escape reasonably well. By the time we reach the bottom, he's recovered enough to push away my hand when I try to steady him. At my direction, the three of us weave through the unmoving traffic to reach the mini-mart. Faith stares around her, wide-eyed, taking in the people caught in private moments of their lives: a man's face twisted in the middle of a sneeze, a recently dropped cigarette floating beside a car, a woman driving with one hand as she reaches toward the back seat to comfort a crying baby.

KJ and Shannon are two steps outside the alley that runs along one side of the mini-mart. They'd frozen only a few seconds before we did, so they must have melted time back here only recently. Shannon is carrying a cloth grocery bag filled with her things. She clutches the small packet against her chest like it holds something precious. KJ, dressed now and wearing the other backpack on his shoulders, is peering back toward the spot where we will momentarily appear. Jack, who should have gotten there first, is nowhere in sight.

"In here," I say, squeezing my way past the dumpster.

"This place stinks." Victor's face has blossomed into a full set of bruises, a bouquet of red and dark-blue smudges that enhances his usual aura of threat. I'm grateful Jack chose somewhere else to reappear. I doubt I could have held Victor back if he'd run across the defenseless frozen body of his attacker.

"It will just be for a few seconds," I say.

Victor backs away. "I need a soda. I'm gonna go in the store and . . ."

"No." The pulse of a headache cuts my patience short. "I'm melting time in five seconds. If you stay out here, the Norms will see you appear out of nowhere." Victor glares at me. I glare back. "They'll think *you're* a spinner."

Faith steps into the alley with atypical assertiveness. Victor, still grumbling, follows her. I don't bother to double-check if anyone is watching. Ducking my head so I'm sheltered by the dumpster's green bulk, I let time slide out of my control. Molecules of trash-scented air expand to fill the space around us.

"Man." Victor makes a gagging sound. "Now it really stinks."

"Wait," I say, breathing through my mouth to avoid the rancid stench, which doesn't really help—instead of smelling the rottenness, I can sort of taste it. "Let the others get a little way ahead, so we don't all pop out at the same . . ."

I should have saved my breath. Victor is already pushing his way out from behind the dumpster. Faith remains behind, crouched beside me in the putrid alley. A bit of the trim on her skirt has come loose and trails in a puddle of muck by her feet.

"Faith," Victor calls. "Let's go."

Instead of getting up, Faith turns to face me.

"You could have left us there," she says.

I shift my weight to ease a cramp in my knee.

"I know."

Faith stands. Bulked up with the heavy pack, she seems less flighty.

"I'm glad you didn't."

I straighten up and follow her into the parking lot. KJ and Shannon are waiting a few feet away in what I'm guessing are supposed to be casual positions, but they just come off as awkward. I tip my chin in their direction. KJ nods back, tight-lipped. Faith moves toward Victor, and the two of them set off down the busy street. Neither one looks back.

"Have you seen Jack?" I ask KJ.

He crosses his arms. "And you care, why?"

"Just because what he did was wrong," I say, "doesn't mean we can leave Portland without him."

KJ's expression remains grim but he doesn't contradict me. We wait. A car pulls into the mini-mart's parking lot and we all watch the driver get out and wander inside. Five minutes later, he emerges carrying a jumbo soda and climbs back in his car. KJ checks his watch. Shannon cranes her neck to peer past the smelly dumpster.

A police car turns the corner, pulling up neatly at the curb by Elmer's front door. KJ tenses and hoists his backpack higher on his shoulders.

"We should go."

We start walking. Quickly, but not too quickly, cutting through residential streets where the cops are less likely to go. KJ and Shannon start arguing about what we should do next. I struggle to follow their conversation. My mind feels clouded. The fear I thought I'd escaped trails after me, soft whispers of doubt warning me about all the dangers closing in around us.

19 ◀◀ *CARSON ROSS*

SHE ESCAPED. WHEN BARNARD CALLED HIM WITH THE news, Ross almost laughed. Alex is such a clever girl. She must have learned to be so wily from spending time with him. He won't let her slip away again.

Ross flicks through the jackets hanging in his closet, selecting a long, nondescript overcoat that should shield him from prying eyes—those of the force (he'd told Chief he had a family emergency) and those of his quarry. Ross smiles at himself in the mirror, then leans forward to study his own bared teeth. It's probably time to whiten them again so they'll show up better in photographs. Chief Graham has the advantage of dark skin to make his teeth look bright, whereas Ross must rely on cosmetics. He smooths his hair, dons a pair of sunglasses and a Mariners baseball cap, then, with one final glance in the mirror, heads out the door.

The day outside glitters with sunshine. Fall is by far Portland's best season—only occasionally too hot, blue sky, and minimal rain. His car chirps as he releases the lock. It's a beautiful car—a Saab, extravagant for a policeman's salary, but then Ross doesn't intend to live on a policeman's salary for much longer. The engine purrs; Ross lets it warm up while he checks his phone.

He'd almost deleted the tracking app when he lost her to the cage in the Center's lobby. Now he's glad he resisted. The map zooms in as it locates the baited business card. Is Alex's refusal to part with it a sign of latent sentimentality? The question barely crosses his mind before a queasy flash brings back her expression when she saw him yesterday. He'd expected her to look surprised. He hadn't expected that much fear. What changed? She used to be so trusting, so faithful. Ross clips the phone into its dashboard cradle. One of the other spinners must have turned her against him. He'll be able to bring her around again, but until then, if she won't work for him out of devotion, he can always use leverage. Alex, he knows, is extremely fond of her friends. Especially KJ.

The Saab rolls smoothly out of the garage, and Ross guides it onto the freeway, heading to a spot near the abandoned warehouse that the app shows as her current location. When he's halfway there, the dot abruptly jumps west. Ross keeps driving, glancing occasionally at the map. The dot starts moving more quickly than a walking pace, which means she must have gotten on a bus. Based on the route, she's most likely heading downtown.

Ross takes the Market Street exit, following a path that will intersect the bus. The dot jumps again. Ross changes course. Sunshine streams through his tinted windows, its warmth balanced by the cooling breeze from the car's air conditioning. Ross turns on the stereo, and the sweet strains of a Vivaldi violin concerto fill the car, the music both uplifting and calming. Ross keeps time with his finger, tapping the steering wheel with steady beats as the gap between him and the wavering dot gets smaller. He turns left on

Tenth. He's driving slowly now, scanning the sidewalk for a glimpse of her. He doesn't see her, but she must see him, because the dot jumps again. Ross smiles to himself and corrects course. He can play this game all day. The more she freezes, the more tired she's going to get. Even if she and her friends take turns, they eventually won't be able to run anymore.

The dot leads him up to NW Twenty-Third, then into the Pearl District, then back near Pioneer Courthouse Square. Every time he gets close, the dot vanishes. Ross hums along to the music. She must recognize the car by now. She must be very scared.

At noon, he stops to pick up a sandwich. Has she eaten? Maybe he should get some food for her, too? He compromises by buying a large coffee. Alex's headache will be blinding by now.

Back in the car, he checks the app again. The dot is not moving. Ross puts the Saab in gear and closes in. It leads him to an Indian restaurant in the heart of downtown. An odd choice. She must have finally lost her strength. Ross finds a parking spot and heads inside. Music continues playing in his head, the notes as glorious as his mood.

"Table for one?" asks a dark-haired woman wrapped in a red and gold sari.

Ross flashes his badge. "I'm following a suspect who I believe may have taken refuge here. Do you mind if I do a quick search?"

The woman's eyes go wide. "Should we evacuate or anything?"

"No, no." Ross smiles. "She's not at all dangerous. A runaway."

The woman, looking relieved, leads him to the back of the restaurant. There aren't a lot of places to hide. Ross tucks his sunglasses into his pocket. The kitchen is much too crowded and busy to offer cover. The small supply closet is empty of anything human. The door to the bathroom is locked, but when he knocks, no one answers. Ross checks the app again. The dot still hasn't moved.

"Do you have a key for this?" he asks the hostess.

The woman nods and hurries off, returning a minute later carrying a single key on a chain that includes a miniature soup ladle.

"Thanks," Ross tells her. "I'll just be a minute. You can go back to work."

The hostess leaves with some reluctance, looking back over her shoulder as she walks away. Ross checks that he has the leash in his pocket while he waits for her to go. Agents are only assigned one leash, which is too bad. Assuming they're all still together, it would be a nice bonus to catch the whole group. Maybe, once he nabs Alex, the others will give up and come with her? This whole day carries the inevitability of destiny. His future is waiting for him on the other side of this door, and he can already taste his success —the flavor is deep and rich, like the tempered sweetness of a dark-chocolate pot de crème.

Ross slides the key in the lock and opens the door. The bathroom smells strongly of potpourri. It's dark, but Ross can hear her breathing, shallow and quick, like the cornered animal she is. Judging by the sound, she's alone.

"Alex?"

He turns on the light. The runaway spinner sits on the floor, wedged next to a small shelf stocked with extra paper towels and toilet paper. One hand holds a large kitchen knife, but the hand is trembling, the knife listing at half-mast. The music in Ross's head ends with an unmelodious screech. The knife isn't a problem. What is a problem is that the person crouched on the floor isn't Alex.

222

"Don't come any closer," Jack croaks, brandishing the knife weakly.

A furious roar replaces Ross's imaginary symphony. Are the fates mocking him? Did Alex think so little of his offer that she gave his card away? Did she give it to Jack so she could trick Ross *on purpose*? Alex's face the last time he saw her swims before him again: her blanched cheeks, her pinched mouth. It wasn't just fear in her eyes, it was something more personal: loathing.

How dare that little brat turn against him? Ross took her under his wing and showed her a whole wide world of possibilities, and she rejected it. Rejected him. Even if he finds her again, he will never be able to trust her. She isn't loyal. She tried to steal his thunder by revealing Sikes's identity. She betrayed him. Alex doesn't *deserve* to be saved.

On the ground at his feet, Jack waves the knife again. Ross studies him with cold appraisal. Jack was his spinner before Alex. He's good at the work, though less pliable and certainly far less interested in solving crimes in the name of justice. But maybe that doesn't matter. A whisper of music rises up in the back of his head. Not the soothing strains of Vivaldi this time—no, this is something stronger, louder, and definitely more militant. The fates didn't lead him astray; what they have done is point out the truth. A sympathetic partner means complications; a pragmatic assistant makes a stronger ally. Ross won't have to play games with Jack. Jack is a realist, and he'll understand the logic of what has to be done.

Ross lowers himself into a crouch, holding out his empty hands to underline his lack of defenses.

"It's OK," he says. "You have nothing to be afraid of. I'm not going to hurt you. I'm here to help."

The knife Jack is holding wobbles. His hand shakes, and his pupils are dilated with terror. Ross edges closer.

"The wipers are going to find you," he says. "They will kill you, just like they are going to track down and kill Alex and Shannon and KJ. I can save you. I can make the fear go away. All I ask in return is your loyalty. Can you promise me that, Jack? Will you do everything I say in order to live?"

Jack stares at him for a long minute, and then, very slowly, he puts down the knife.

20 ◀◀

AT THREE O'CLOCK IN THE AFTERNOON, KJ, SHANNON, and I stand in front of Room 217 at the Pegasus Motel. Plunked down between a Chinese restaurant and a place that sells discount tires, the Pegasus promises anonymity and not much else. Thirty rooms share a bunker-like concrete building that's bent in an *L* shape around a potholed parking lot. Guessing by the number of cars, business isn't booming. Our second-floor room is off an open-air hallway. I avoid touching the railing. Its aqua-blue paint is rippled with flakes, and the whole thing looks like it's rickety enough that one good shove would knock it over.

KJ swipes the key card and pushes the door open. The room is dim, its sole window almost completely blocked by slumping, dust-colored curtains. Two double beds fill most of the space, facing a laminate dresser and a TV bolted to the wall. A second door in the back promises the first shower we've had in a week, a prospective pleasure that's dimmed by the nasty smell permeating the air. Instead of the squat's organic mold smell, this room reeks of old cigarettes mixed with a harsh chemical stink that, as Shannon points out, makes you wonder what kind of vile spill needed something that toxic to clean it up.

"They didn't ask for ID," I say, tossing my backpack on the bed closest to the door. The bedspread has a swirled orange print and feels like it's made from woven plastic bags. I flop down anyway. I'm exhausted, my feet hurt, and my shoulders have bruises from carrying a pack all day.

KJ sits down on the other bed. He picks up a TV remote from the side table and starts clicking through channels, stopping when he finds a news station. All three of us watch the announcer for a few minutes as he drones on about forest fires in California. When the show cuts to commercials, KJ snaps it off.

"Guess there's no breaking news about escaped spinners." A yawn stretches the end of his sentence into near-nonsense. He shakes himself. "Who wants to shower first?"

"You go ahead," Shannon says. She's perched on the room's single chair, her bag of belongings spilling out on the dresser top. Her prissy schoolteacher outfit has lost its freshness. Her blouse is wrinkled, the sweater blotted with a drip of ketchup from the burgers we ate for lunch.

"Take the stuff from the drugstore," I remind KJ, sitting up so I can toss him the sack with the hair dyes and clippers we'd picked up earlier. KJ catches the bag, grabs his pack, and heads for the bathroom. Seconds later, I hear the hiss of running water. I lean against the headboard and study the ugly dresser. It's unlikely we'll stay here long enough to make it worth unpacking.

Shannon glances toward the bathroom door to make sure KJ isn't around before asking, "Do you think we should call Jack?"

"Oh, yeah, right." I drag myself off the bed and dig through my backpack. I canceled my old phone's service right after we left the squat, but the replacement I bought is still sitting in its fancy box. I tear open the plastic seal and dump the contents in my lap—phone, charger, directions. I open the latter and skim the Get Started section.

"It's probably better we didn't spend the day together." I turn the phone over and hold down the on button. "He needs time to cool off."

"Do you think he's all right?"

"Jack?" I rub my eyes, gritty with lack of sleep. "Knowing him, he's probably all snuggled up in some fancy downtown hotel eating room service."

The directions are frustratingly unclear. I flip the page and look for something that tells me how to program in my old phone number.

Shannon shifts in her chair. "Do you really think leaving Portland is the right decision?"

I sigh. Of course I think it's the right decision. We've been talking about it all day.

"It's not safe for us to stay here anymore," I say, for the millionth time.

"Yeah, I know." Shannon rubs at the stain on her sweater with her thumb. "It's just . . . well, that assumes we don't want to go back."

Fatigue settles over me like a heavy blanket. I put down the confusing directions to tackle later.

"You're still not convinced the Center is evil?"

Shannon scrubs at her stain more vigorously. "All we have to go on is what you've told us."

"And that's not enough? Shannon, when I was back there yesterday, Barnard said he was going to take me to the Central Office."

"So?"

"So, he practically said he was going to kill me."

"*Practically* said." Shannon gives up on the sweater. "Why do you assume the Central Office is so terrible? It's just the place they take people when they're really, really sick."

"And you think I'm sick?"

"You can't tell me Jack was acting normally this morning. You've never been that bad, but sometimes you do seem—I don't know—off. And you have to admit, your skills have mutated."

"It's not a mutation." I stack up two of the flat motel pillows so they make a reasonably decent mound and lie down. I can't believe after all that's happened, I'm still having this same conversation with Shannon. "Look at KJ—he's fine now. This is how we're supposed to be."

"Maybe. Or maybe it's just a late stage of the sickness. How can we know if we don't see an expert?"

"If you want to see an expert, go ahead." I close my eyes. "I'm staying here."

There's a long pause. I hear the water in the shower being turned off. A few minutes later, the whine of electric clippers slides through the closed door.

"I can't go anywhere." Shannon's voice is so soft I barely hear it over the clippers. "I can't leave KJ."

An uncomfortable feeling crawls over my skin.

"You've only been together a couple weeks," I say.

"I know." Shannon sounds wistful. "When we were at the Center, I liked him for ages, but he always hung out with you and I thought . . . I mean, everybody said he liked you. And then things changed. He chose me. KJ made me feel like the things I did at the Center—helping the Youngers, working in the Clinic—made a difference." She gives a small sniff. "I love him. I think I'd risk anything to stay together."

The uncomfortable feeling seeps down into my gut. I remember the way KJ hugged me when he rescued me from the Center. I also remember KJ saying how grateful he was to Shannon for staying with him while he was sick. The two memories pull at me. I lie very still and hope Shannon thinks I'm drifting off to sleep. Behind my closed lids, her words bounce around my brain: *He chose me.* Did he? Was his relief in my escaping the Center just a friend's relief?

The bathroom door bangs open.

"Ta-da!" KJ says. "What do you think?"

I open my eyes. KJ has buzzed his long hair military short. Removing the sheltering strands exposes the sculpted lines of his face. His high cheekbones, extra prominent thanks to the weight he's lost, give him a hint of the exotic. He has shaved, too, smoothing his cheeks but leaving the early growth of a mustache and a patch of hair on his chin. He looks older and unbearably handsome.

"Oh, my gosh," Shannon squeals, jumping up from her chair. "You're gorgeous!"

"Thanks." KJ rubs the back of his head and shifts his gaze to me. I stare back. It's like a new person stands before me. Someone I'm not sure I know.

Shannon dances across the room and wraps her arms around his neck.

"My guy." She strokes his fuzzy hair, then draws his head down for a kiss.

I stand up. "I think I'll take a shower."

KJ lifts his head. Even under his dark skin, I can tell he's blushing. "What do *you* think?" he asks me.

"It's good," I say. "You'll be much harder to recognize."

I slip past them to reach the bathroom. As soon as I close the door, I turn both the shower and the fan on full blast. The walls in this place are thin, and I don't want to hear anything from the other side.

I stay in the shower a long time, letting the hot water run while I wait the twenty minutes it takes for the dye to set. By the time I get out, my skin shines with an unnatural pink. I grab a towel and wipe away the fog covering the mirror. My face stares back at me, familiar features now framed by startlingly red hair.

Digging through the bag KJ left on the sink, I pull out a pair of scissors. Wet strands drop to the floor, mingling with the black ones already littering the tiles. When I'm done, my hair hangs in a straight bob that ends at my chin. I look different, but unlike KJ, I haven't transformed into a more beautiful version of myself. I just look tired, plus my new hair color washes out my skin.

I put the scissors down and leave the bathroom. KJ and Shannon are sleeping side by side on one of the beds, their hands joined in a loose clasp. They seem peaceful. I watch them for a minute. Twenty-four hours ago, I thought I was about to die. Now, I have another chance to make the right decisions and do some good, and I am determined not to blow it. KJ is my friend. That has to be enough. I lie down on the other bed and shut down the chaos in my mind, waiting for sleep to claim me.

The sky, when I wake up, hovers somewhere in that hazy divide between night and day, when nothing feels quite real. I peer at the digital clock on the night table: 5:30 a.m. We've slept for over twelve hours.

I roll over and knock something hard with my leg. I fumble around in the dark until my hand lands on the cell phone. Shoot. I never did program it. I turn on the bedside light. A night's sleep has done wonders for my reading comprehension, and I figure out how to tie the new phone to my old number with only minimal frustration.

The directions say it might take a few minutes to fully sync, so I turn off the light and grab my clothes, tiptoeing past Shannon and KJ, who are still sacked out on the other bed. The bathroom tiles chill my bare feet. The room's air conditioner was cranked up all night and the room is freezing. I splash water on my face and finger-comb my red strands into submission.

The tiny beacon of a message light catches my attention when I reenter the main room. I snatch up my phone and thumb Jack's message open. It's date-stamped four yesterday afternoon.

Where are you?

Relief spreads through me like the warm rush of a gulp of hot coffee. Yes, what Jack did to Victor was wrong; yes, he can be a pain, but he's one of us. Spinners are stronger when we stick together.

I hit the reply button.

A motel, I type. *You?*

The little icon whirls as the message shoots out into cyberspace. I hold the phone against my chest. Maybe this is a sign. Maybe luck is finally turning our way. I study the little screen, hoping for a reply, even though I know it's unreasonable. Jack is surely sound asleep.

"Hey," a voice says softly.

I turn around. KJ is sitting up in bed. The hazy motel light outlines the familiar shape of his shoulders and masks the changes he's made to his face.

"Hey, yourself," I whisper. I hold up the cell phone. "Jack texted."

"That's good." KJ stands, careful not to disturb Shannon. "What'd he say?"

"Just asked where we were."

KJ crosses the room and leans over my shoulder so he can see the phone.

"Did you answer him?"

"Yeah." The flowery scent of shampoo fills the small space between us. I busy myself connecting the phone to the charger. The thing must not have come with a full charge because the battery is already down to less than 10%.

"I like the hair." KJ reaches out and slides a loose strand behind my ear. "Very stylish." The brush of his fingers wakes every nerve along my cheek.

He's your friend, I remind myself, *that's it.*

"It's kind of crooked." I cross over to the window and part the curtain a few inches. The parking lot outside is so quiet it could be frozen. The only thing moving is a blackbird, picking at a bag of chips lying next to a rusted Chevy.

"Alex," KJ says, his voice barely more than a murmur. "Can we talk?"

I glance over at Shannon. In the pale light leaking through the parted curtains, I can see her blankets rising and falling rhythmically.

"Yeah." I try to infuse my whisper with briskness. "Now that we've contacted Jack, we should meet up somewhere and head out of town. Did you and Shannon find any places we could stay?"

KJ sits down on the edge of my bed. Not having any place else to sit, I lower myself down beside him.

"That's not what I meant," KJ says. "I want to talk about . . ." He stops. I study my ragged nails. "Alex, I've been wrong, and I'm sorry. Being so close to dying messed me up. When I first recovered, I just wanted everything to be simple. I didn't want to deal with all these new complications—the Center closing, the idea that we might get caught, my relationship with Shannon. But then you got trapped in the Center and I thought you might be gone for good."

I shiver. I've been trying very hard not to think about how close I was to dying.

"Are you cold?" KJ pulls the rumpled sheets from my bed up around both our shoulders, enveloping us in a cocoon. The skin of the arm he leaves draped around me feels hot against my neck.

"You believe me, don't you?" I ask. "That the Center is trying to kill us and that Barnard is a monster?"

"Of course I do."

KJ's side is touching mine. Every time he speaks, the rumble of his voice vibrates against me. I pick at the edge of the sheet.

"Shannon doesn't," I say. "She still thinks there might be a chance I'm making it up." I'm afraid to stop talking. If I do, there will be silence, and then there will be nothing for my brain to do except think about how close he is and how much closer I want him to be. "She's worried that we'll all go crazy without Aclisote. The only reason she's here at all is because of you. She told me . . ."

I can't say it out loud. I can't say that Shannon told me she loves him. Silence hangs between us, the quiet thick with unsaid words. My awareness of KJ's body expands to fill all the parts of my brain capable of creating rational thought.

The quality of the hush around us abruptly changes. It's not the quiet of words not spoken, it's the silence that comes with the absence of sound. It's the silence of a freeze. KJ clears his throat.

"Shannon believes a lot of things that aren't true."

His hand tightens around my shoulder. Even through my sweater I can pinpoint the exact spots where each finger touches me.

"When I thought you were going to die," KJ says. "I realized I couldn't pretend anymore. I want . . ." His voice catches. "I mean, if you still want . . . ?"

I lift my head. KJ is staring at me like he did the night before we left the Center. I think about Shannon saying she would do anything to stay with him, and I know I should say we have to wait. I don't. Tenderness melts the planes of KJ's face, or maybe it's just my own vision gone fuzzy. I push aside guilt and responsibility and the pressure to do the right thing. Instead, I ask the only question that matters:

"You're not in love with her?"

"I've only ever loved you."

When I move my lips toward KJ's, he meets me halfway.

Kissing KJ is even better than it was the first time. Familiarity tinges the newness with something precious. My mouth moves with its own rhythm, taking in his sweetness. Comfort and longing race side by side with the beating of my heart. KJ wraps both arms around me. I twist toward him. The sheets slip from my shoulders when he pulls me into his lap.

Minutes pass. KJ's hands slide under my sweater, stroking my back with trails of heat. I kiss his lips, his cheeks, his newly bare forehead. KJ kisses my neck. I lift my chin to give him more room.

"Alex," KJ murmurs.

My limbs feel like they're made of syrup, heavy and liquid. I open my eyes so I can see KJ's face. I want him to fill my vision the way the touch of his hands fills every one of my nerve endings.

The glimmer of a sunrise peeks around the curtains, washing the motel furniture with rose and softening its edges. The whole room glows—the ugly dresser, the rumpled pillows. Even the gentle sway as the air conditioner flutters the heavy curtains adds to the sensation, like the sun is winking at us with pleasure.

Wait. The curtains are *fluttering*? I reach for time and feel its eternal motion ticking forward. KJ must have stopped paying attention.

All that kissing... My head whips around to the girl lying in KJ's abandoned bed. The girl who is no longer asleep. My body stiffens.

"What's wrong?" KJ asks.

I open my mouth, shock and shame taking away my ability to speak. KJ must register the direction I'm looking in, because he spins around, standing so abruptly he knocks me to the floor.

"Shannon." His voice quavers.

I breathe in rancid carpet stench and wish there was any scenario that made crawling under the bed OK. I could freeze time, just long enough to get my bearings, but I don't. It feels like cheating. My legs shake as I straighten to standing.

Shannon emerges from the other bed. Anguish strips her cheeks of color. Her eyes look huge beneath the tumbled curls of her hair. KJ takes a few steps in her direction, but Shannon puts up a hand and he stops.

"What are you doing?" she asks. The T-shirt she'd slept in slips off one shoulder, exposing the thin line of her clavicle.

"I'm sorry," KJ says. "I should have told you."

"You should have *told* me?" Shannon's words bounce against the motel walls like sharp objects. "Told me what? That this was all a joke?"

"No." KJ takes another step toward Shannon. I fold my arms around my chest, trying to hold onto the warmth KJ left behind. My stomach roils. Despite not having eaten in hours, I want to throw up.

"I meant everything I ever said to you," KJ is saying. "I really do care about you. It's just..."

"You *care* about me?" Shannon collapses back onto the bed. I force myself to watch as her face crumples, as the tears start streaming down her cheeks. "All this time I thought we were together, you and

235

she . . ." She flicks a hand in my direction as if she's shaking mud from her fingers.

"It's not like that," KJ says. "Really. This is the first time anything happened."

Shannon's head snaps up. "And that's supposed to make me feel better?"

I hug myself tighter. My skin feels coated with Shannon's imaginary mud. Watching their exchange feels intrusive, but the urge to leave beckons with something too much like relief. Witnessing this is much harder than leaving, and I deserve hard.

KJ hangs his head. "I'm sorry. I'm so sorry."

"Sorry?" Shannon yells. She's on her feet again, body shaking with anger. "I left everything for you. My home. My friends. I stopped taking Aclisote and let time *mutate* me." Before my eyes, Shannon disappears, reappearing instantly a foot in front of KJ. He flinches, and I wonder if she slapped him while he was frozen. "I listened to Alex's ridiculous lies. I stayed because I believed . . ." She turns her head. "Oh, god."

"Shannon." KJ puts a tentative hand on her shoulder. She wrenches herself away.

"Why can't you see that Alex is crazy?" Shannon smears the tears running down her face. "The way she rants, the paranoia. The Center is our *home*. They take care of us. I know you don't want to believe we have to die, but it's true."

"We have proof," KJ starts.

"Proof." Shannon's mouth twists. She drops her eyes to the floor, as if the sight of us is more than she can bear. "I can't stay here."

Cold that has nothing to do with the air conditioning tickles the back of my neck.

"You can't go back to the Center," I say. "It's not safe."

Shannon raises her face toward mine. She looks broken, like a doll that's been smashed and pasted back together without skill.

"Shut up."

KJ reaches toward her again. "She's right, Shannon. You can't go back there. We'll work something out. It will be OK."

Shannon draws herself to her full height, a righteous queen blazing with scorn.

"No," she says, "it won't."

For a moment, the three of us stare at each other. Then, as quick as a candle going out, Shannon vanishes.

21 ◀◀

KJ SPINS IN THE EMPTY ROOM.

"Shannon?"

The dresser, crowded with her grocery bag of stuff, gazes back accusingly. Cold sinks deeper into my body. The sun sliding through the heavy curtains no longer offers the promise of a new day. Instead, I see the shadows the light pushes ahead of itself, the patches of darkness reaching toward us like fingers. Shannon could be in the Center's lobby at this very minute, Dr. Barnard running to the sound of her voice. He'll make her freeze time again. In seconds of real time, they could be back.

"We have to get out of here." I touch my wrist, half expecting to feel the buzzing clasp of a leash.

"Shannon wouldn't turn us in," KJ says, in a voice that reveals his doubt.

I scramble over the bed and snatch KJ's arm. Time yanks to a stop. "She wouldn't see it as turning us in. She'd see it as saving you."

We pack our stuff without speaking, moving carefully so we won't accidentally brush against each other in the cramped space. The fleeting intimacy that passed between us feels tainted. Perfect joy erased by bitter consequence.

We trudge away from the motel through gray, frozen air. Hardly anyone is outside this early on a Thursday morning. We pass an unmoving delivery truck, a jogger in a reflective yellow slicker hovering above the sidewalk, a rat frozen in a gutter. We keep walking. It's KJ who breaks the silence.

"It's my fault," he says.

I settle the backpack more firmly on my shoulders. "It's mine, too. I knew how much she liked you."

KJ kicks a plastic water bottle lying on the curb. "I should have talked to her right away, told her it wasn't going to work out."

We turn a corner, moving off the wide frontage road and onto a smaller commercial strip.

"We can't leave her in the Center," KJ says. "They'll take her to the Central Office, just like they were going to take you."

"They might not." I rip a handful of leaves off a roadside shrub. They're dusty and smell like car exhaust. "She *wants* to be at the Center. She'll take Aclisote willingly."

KJ shakes his head. "She still knows too much. If she tells the other spinners what we told her, some of them might believe her. Plus, they're transferring everyone soon, which means the information could spread. There's no way Barnard will risk that."

I tear the leaves into tiny pieces, sprinkling them on the ground as we walk.

"Maybe she won't be able to find her way back. She doesn't know the city very well."

"There's a reassuring picture. Shannon wandering around the city alone and completely lost. She'll be terrified."

Logic tells me the accusation in his voice is mainly aimed at himself, but his anger hurts anyway.

"Let's get something to eat," I say, "and we'll decide what to do."

KJ grunts his agreement. I adjust my pack again. The straps settle onto my day-old bruises like I never took them off. The sweetness of KJ's kisses and the wonder of us as a couple once again lie in tatters. It's almost like nothing ever happened between us. Except something did happen, because if it hadn't, there wouldn't be another spinner at risk of dying because of me. In the death of Austin Shea, I can claim ignorance. With Shannon, I knew exactly what I was doing.

The first pulse of a headache blooms behind my eyes. I let the bits of shredded leaves flutter from my hand, a trail of broken green leading back to all the places where we can never return.

We walk about a mile before we find a diner serving breakfast. KJ wanted to grab something from a corner store, but I insisted we get a real meal. My headache has grown to a steady throb, and I melt time with relief.

The diner clangs with dishes and conversation. Perspiring waitresses thread their way through a room packed with tables and booths, coffeepots raised above their heads like truce flags. A waitress with a name tag identifying her as Tammi herds us into a booth by the front window. I check our surroundings before we sit down. In the booth on one side of us, a heavy-set white man works his way through a pile of eggs while scanning the sports page. On the other side, three Hispanic men chat in rapid Spanish. No one seems to be paying us any attention. I slide onto the red plastic seat and pick up the menu.

Fifteen minutes later, we're facing our own platters of food. We both chose a full breakfast: fried eggs, toast, a heap of steaming potatoes, bacon, and a short stack of pancakes. KJ nibbles his toast. I work steadily through the whole pile. Whatever comes next is going to require energy.

"Maybe the Center hasn't fixed the window you broke," I suggest, wiping a piece of toast through the egg yolks and grease. "We could bring a ladder over again."

"They wouldn't be that careless. Either they fixed it, or they put one of those zapper things in there."

Tammi comes by, and we stop talking while she refills our coffees. I let my gaze roam around the diner. The crowd has thinned a little. The hefty guy reading the sports page behind KJ is gone, and the hostess is ushering a new man into his place. I study his back as he settles in. He's middle-aged but still fit, dressed in a heavy rain jacket, khakis, and a dark green baseball cap.

KJ picks up the thread of our conversation as soon as Tammi moves on. "That zapper thing is probably our biggest problem. If our freezes can be broken at any moment, it makes getting anywhere near the Center riskier."

"I think we'll be OK." I take a swallow of fresh coffee. Each dose of caffeine does its bit to ease my headache. "I'm pretty sure I can tell when I'm near one." I explain about the dread that crushed me both times I'd been close to a zapper. KJ listens, nodding attentively.

"That helps," he says. "What if we try staking out the Center today? Find somewhere we can watch who comes and goes."

"I don't know . . ." I start, about to say I think we might stand out too much, when something roars outside our window. I jump. KJ slams his hand onto mine. We both turn to the glass. An ancient truck revs its engine again before backing gingerly onto the street. I heave a sigh of relief.

"Did you drop this?" a voice asks.

I turn my head. The man from the next booth is standing beside us, offering KJ a hat. I shake my head.

"No," KJ says, "thanks, though."

"You sure?" The man is smiling. There's something familiar about him, but I can't place it because I'm distracted by the hat. It's green and looks just like the one that was on his head a minute ago. He knows the hat isn't ours.

I flip my hand over to grab KJ's fingers, hoping he'll recognize the pressure as a warning. Time pulses around me. I let the strands run through my mind, skeins of silk sliding on the edge of control. The hat slips from the man's fingers. His hand swoops toward KJ's and mine with the swiftness of a hawk snatching its prey. Our three hands slam onto the table at the same instant that time screeches to a halt.

Silence hits the diner like a bomb. I hadn't appreciated how loud the rumble of voices and rattling dishes was until it stopped. The people around us have turned to statues, forks halfway to mouths. Coffee hangs in impossible suspense from the lip of a pitcher.

The man lifts his hand, and in that moment, I remember who he is. He's the man on the motorcycle who almost trapped me on the bus. Horror encircles me like a noose.

"Quick," I say to KJ. "Melt and refreeze."

KJ's face quivers.

"I can't," he says. "It's not my freeze."

"But . . ." I reach out. The time strands are blocked, completely immobile, and utterly out of my control. KJ and I gape at each other. Then we both turn to the man standing beside our table.

"Sorry." He gives an apologetic shrug. "It's mine."

I stare at him—at the laugh lines emerging around his eyes, the sprinkling of gray mixed with his thick dark hair. He's a spinner. An *old* spinner. The man slides into the seat next to me, blocking me from leaving the booth.

"Miguel Hernandez," he says, holding his hand out. Not knowing what else to do, I shake it. So does KJ. Miguel's handshake is firm, his palm warm and dry. "You two are hard to track down."

My feet feel like I just stepped into an ice-cold creek.

"You've been searching for us," I say. A statement, not a question.

"Ever since you left the Center."

My breakfast sits in my stomach like a pile of concrete. This must be how condemned prisoners feel after eating their last meal. The numb feeling in my feet spreads to my knees.

"You're a wiper, aren't you?"

Miguel blinks at me. "Me?"

"Yes, you." The weight of our failure pins me to my seat. My brain empties itself, unable to come up with even a hint of an escape plan. "The guy who's been chasing us all over the city."

"I've been chasing you," Miguel says, "but I'm definitely not a wiper. I'm not even a cop. I'm a spinner like you." Neither KJ nor I move. "If I worked for the Center, I'd have already slapped you with a leash." Miguel stands up from the booth, spreading his arms wide. "I don't have one. You can search me."

KJ hesitates only a moment, then stands and begins patting Miguel down. Besides a wallet, which KJ tosses to me, Miguel's pockets are empty. The chill wrapping my legs recedes only slightly.

"If you're not a cop," I ask, flipping through Miguel's wallet. "What's this?" I hold up an ID tucked inside one of the wallet's plastic windows. It shows a picture of Miguel next to an official-looking seal.

"It's my license," Miguel says, reclaiming the wallet from me. "I'm a private investigator. It's a good job for a spinner." He stuffs the wallet into his pocket and slides back into the booth. "That's not why I'm here, though. I'm here for my volunteer job—with the Society for Spinner Rights."

"The Society?" I make no effort to hide my disgust. "Those people are idiots. All they want to do is bring entertainment to the Center."

"That's just our public face." Miguel winks at me. "People like me carry out the real work. I'm the lead trawler for the western region."

He says this as though we should be impressed.

"You're the what?" KJ asks.

"Lead trawler." Miguel beams. His long hair, freed from the cap, dances around his shoulders. "Like the fishing term? We try to bring in all the rogue spinners."

"*All* the rogue . . . ?" KJ gapes at him. "How many are there?"

"A few. Occasionally people escape, like you. Then there are the ones that never got identified in the first place—inaccurate test results, sympathetic nurses, or parents who refuse to let their children even get tested."

"Like Austin Shea," I blurt.

"Yes." Miguel sounds surprised. "How did you know he was a spinner?"

Words catch in my throat, which has grown painfully tight.

"Someone told me," I mumble.

Miguel shakes his head, his chipper spirits momentarily dimmed. "Austin's death was a real tragedy."

I pick up my coffee, burying my face under the pretense of taking a sip.

"After you round us up, what do you do with us?" KJ asks.

"Do with you?" Miguel echoes. "Nothing. Our goal is to keep

everyone free. Underground, of course, but free. No missions, no leashes. We start by taking folks to one of our refuges. It's a great place to get settled, figure out your options, and learn the strategies you'll need to survive on your own."

Miguel's words float around inside my head like confetti, light and impossible to grasp hold of. "There's a whole *refuge* of spinners?"

Miguel nods. "There are seven refuges, actually. The nearest one to us is in Eastern Oregon. It serves Oregon, Washington, Idaho, and most of Northern California."

"That's not possible." KJ crosses his arms. "Someone would notice."

"We have a legitimate cover story," Miguel says. "We're set up as a camp for troubled youth, plus my wife and I are licensed foster parents. The place is way out in the boonies. We don't get a lot of visitors."

Miguel chatters on, blathering about how this refuge is the best in the nation, and the place he still lives when he's not out working. He promises we won't have to run anymore. I barely listen. I've been so careful, even paranoid, as Shannon repeatedly pointed out, and now, when it mattered, I let my guard down. How much longer do we have before we end up in the Central Office? Or somewhere worse. Maybe Miguel is a scientist, and this camp is a lab to test ways to exploit our skills?

Miguel's shower of words slows into silence.

"You don't believe me." His mouth droops, as if our doubt hurts his feelings. "I should have expected it. You've been out, what, a week? Have you been freezing a lot?"

I shrug. My water glass left a ring of condensation by my plate. I rub at the spot, smearing the water into a thinner and thinner pool, until all the liquid disappears.

"You're probably feeling pretty suspicious by now. Thinking everyone is watching you? Getting angered easily?"

My skin prickles. I scramble as far away from Miguel as the narrow booth bench allows. "Who are you?"

"I told you, I'm a spinner like you. I know the symptoms of overusing your skills. I've been there, too."

I tighten my hold on the coffee cup. The ceramic is heavy. If worse comes to worst, maybe I can throw it at him.

"Spinners aren't paranoid." I recite the words like a talisman. "That's what Norms say. It's propaganda to make them hate us. Just like saying we're violent."

"You haven't felt flashes of rage since your skills changed?" Miguel asks. I shift uncomfortably, thinking of the times I lashed out at Shannon. KJ meets my eyes across the table. He doesn't have to say anything. Images of Jack standing over Victor's broken body hang in the air between us. I look away.

"It's not the freezing," I say. It can't be the freezing. If it is, then the Norms are right about us. "It's just that we're scared. I've actually been a lot less suspicious the last couple days."

"You were back in the Center recently, right?" Miguel touches my hand, the gesture almost apologetic. "Did they give you Aclisote?"

I clutch the mug even more firmly. "One dose. It wasn't enough to change my skills back."

"No," Miguel agrees, "but it was probably enough to ease your symptoms."

"I don't have symptoms." I pull my hand away from his. "I'm not sick."

"We know Aclisote kills us," KJ says. "When Shannon stopped giving it to me, I got better. Same with Alex."

Miguel sighs. "It's not that simple. Working with time is incredibly stressful for the body, and the brain reacts in ways that aren't always healthy. Paranoia is the most common reaction, followed by intense anger. Violence isn't unusual. The more you freeze time, the more intense the symptoms get, and those symptoms will only get reduced through chemical intervention. Some of history's most notorious criminals really were spinners, just like the Norms say—Jack the Ripper, Billy the Kid."

"But . . ." I say. Miguel holds up a hand.

"Let me finish. Like most medicines, Aclisote is derived from a natural plant, in this case *Rubiaceae*. It's a tropical plant, in the same family as quinine and coffee beans." He gestures to the cup locked between my palms. "That's why caffeine helps your headaches. Early spinners in South America and the West Indies discovered centuries ago that if they consumed these particular plants regularly, they could control their symptoms and still manipulate time—not every day, but enough to maintain their positions as shamans and wisewomen. Since *Rubiaceae* is a tropical plant, spinners in northern countries suffered much more than their southern cousins. They were a genuine threat to the rest of society.

"Then in the 1500s, the Europeans 'discovered' the tropics and the local medicines. They brought the plants north and started experimenting. Eventually, they figured out how to increase the plant's natural potency, bringing the concentrations up high enough to render spinners' skills ineffective."

Across the table, KJ starts twirling a spoon between two fingers. Light glints off the metal in regular bursts that hurt my eyes.

"They don't render our skills *ineffective*," I say. "They kill us."

"Sure," Miguel says. "But even aspirin can kill you if you overdose.

Used sparingly, Aclisote is extremely useful. I take a version of it every day."

KJ's spoon hits the table with a bang. "You do?"

"In much lower doses than the Center was giving you, of course. And I modify it based on need. Right now, I'm on a higher dose so that my freezes don't stick. It makes it easier to have conversations like this." He gestures around the stalled diner. "When I melt, everything goes back to how it was before. We don't have to worry about how much we move during the freeze. Plus, if anything goes wrong—if you run away while we're talking, or you try to hurt me—I can always get back to the beginning."

I tip my coffee cup to my lips without drinking any. My mind holds too much information to process it coherently. KJ picks up his fallen spoon and sets it down in perfect alignment with his butter knife.

"How did you find us?" he asks.

"Whew." Miguel grins to himself, as if remembering a particularly exciting adventure. "You sure didn't make it easy."

KJ doesn't return Miguel's smile. "Tell."

"We heard about your escape as soon as Charlie got off shift. He goes to the same pub every night after work for a beer. The bartender is one of ours, and he always pumps Charlie for any news."

"There's a spinner bartending a few blocks from the Center?" I ask.

"He's not a spinner," Miguel says. "Just a sympathizer. Anyway, when Charlie told him Alex had disappeared in the middle of the lobby, and that three other kids were unaccounted for, the bartender called me right away. I got into Portland Thursday night.

"At first I was afraid you'd left town, but then Sonya reported seeing you at the farmers market. I tracked you as far as the bus, but unfortunately, you ran off before I could talk to you."

Rabbit Lady! My mind reels back to that day, remembering my blind terror, my desperate fear of the motorcyclist boarding the bus. What if I'd asked Sonya a few more questions and ended up talking to Miguel then? He would have found us before KJ woke up, before I got trapped in the Center, before Jack beat up Victor. Before Shannon fled.

"The rest," Miguel continues, "was pure detective work. I told you that's my day job. I've been cruising around the city, asking at all the places that help homeless kids. A couple times I thought I saw you, but I never managed to connect. I also left your picture at the front desks of motels I knew were unlikely to check ID, telling everyone you were runaways and I'd been hired by your parents to find you. The manager of the Pegasus has a soft spot for troubled kids, so he called me as soon as he heard that three rather bedraggled-looking young people had checked into a room yesterday. That was at six this morning. I came over immediately. The curtain of your room was open just enough I could see the place was empty. Luckily, there aren't many restaurants nearby." Miguel motions around the crowded diner. "This is the first spot I tried."

I realize I'm staring at Miguel with my mouth slightly open. KJ scratches his cheek. "Wow," he says to Miguel. "You're good."

"Thanks." Miguel ducks his head. "So, I've been meaning to ask, where are Jack and Shannon?"

KJ starts fiddling with the spoon again.

"Jack is staying somewhere else," I say. "We think downtown. Shannon . . ." I swallow. "Left this morning." KJ lets the spoon droop between his fingers.

"An excellent safety precaution," Miguel says. "It's a good idea to separate. Less likely you'll all get caught."

I shake my head. "We think Shannon went back to the Center. She never believed they meant to hurt us."

"Oh." The cheer on Miguel's face fades. "I'm so sorry. It's not that unusual, though. Reality is too much for some kids to accept. What about Jack? Do you know where he is? We can pick him up before we head to the refuge."

"Right now?" I ask.

"Of course." Miguel slides out of the booth, smoothing the creases out of his pants. "I'm not the only one out here showing folks your picture. The Pegasus guy may like kids, but he also likes money, and the wipers offer generous rewards for lost spinners." He shakes his head. "Wipers are very committed to making sure no free spinners survive."

Outside the window, the truck that had startled us earlier is still visible, red taillights barely a block away. Miguel seems legit, but can we trust him not to lead us into another trap? I clench my fist and feel my own pulse throbbing in my veins. My eyes seek KJ's.

He isn't looking at me.

"We need to get Shannon out," he says to Miguel.

Something heavy shifts in my stomach. Shannon is probably locked in the room I left only the day before, though I doubt they'll grant her even the limited freedom they gave me. She'll be sedated, leashed, and probably guarded by a buzzing zapper. The still sunlight around us seems to fade. How long before her time skills "normalize" and Barnard can whisk her away?

"Oh. Well. Shannon." Miguel places his hands together, palms touching. "I'm afraid I can't help you there."

KJ frowns. "Why not?"

"It's our policy. We never interfere directly with the Center."

"But you rescue spinners."

"Only the ones that are already out." Miguel claps his hands together without making any sound. "Right now, we fly pretty far under the radar. If we started breaking people out, they'd be on us faster than metal to a magnet."

KJ's jaw twitches. "We can't leave Shannon there. She'll die."

"Which is heartbreaking," Miguel agrees. "And I'm sorry, but we can't save everyone. We're doing what we can."

KJ crosses his arms over his chest. His mouth is set in that stubborn line he gets when he thinks people are being unreasonable.

"What if we don't go with you?" KJ asks.

Miguel sighs.

"I won't force you, but please think through your decision carefully. Your chances of surviving out here alone are extremely slim. Your fear and paranoia will grow every time you use your skills, until eventually you'll do something that will make it easy for the wipers to track you. It always happens." He shakes his head. "All the free spinners I know have access to Aclisote. No escapee from the Center has ever survived unless we've gotten to them first."

"I'm not leaving Shannon there," KJ says. "It's my fault she went back."

"It's a miracle you managed to break out of the Center twice," Miguel says. "There is no way you can do it a third time."

KJ's expression doesn't change. Miguel turns to me. "What about you?"

For one shining second, I picture standing up and walking out of the diner with him, but even as the image flashes in my head, the picture dims. Miguel is offering the kind of support I never imagined was out here, but how can I accept it when there's even a slim chance we can rescue the others? My dream of leaving the Center has never been about creating some new life for myself. It's about setting every single one of us free.

"No," I say. "I'm staying too."

Miguel's face wilts.

"It's your choice." He picks up his hat, lying all this time on the edge of the table.

"Wait," I say. "What if we want to find you?"

"I can give you my cell number." Miguel recites a number and makes us repeat it back three times to make sure we've memorized it. "But you should know I'm leaving town in the morning, heading out to Idaho Falls. I can try and come back to check on you next week, but . . ."

I pick at a chip on the rim of my coffee cup. I know how his unfinished sentence ends. Miguel doesn't believe we have a week. If we don't go with him now, he thinks we won't make it.

"You better not stay here much longer," Miguel says, gesturing around the diner. "If I found you, the wipers may come here, too." He gives us both a final, searching look and sighs. "When time starts again, it will be safer for me if you act like we don't know each other. I don't want anyone to link us together, in case someone comes asking questions."

KJ and I both nod.

"OK, then," Miguel says. "You ready?"

The room spins. My body shifts, and the silverware on our table blurs, as everything returns to its prefreeze position. The reel of life picks up where it left off. Noise erupts around us. Forks make their way into mouths, coffee splashes into cups. Miguel lifts his hand from on top of our re-clasped fingers.

"Sorry," he says in the neutral tone of someone talking to strangers, "must have tripped." He straightens up. "Well, if it's not your hat." He picks up the cap and plops it on his head, then saunters toward the register, taking with him the brief mirage of his promised refuge.

KJ clears his throat. "You don't have to stay just because I am."

"I know."

KJ unclasps his fingers from mine. "There's no need for both of us to risk our necks in an impossible scheme."

"No." I put both my hands over his, trapping them on the tabletop. "We agreed when we decided to break out—we're in this together."

From behind me, a bell jangles as the diner's door closes on Miguel. I don't turn my head. Instead, I close my fingers around KJ's and hold on very tightly.

"You two ready for your check?"

Tammi waves her order pad at us.

"Yeah," I say.

Tammi rips out the bill and drops it beside KJ. "You pay up front when you're ready."

"You think Miguel's telling us the truth?" I ask KJ, once Tammi threads her way back to the kitchen. "That this mythic refuge exists?"

"If he was working for Barnard, he would have agreed to help us get Shannon. It would have been an easy way to get us to go back. Plus, he was right when he said he could have just slapped us with a leash."

I let go of KJ and dig my cell out of my pocket. "We should call Jack. Tell him about Miguel's offer." I thumb the phone on. The message light blinks with another text from Jack. *Which motel?*

"There's got to be a way to get Shannon out." KJ drums his fingers on the table.

I scroll down to press Jack's number. The phone buzzes before I've placed the call.

"Jack! I was just calling you."

"Alex?"

It isn't Jack. The voice is wobbly, whispery, and female.

"Shannon?"

KJ's head snaps in my direction. I press my fingers against my other ear to drown out the hubbub in the diner. "Where are you?"

"It's not Shannon," the voice whispers, "it's Yolly. Shannon . . ." Yolly's voice breaks. "Shannon's gone."

"Gone?" I repeat. KJ leans forward. I shake my head, trying to focus. "You mean she's not with you?"

"She was." Yolly sniffs. "She came in this morning. I was so happy. She wasn't sick or anything." Yolly is crying now, her words a teary jumble that makes them hard to understand. "Then Dr. Barnard came in, and, oh, Alex, they took her."

"Who took her? Where?"

Yolly only sobs. KJ mouths *What? Took who?*

It's Yolly, I mouth back. KJ's body stills.

"Please," I say into the phone. "Tell me what happened. Where is Shannon?"

"Barnard said . . ." Yolly sniffs again. "He said they were taking her to the Central Office."

22 ◀◀

I CAN'T BREATHE. THE BLOOD SEEPS AWAY FROM MY FEET again, turning my toes into blocks of ice.

"When?" I ask.

"Just a few minutes ago," Yolly says. "Barnard called some kind of Central Office security agents, and they drove her away. But Shannon was *fine*; she was perfectly healthy."

"I know," I say.

"And you were right." Yolly makes the odd gulping sound of someone holding back tears. "About the files. I checked them like you asked. The dosages do get higher before people die, and everyone's chronotin levels are really, really low at the end. And Shannon—I checked her blood when she first came in, before Barnard got here. Her chronotin reading was 308. But she wasn't sick."

"I know," I say again.

"Nothing makes any sense. Everything is crazy here. The kids are crying, there are boxes everywhere. And they won't let me go with them, even though I volunteered."

"Go with them?" I interrupt. "Go where?"

"Haven't you heard?" Yolly draws in a shaky breath. "The Center. They moved up the closing date. They're taking everyone to the Central Office first thing tomorrow morning."

The chill in my feet spreads higher. Goose bumps dot my legs.

"Tomorrow?"

"What's she saying?" KJ asks, out loud this time.

I smash the phone harder against my ear, straining to hear Yolly over the diner's clatter. "I thought it wasn't closing until the end of the month?"

"Dr. Barnard said something about a research project," Yolly wails. "None of this makes any sense."

It makes perfect sense to me. The research project may be legit, but it's also an excuse—the Center's higher-ups are not going to keep a facility open if its spinners are escaping.

"What's going on?" KJ raises his voice. I glance around the diner. A couple at a table near ours turns to watch us. I hold up a finger in KJ's direction. One minute.

"Yolly," I say. "We'll help—I promise—but I need to think. Can I call you back at this number?" Yolly mumbles something like agreement. "OK," I say. "In the meantime, don't talk about this to anyone. *Anyone*. Not the kids, not the staff, not your best friend. And don't ask Barnard any questions when he comes back. He can't think you're suspicious. OK? Promise? I'll call you back soon."

I hang up. KJ is leaning across the table, his arms stretched even closer as if their proximity might help him hear better.

"What's going on?" he asks again.

The couple at the other table are still casting surreptitious glances in our direction. The woman wears a small frown. I give her my best reassuring smile.

"Let's get out of here," I mutter to KJ.

Five minutes later, alone on the empty sidewalk, I tell him Shannon is gone.

"We have to save her." KJ strides down the street so fast I start trotting in order to keep level with him.

"How?" I ask. "She's in a car with a wiper right now."

"We'll follow them."

"We don't know where the Central Office is."

"We can ask Yolly. Or break into the Center and search Barnard's office."

"It's not just Shannon." Greasy breakfast and bad news swell my insides. If KJ doesn't slow down soon, I'm going to puke. "Barnard moved the date up. He's closing the Center tomorrow and sending everyone to the Central Office."

KJ stops walking so suddenly that I've gone three steps past him before I realize he isn't there. I turn around. KJ is standing stock-still in the center of the sidewalk. He's the picture of dejection: shoulders slumped, arms dangling by his sides, hands loose and empty.

"So he's murdering them." KJ stares at the ground, his voice so flat it sounds as if he's reading the words off the sidewalk.

"He won't kill them right off the bat," I say, aching for the words to be true. "Maybe this research project is just a small thing, and then when he's done, he'll send them back."

KJ shakes his head. "He's never sending them back. The Center has to be crawling with rumors. Aidan saw Jack vanish the day you got us all out, plus you've popped in and out of there, what, twice? If the other kids know the truth, or even suspect it, they can never be part of a new Center."

A truck rumbles past, blasting warm diesel air. The smell coats the inside of my nose. It tastes like ash.

"KJ."

He raises his head. His eyes are pure black, as if everything that usually lies behind them, all the joy and life that is KJ, has winked out, leaving only darkness behind.

"She's going to die," he says. "They all are. Because of us."

My stomach twists. KJ said *us*, but I know most of the blame is mine. I'm the one who "popped in and out" of the Center. I'm the one who made Jack disappear.

The three-step separation between me and KJ yawns like a chasm. I want to close the gap—hug him, soothe his hurt—but I know I can't. Our last embrace led us here. The only reason we are alone together is because Shannon is gone.

"We'll get them out tonight," I say. "All of them."

"How?"

A fierce energy bursts open inside me. The odds are against us, and we have two choices: crumble and die or gear up for a fight. If I'm going to choose a fight, I'm going to make it a good one.

"Yolly," I say, putting a plan together as I speak. "When Miguel said we'd never break out a third time, he didn't consider that we might have an inside helper."

There's still no flicker in KJ's eyes, no spark of hope or enthusiasm. He just studies me for a while. Then he nods.

THE BRAZENNESS OF ALEX'S PLAN TAKES ROSS'S BREATH away. Does she really believe she can walk into the Crime Investigation Center and waltz out with twenty spinners? Her skills change her chance of success from impossible to unlikely, but that's still too much risk. Twenty-plus unmedicated spinners roaming around on their own would be a disaster. There is no way the Center can cover up all the mistakes they're bound to make, and if their secret skills are exposed, all Ross's plans would implode. Just thinking about it makes him feel twitchy.

"I think your best bet," Yolly says to Alex, "is to come in through the underground parking garage as I go out."

Yolly's voice over the phone sounds muffled, as if she's talking in a closet, or else has her hand cupped around the mouthpiece. It doesn't help that the officers who share the office with Ross seem to be confused about the difference between *talk* and *yell*.

Ross adjusts the volume on the headphones plugged into the laptop he's using—the one loaded with the precinct's finest wiretapping software. He'd pulled Alex's phone number off Jack's cell yesterday afternoon and asked Chief to approve a rush court order to track and tap it. Chief agreed when Ross claimed that the number was the final piece he needed to close out the rewound murder case, but the "rush" still took over twelve hours. Ross's original goal was merely to catch the girl who betrayed him so he could turn her in to the Center; he never expected to uncover a full-fledged rescue plan.

"What about the inner door?" Alex asks. "The one from the garage into the Center?"

"I'll leave that one propped open," Yolly says.

"Better to leave us a key card. That way, if something goes wrong, they won't suspect you of helping us."

If something goes wrong? The pen Ross is using to take notes slips, making a blue slash across his notepad. The question can't be *if*, it has to be *when*.

Yolly warns the runaway that Dr. Barnard slept in his office the past two nights, and that he's added extra security guards—one per floor, plus a guy that walks through the whole building in a circuit. She and Alex hash out a plan while Ross writes down every detail. Key card. Rental van. Room keys. Staff lounge. Alex promises she'll be at the Center when Yolly's shift ends at eleven p.m., and they both hang up.

Ross slides his headphones down around his neck and sips from the mug of coffee cooling at his elbow. What he'd really like to do is catch her in the act. It would make Ross a hero, but unfortunately, it's not a realistic plan. It would be impossible to feign innocence of the spinners' true skills if Ross inserts himself in the middle of their escape. He'll have to settle for catching her privately and then turning her over to Barnard in the morning. Her *and* her friend KJ. He'll say he found them sleeping, or that they turned themselves in. Barnard won't ask too many questions as long as he gets what he wants.

Which still leaves the problem of coming up with a way to "prove" that Jack has either fled town or died. Ross turns the mug in his hand and thinks about the boy locked away in his forest hideaway. Jack had been quite meek once he'd relinquished his knife and come with Ross the day before. Ross had spoken soothingly to him the whole drive out to the secret house. Once inside, he'd made the boy a hearty lunch, which included a drink laced with both Aclisote and a sedative. When Jack woke up, hours later, he'd been calmer but also leashed and the bearer of a brand-new tracking device, one of the modern near-microscopic ones, which Ross had inserted not under the thin skin at the back of Jack's neck, but deep in the fleshiest part of his thigh.

The conversation that followed was short. Ross was very clear about what he could offer and what Jack had to do in return. He told Jack he could save only one spinner; if Jack didn't want the deal, then Ross would find someone else. Turning in the escapees wasn't treachery, he told the boy, just a shortcut to their inevitable end, and having Ross bring them in was more humane than letting them be hunted down by the wipers. Jack didn't look happy about this bargain, but as Ross predicted, he understood it. The boy still shuddered every time Ross said the word *wiper*.

Ross puts his coffee down and picks up Jack's phone. It has only one number saved in the contacts. Ross clicks on the text icon and taps out a message to Alex.

Where is your motel?

Within seconds, the phone in his hands buzzes to announce an incoming phone call. Ross hits reject and types another message.

Can't talk right now. Text me.

Alex's answer comes quickly.

Shannon caught by Barnard. We're going to break them ALL out tonight. We met a guy who can get us somewhere safe.

Ross squints at the message. They met a guy? She hadn't mentioned that part to Yolly. Alex must be more desperate than he thinks. Didn't all those years working vice teach her not to trust strange men who offer protection? He shakes his head. He's seen what happens to girls like that. Bringing her back to the Center will be doing her a favor.

Who's the guy? Ross taps out. *Where is he taking you?*

Out of town, Alex types back. *Meet us tonight and we can all go together.*

Ross tries to think like Jack. He'd be suspicious, right?

Let's talk in person. Where are you?

Better to stay separate, Alex replies. *And DON'T freeze. That's why we've been so paranoid.*

Ross frowns at the message. It's inconvenient that Alex knows about freezing's side effects; it might make her more cautious. That boy KJ must have helped her figure it out. He was always a little too clever for his own good.

Breaking others out sounds too risky, Ross writes. *Meet me and we'll run for it.*

No. We have to help them.

Where are you??

Phone dying. We're leaving from the Sick. Meet us by the garage gate at 11 p.m.

The officer across the room laughs a loud, honking laugh. Ross bends over the phone and types quickly.

I'll help you plan. Just tell me where you are.

No answer. Ross checks the phone tracker. There's no signal, which means Alex's phone must have powered off. Ross tosses Jack's phone on the desk. So much for the idea of tricking Alex into telling him her location. He drums his fingers on the desk's cheap laminate top. He could go with Jack to meet up with the other kids at eleven, and then nab them in a freeze, but that's risky. The best way to contain the spinners is to handcuff them to the rail inside his police car—even if they froze time they'd be helpless— but he only has one leash, so he'll have to take them one at a time. It will be a lot safer if that whole operation happens some-where more sheltered than a public street. Ross doesn't want to chance more unexplained disappearances, much less get caught himself as a flicker on the Center's surveillance video. Besides, thanks to Alex's phone call with Yolly, Ross knows exactly where they're going to be and how to intercept them. This time, Alex won't be able to escape him, because this time, the odds will be even. This time, Ross will have a spinner on his side.

Ross slips Jack's phone in his pocket next to his own and heads out of the precinct. He'll pick up something hearty for him and Jack to share for dinner when his shift is over. They'll need it. The two of them have a long night ahead.

24 ◀◀

WAITING IS HORRIBLE. KJ AND I WALK DOWN RANDOM streets, ending up sitting on metal bleachers next to an empty baseball field. We work through the details of our plan until the cold settles into our bones and the only thing left to talk about are all the ways things might go wrong.

"There could be zappers set up all over the place," I say.

"You said you can sense them."

"Yeah, but we still can't get near them."

KJ blows on his fingers, then shoves his hands into his armpits.

"It's too risky for Yolly," he says. "If she gets caught helping us, she could go to jail."

"It's her choice," I counter. "She offered."

A dog across the field starts howling. I chew on the last fragment of fingernail I have that sticks even slightly above the line of my skin.

"Our biggest weakness is us," I say. "It's going to be hard to hold time long enough to get that many people out."

"So we run off to safety and leave them all to die?"

We give up on talking and walk aimlessly around the city instead, afraid to freeze time, afraid to stay anywhere too long. I suggest we find somewhere to take a nap, but the suggestion is half-hearted, as we both know we won't be able to sleep. Besides, where could we go? We end up killing most of the afternoon in a library. I flip through book after book without absorbing a single word. KJ sits at a table with a magazine and doesn't turn the pages. At least the place has electrical outlets. I plug in the phone charger and sit on the floor in front of it so the librarian doesn't see. When I check later, I don't have any messages.

Day fades into night. Lights blossom behind shaded windows; neon springs alive in the shops. We take a bus downtown, then find a coffee shop a few blocks from the Center. My nerves are jumping so much I don't need the caffeine, but I'm hoping the preemptive dose might slow down the headache waiting in my future. At 10:55, we dump our cups into the dirty-dish bin and head outside.

The bite of coming winter slides through the seams of our clothes. Night presses down from a starless sky, darkness kept at bay only by the mustard gleam of streetlights.

KJ and I turn up the street that flanks the north side of the Center, staying on the opposite sidewalk, out of range of the Center's security cameras. The street is empty except for a U-Haul truck parked at the end of the block. On the side panel, a banner screams *Venture Across America* in bright letters over a picture of a wide-eyed green alien. Underneath, it says *New Mexico. What happened in Roswell?* The alien looks like he's laughing at me.

I check my watch: 11:00.

"Jack's not here," I say.

"Did you expect him?" KJ asks.

"Sort of."

KJ shrugs, an uncharacteristically callous gesture. "Jack will take care of himself. He always does."

I swallow my disappointment, take out my phone, and dial Yolly's number.

"Alex?" Yolly's voice cuts through the first purr of the phone's ring. She must have been holding her cell in her hand.

"I'm here," I say.

"I'm scared."

"Don't be. Either we'll be with you in a few minutes, or we won't, and then you just drive away and no one will ever know you tried to help us."

Yolly makes a whimpering sound. "Remind me what I'm supposed to do."

"It's easy. Go to your car and get your overnight bag and then walk out through the parking garage so the gate opens. You mentioned to someone that you were helping your cousin move this weekend, right?"

"I told Charlie."

"See? You're covered. No one is going to suspect anything. When you leave the Center, go to the U-Haul. Did you hide the keys for us?"

"Yes," Yolly says. "They're in the staff lounge, like you asked. I put them under the spider plant on the windowsill."

"Perfect. We'll see you soon, OK? Everything is going to be fine."

I click the call off.

We wait. A taxi slides past, the yellow light on its roof shining like the eye of some urban predator. When it's gone, KJ takes off his backpack and stashes it at the foot of a parking meter. I do the same. If the night goes well, we can pick them up later, and if it doesn't, their contents won't matter. All either of us grabbed from the squat was a change of clothes and some toiletries. KJ pulls the hood of his sweatshirt over his head. I take the cell phone from my pocket and drop it down a sewer drain. Miguel's is the only number I need, and I have that one memorized. All my phone can do now is expose Yolly.

From across the street, the Center watches us with the blank stare of a fortress. There's no hint of the uproar taking place inside those stone walls. Packing boxes, questions, and fear must be clogging the hallways. I wonder how many spinners lie awake behind the dark windows. There's no way to tell. The Center keeps its secrets.

A breeze ruffles the trees lining the sidewalk, sending a flurry of dead leaves down the street. I shift my attention to the underground garage. The driveway sinks into a dark tunnel, its entrance protected from the street by a sliding gate made of crosshatched metal bars. As I watch, a light, faint and wobbly, drifts up from the depths of the garage. KJ and I draw closer together. The light gets brighter; the gate clicks and starts slowly grinding its way upward.

I hold out my hand, and KJ takes it. His palm feels dry and impersonal. When the garage gate is four feet off the ground, I stop time. KJ lets go of my hand as soon as it's done.

"All right," he says. "You ready?"

I rub my empty palms together and look up and down the street again, hoping against hope I'll see a frozen Jack hovering on the sidewalk. He's not there. The tension of this long day winds a little higher. If we leave Jack in Portland, will we lose him forever?

"Come on," KJ says.

The two of us troop across the street and duck under the entry gate. Yolly stands on the other side, a flashlight in one hand, a small rolling suitcase gripped in the other. The ramp beyond tilts sharply downward, dark and unwelcoming. We walk in silence until we reach the bottom. Down here, it's brighter. The garage has lights ringing the interior, one bulb set between every other parking space. Only a few cars are parked, most presumably belonging to the guards. I search for Barnard's beige sedan before remembering he totaled it when he tried to take me to the Central Office. Any one of these cars could be his.

"Do you see the key card?" I ask.

KJ shakes his head, and the two of us spread out across the garage, faces bent toward the floor. The card releases the electronic locks on both the garage door that leads into the Center and the door to the staff lounge where Yolly left the other, nonelectronic keys we need—one to open the spinners' bedroom doors, and one to open the back of the U-Haul that will transport us out of here.

"Here it is." KJ squats down near a blue Honda, then stands up waving a small rectangular card. "She must have let it slip when she got her luggage out of the car. Very natural."

The entry door to the Center is painted off-white, the bottom section marred with scuff marks. A wire-enforced glass panel on the top half allows me to peer inside. A hallway stretches beyond it, shadowed and empty.

"Ready?" I hold out my hand. We'll have to melt time for a second so we can release the lock.

A furrow pinches KJ's brow.

"If the guard's watching the monitors," he says, "he'll see us open the door."

"He won't have any reason to be watching the monitors in the garage now that Yolly is gone," I say, with more confidence than I feel. "And if he is, we'll only show up for a couple of seconds. Even if he comes down to investigate, we'll be long gone and the door shut tight by the time he gets here."

KJ's frown doesn't lighten. I don't blame him. Of all the dozens of rescue-destroying scenarios we have imagined, this is not one of them.

"Come on." I flick my fingers impatiently. "Let's just do this."

KJ's hand clasps mine as he places the key card against the reader. I tilt my face away from the security camera perched over the doorframe and let time slip forward. I wait one heartbeat after I hear the click of the door's electronic release, to make sure it caught, and then slam time to a stop again.

For a moment, we stand there, hands linked, staring at the closed door.

"Think that worked?" I ask.

"We'll see." KJ pockets the card and grabs the handle. When the door swings open, I release a shaky breath.

The two of us step over the threshold together. KJ pulls his sweatshirt off and wedges it between the door and the frame to keep it from closing all the way. We huddle in the hallway, peering around the darkened space. The black cavern of the cafeteria opens off to our right. Up ahead lie the double doors to the gym. Just before it is the stairwell that leads to the lobby. The lack of light makes the once-familiar spaces seem foreign; the usually comforting silence makes them eerie.

"What now?" KJ's voice booms in the quiet.

"We get the keys," I say. "Then we start waking up the kids."

"Let's check the guard station's monitor, too," KJ says. "If we rewind, maybe we can tell if he saw us open the garage door."

We walk down the echoing hall and climb the stairs to the main floor. The lobby's overhead lights are blinding after so much time in the dark. It's not a big lobby, maybe fifteen feet wide. Barnard's office is on the other side, the front door is to our left, and to our right is the main staircase—a last remnant of the building's glory days as a grand hotel—leading to the upper floors. The guard station stands halfway across the room, tucked against the bend in the stairs' elegant curve.

Off to the side, near the front door, piles of boxes are stacked like oversized blocks. Neat writing identifies each one's owner: Yuki Ota, Emmaline Smith, Emilio Montero. Fear nips at my heels. We won't have a second chance at this rescue; there is no room tonight for errors.

"Guard station first?" KJ asks.

I nod, and we cross the threshold into the lobby.

Dread catches me before I've taken three steps. I jump back, panicked. On the other side of the tiled floor, the door to Barnard's office radiates a familiar ominous warning.

"Stop!" I call to KJ.

"What's wrong?"

I point. "The zapper's on. Can't you feel it?"

KJ follows the line of my finger. "Feel what?"

"It's like . . ." I struggle to find the right words. "Like something huge and hairy is about to jump on top of you."

He shakes his head. "I can't feel it. Maybe 'cause it's not my freeze?"

"Yeah." I stare at the closed door. The terror has lessened now that I've backed away, but just knowing it's there makes the wood seem like it's pulsing with evil. "Stay away from Barnard's office. We don't know how it works. Maybe any spinner getting near the zapper is enough to break the freeze."

KJ edges his way to the front of the guard station and sticks his head inside the sliding glass window so he can see the video monitors.

"Rewind for a bit," he calls. I reach for the strands and pull time backward a few minutes, slowly, so KJ can watch the feed and the

270

guard's reaction at the same time. It's awkward; the danger emanating from Barnard's office rattles my concentration.

"We're good." KJ straightens and heads back in my direction.

I wipe away the sweat dampening my upper lip. The farther KJ gets from the zapper, the easier it is for me to hold time.

"Let's go to the staff lounge," I say.

The light from the lobby doesn't reach very far down the hall, so by the time we get to the lounge it's nearly pitch black. KJ fishes the key card out of his pocket and holds out his hand. I take it. Air shifts around us as time moves forward. The door clicks. I wait, just for a second, to make sure the lock unlatched.

The hall vanishes. I blink, change hitting me so hard my brain has trouble making sense of it. I'm inside the lounge. The lights are on. Time is frozen, but I know it's not my freeze. My body is off-balance. I stumble but don't fall because someone is holding my wrist in a very tight grip. It's Jack. He's standing in front of me, and smiling next to him, one hand firmly clasped around Jack's bare forearm, is Carson Ross.

25 ◀◀

"HELLO, ALEX," ROSS SAYS. "WELCOME BACK."

The coffee I'd drunk earlier burns my stomach. I rip my arm free from Jack's hold and spin around. KJ is propped against the wall behind me, frozen, his hand still clutching the key card, though he's no longer facing the door. Jack must have been listening for the click of the door's release, freezing time as soon as he heard it. The room wobbles. I put out a hand to steady myself, but there's nothing nearby to grab hold of.

"Sorry about this," Jack says.

"I don't understand." My brain feels sluggish, as if my thoughts are moving through glue. "Why is Ross here?"

"You turned down his offer," Jack says. "So instead he asked me."

"You're going to work for Ross?"

Jack fiddles with the sleeve of his jacket—the fancy one we bought the day we stole all that money. The animal smell of leather drifts into my nose, bringing back memories of us standing together, laughing over fistfuls of cash. The sludge in my brain grows thicker.

"Why?"

Jack looks away. "I don't have a choice."

"Of course you have a choice. You're making the wrong one."

"We'll never survive out there alone," he says. He's pulling on his jacket's zipper, sliding it up and down with quick jerks, making an erratic zzzz sound that fills the space between us. "You saw them. The wipers were everywhere. Ross is the only person who can keep us safe."

The words, I'm sure, are Ross's. They smack of his egotism, plus the man himself is beaming at Jack, a proud mentor watching his protégé.

"Ross is a liar," I say. Miguel's offer hovers on the tip of my tongue, but I know I can't reveal it in front of Ross. Too many other spinners rely on Miguel's protection. "Whatever he promised you is not going to happen."

"It already has," Jack says. "I'm free. Ross even got me a guitar. I start lessons on Monday."

The room feels crowded. The presence of Carson Ross sucks up all the vacant space. I know all about his earnest expression, his reassuring tone. Ross is easy to believe—until he isn't.

"What about everyone else?" I ask. "Do you know that's why I came here tonight? To rescue them all?"

Jack's shoulders hunch under the heavy jacket, though his hand doesn't stop its restless motion. "Getting out of the Center won't help anyone. They'll just get caught again. It's cruel to give them hope when they aren't going to get to live."

The jagged whir of Jack's zipper is as bad as a leash. I can't think with the annoying white noise filling my head.

"They *will* make it. We all can. I know a place where we can go. Jack, please."

For the first time since I appeared in the lounge, Jack looks straight at me. Something flashes in his eyes—a question, or a glimpse of hope. I hold my breath, trying to telegraph the future I can see in my head: all the spinners away from the Center, united and strong. It doesn't work. The light in Jack's eyes is brief and quickly snuffed.

"Face it," he says, "only one of us is going to make it. Why shouldn't it be me?"

The vision in my head shatters.

"Jack . . . !"

"He's made his decision, Alex." Ross puts a hand on Jack's shoulder. "I think you've tortured him enough."

I whirl to face my former agent. "You just want to use him," I say, "use his time skills to manipulate people so you can get what you want."

"And what's wrong with that?" Ross moves toward me, away from Jack. "You have this power no one else does; why are you so afraid to use it when it can do so much good?"

"You used me to *murder* someone, Ross."

"Someone who you know killed a bunch of other people. How is it wrong that he got paid back?"

"You can't just decide who's guilty all by yourself."

Ross sighs, the annoyed huff of a teacher dealing with a tiresome Younger.

"Our judicial system is broken. The wrong people get arrested every day. My goal has always been to make sure there is true justice."

There's a hungry, hopeful expression on Ross's face, and in that second, I know that if I said I would join him, I could be the one to walk out of here tonight instead of Jack. I step back.

"The system might have flaws," I say. "But they're not as big as yours."

The light in Ross's eyes turns dark. He reaches into his pocket and pulls out a leash.

"Come on," Ross says to Jack. "It's time to stop this nonsense."

The metal bracelet dangles from Ross's fingers like a hungry jaw.

"Jack," I say, not taking my eyes off Ross. "You're the one in control here. You can end this."

"No," Jack says. He stops messing with his zipper. The silence it leaves behind feels ominous. "I can't."

Ross makes an impatient gesture. The leash clanks in his hand, and I instinctively jump away from him. Pain lances my leg as the corner of a table drives into my thigh. I hold up my arms, braced to fend off Ross, but he hasn't followed me. He's reaching for KJ, and in one quick move, he snaps the leash around KJ's wrist.

"Take Alex's arm," Ross tells Jack. "I don't want you letting time go for even a second until she's handcuffed to the rail in my car."

The hard bulk of the table presses against the backs of my legs. KJ hovers to my right, the door to the hall beside him, but Ross stands firmly between it and me. Thoughts slog through my head without any coherent pattern. *Think!* I have to think.

Jack's fingers close around my upper arm. Ross moves away from the door, grabs the other one, and yanks it behind me with so much force I can't help the cry of pain that bursts from my lips. Jack flinches but Ross doesn't hesitate. He pulls a pair of handcuffs from his belt and locks both my wrists behind my back with the efficiency of long practice. Shock leaves me momentarily immobilized. I've seen Ross handcuff people dozens of times; I never imagined he'd handcuff me.

"Come on," Ross says, gripping my arm above the elbow. Jack takes his place on my other side and the two of them march me across the room.

Wild plans skitter through the chaos in my head. I could kick over the bookcase and smash all of the ceramic figurines resting on its surface, creating an anomaly someone would have to explain when time melted, but would that help anything? We're two steps past the bookcase before I can decide. My feet stumble as we start down the hall. Time isn't moving and it's still running out.

The lobby, with its piles of boxes, opens before us. We step out onto the brightly lit floor and Jack stiffens.

"There's something wrong," he says.

I glance over at him. A sheen of sweat moistens his brow. The haze in my brain sharpens into focus as the explanation dawns on me: we're within range of the zapper. I never told Jack about it, and Barnard would have no reason to tell Ross since he doesn't think Ross knows the truth.

My brain starts spinning out possibilities as fast as I can think them. Now that it's not my freeze, the dark wood blocking Barnard's office seems like any door to me, but I know to Jack the whole lobby must be oozing dread.

Ross tugs me forward.

"Nothing's wrong," he snaps at Jack.

Jack's eyes dart around the lobby, searching for the unseen threat. I pick up my pace. Jack's hold on my arm loosens slightly. We're nearly at the guard station. This is it. My only chance of escape.

I run as hard as I can straight for Barnard's office door, dragging my captors with me so that all three of us stumble forward. The door is almost near enough to touch. Even without being the one holding the freeze, this close I can feel the zapper, its buzz like the angry whine of a dentist drill working its way into my brain. Jack moans. I twist my head to look at him. Whatever disruptive waves squeeze my head, I know they are hurting Jack a hundred times more. It's his freeze, and right now it's being ripped out of his control.

Moving air brushes my cheek. The overhead lights brighten. A snatch of music drifts from the guard-station radio. Jack's hand slips off my arm. He's blinking, his face mirroring the dizzy sickness that I remember from my own experience with the zapper. Ross's head jerks around to look at Jack. Taking advantage of his moment of confusion, I spin toward Ross and drive my knee as hard as I can into his crotch.

Ross groans. I rip my arm out of his grasp and scramble out of range of the zapper, so I can stop time.

Silence descends. I stand on the threshold and look back. Jack's body hangs in an awkward crouch, hands wrapped around the agony that must be in his head. Ross is bent forward with his face clenched in pain. The guard in the security station has half-risen, his head almost at the station window as he cranes toward the flash of commotion.

I race down the hall, my bound arms flopping awkwardly against my back. When I reach KJ, I twist my body so that I can touch my bare hand against his. Melt time. Freeze time.

KJ starts. His eyes flash from my cuffed hands to his leashed wrist. "What happened?"

"Ross." I struggle to keep my voice steady while I explain. KJ's brows draw lower and lower until they are a solid line across his forehead.

"Jack's a spinner!" KJ bursts out when I finish. "How could he side against us like that?"

"He truly thinks the offer is legit. Ross can be really convincing. Plus, Jack must have been a mess when Ross caught him. He'd frozen way too much. You haven't felt it. It makes you crazy."

"You're defending him?"

"Yes. No." A headache blooms behind my forehead, its soft pulse counting down the minutes I can still hold time. A welter of panic bubbles inside me. I can't be getting tired yet. We haven't even started taking out the other spinners.

"It doesn't matter right now," I say. "What matters is that you're leashed."

The black line across KJ's face draws even straighter. He holds up his arm, pulling against the leash in a useless effort to slide his hand through the narrow opening. He's lost the blank stare that haunted him all day. Instead, he exudes the shocked alertness of someone recently doused with a bucket of ice water.

"Ross will have a key," he says. "To this and those cuffs."

We make our way back down the hall, and I wait at the lobby's entrance while KJ approaches the hunched figures of Jack and Ross. Fear laps at me from across the room. I curl my toes away from the lobby floor, the smooth linoleum as threatening as a pool of venom. KJ moves steadily closer to the two guys. Time wobbles in my hold, an external pull that drags at the ephemeral force I control.

"KJ," I shout. "I'm losing it. Get away from there. Now!"

KJ leaps back, making a quick grab to yank Ross's inert body as he moves away from the office door. The pressure in my head lessens. KJ drags Ross across the lobby, then goes back and does the same with Jack; he's panting with the effort by the time he reaches the steps. I wriggle my arms impatiently while he searches through Ross's pockets: wallet, badge, phone, lock picks.

"There!" I say, pointing with my chin when he digs out a key ring. I turn around and feel a rush of relief as my wrists are freed.

"Now me," KJ says. He hands over the keys and holds out his wrist. I search through the rattling chain. None of the keys fit the leash.

"He must have left it in his car," I say.

"Can you pick it?" KJ asks.

I study the leash's locking mechanism. The slot looks nothing like a door's. I try anyway, sliding in the pick and wiggling it the way Ross taught me. My head aches.

"It's not working," I say.

"Forget it." KJ pulls his wrist out of my hands. "Let's put these two somewhere and then go search Ross's car."

I nod, trying not to think of the growing pressure in my head and what that means for the others' rescue. KJ shoves Ross's belongings into his own pocket, before grabbing Ross under the arms. I do the same with Jack, and we drag their bodies down the hall to the janitor's closet.

The door has a regular, physical lock, but my hands are shaking so much it takes me four tries before I manage to pick it. The smell of cleaning solution fills the stale air. KJ and I stuff Ross and Jack inside. There isn't a lot of room. I roll Ross onto his side and handcuff his arms just like he did mine. KJ grabs some clean rags from one of the storage bags; he uses a pair to tie Jack's arms behind his back and another to gag them both. I stare down at Jack, crumpled in a corner, one leg flopped over Ross's, the other balanced on an upturned bucket.

"So we're just going to leave him here." I say the words slowly, as if tasting them to see what they're like.

KJ's tone is grim. "He made his choice."

KJ slams the door shut and I relock it with the pick. The pins fall into place with the dull click of a bullet locking into the chamber of a gun.

"Where do you think Ross parked?" KJ asks.

I touch my forehead. I can feel time pulling at me, the strain of so much freezing wearing down my abilities with every second that doesn't pass.

"KJ," I say. "We aren't going to have time."

KJ turns to me. "What are you saying?"

"I didn't see a police car outside when we came in, which makes sense because Ross will have parked somewhere far away. I won't be able to hold time long enough if we have to run around looking for it." I hold out my hand. "Give me the key card to the lounge and run for the U-Haul. I'll meet you there."

"You can't hold the freeze long enough to get them all," he says. "Not if you're taking other people with you."

"I can try."

"Keep me with you and I'll carry out kids frozen. Some of the Youngers are pretty small."

I shake my head—a mistake, since the movement makes it feel like my brain is slamming against my skull. "It won't help. I can't bring more than two people in a freeze. If you're one of them, it means I can only take one other spinner. Even if you carry another person, it won't get the kids out any faster."

"There's got to be another leash key somewhere. What if we searched . . . ?"

Pain spasms across my head. The invisible clock that controls my skills is ticking down.

"There's no time," I say. "You have to go, KJ. I'll count out two minutes; you run as fast as you can toward the U-Haul. After that, I'm melting time and taking out the other kids."

KJ bites his lip. He looks feverish, his pupils wide, his face flushed. "You can't do this by yourself. You're already feeling the strain. I can tell."

I rub my temple. "You have a better plan?"

"We can tie up the guards. Lock them in a room. Take the kids out in real time."

"It won't work," I say. "Barnard would hear us. And there's no way we can touch him with that stupid zapper in there."

KJ grabs my arm. "You're not going to be able to rescue them all."

He sounds angry, and I wonder if he, too, is thinking about Shannon.

"I'll save as many as I can," I say.

"It's not fair." KJ's grip tightens.

No, it's not fair. Not for Shannon. Or Shea. Or all the kids I won't be able to save. All the deaths laid at my feet.

"Give me the key card and run, KJ."

"No."

"I'm counting now." I shut my eyes. "One. Two."

"I won't just do nothing!"

"Three." I raise my voice to drown him out. "You better hurry. You have to get to at least the basement in two minutes or someone will see you. Four." KJ lets my arm go like he's throwing it away. "Five." He shoves the key card into my palm. "Six." Footsteps thunder down the hall. I keep counting, hiding behind my closed lids. At one hundred twenty, I open them. Even though I heard him leave, the reality of KJ's absence hits like a punch to the gut.

I run the short distance to the lounge and release time just long enough to open the door. Without the drag of carrying an extra person, my headache lightens a little. The two sets of keys are resting just where they're supposed to be under the spider plant. I don't think about Jack's frozen body, bruised and stuffed in a closet. I don't think about the laughing boy who helped me rob a truck. I just take the keys and walk out the door.

I start on the second floor, which is where the Youngers sleep. There's a man I've never seen sitting in the hallway. He's perched on a metal folding chair, dressed in a green uniform, with a nightstick dangling from a loop in his belt. The freeze caught him with his head tipped toward his phone, one finger tracing the screen as he outmaneuvers an electronic opponent. I walk past him and unlock the first door at the end of the hall.

Kimmi and Claire lie peacefully in their bunk beds, their eleven-year-old selves slight beneath mounds of blankets. I dig one of each girl's hands free, stretching my arms wide so I can touch them both at the same time. The silent darkness fills my lungs. I gather myself for the task ahead and try not to think about KJ's race toward safety.

Melt time. Freeze time.

Kimmi jerks her hand from mine and sits bolt upright, smacking her head on the underside of Claire's bunk. Claire mumbles something incoherent and nestles deeper into her sheets.

"Who's there?" Kimmi asks, rubbing her head and squinting into the unlit room.

"It's me," I say.

Claire's bed rustles.

"Alex?" Claire's voice is slurred with sleep.

Kimmi reaches out and clicks her bedside light. Nothing happens.

"Time's frozen," I say.

"They said you got sick," Kimmi says, her dark eyes narrowed with suspicion.

"They lied. You have to get up now. We're leaving the Center."

"Now?" Claire blinks at a digital clock beside their beds. The glowing numbers read 11:07. How far did KJ get before I froze him?

"I'll explain as we go, but you have to hurry."

I step back, hoping my example will push them to their feet. It only half works. Claire yawns and slides obediently down to the floor. Kimmi, however, pulls the blankets more closely around her shoulders.

"Dr. Barnard said we were being transferred to another Center," she says.

The distrust in her tone makes my head hurt worse. I try to keep my voice calm.

"The plan changed. Please, Kimmi, I need you to get up right now."

Kimmi's eyes narrow. "But time's frozen. How can we go anywhere?"

"Like this." I grab Claire's hand and pull her next to Kimmi's bed so I can more easily touch them both. I melt time long enough for them to sense the difference, then freeze it again. Kimmi's mouth falls open in a soundless *oh*.

Claire gasps. "How did you do that?"

"My skills changed when I stopped taking Aclisote." I strip the blankets off Kimmi's legs. "Yours will too."

The two girls gape at me in stunned silence. I snap my fingers at Kimmi and she stumbles to her feet. I keep talking as I get them into their shoes and guide them out the door. When we reach the hall, I relock the dorm's door.

The girls keep up with me as I dash down the Center steps. I tell my story simply, sticking to the basics: the Center is bad and I can get them somewhere safe. I'm not sure how much they believe me and how much they're following me because they're in a groggy half-sleep. As long as they come along, I don't really care.

"Is Shannon with you?" Claire asks when we reach the bottom of the stairs. "Raul said he saw her here this morning."

"No." I glance across the box-cluttered lobby. Barnard's office door is still shut and radiating menace. I hurry around the corner and start down the stairs to the basement. "I don't know where Shannon is. We got separated." Accurate, if not completely true.

"What about KJ and Jack?" Claire twists her head, as if hoping one of them might pop through the cafeteria doors at any moment. "They said you all got sick the same day. Have you been together all this time?"

I do my own search of the poorly lit hallway leading to the garage. KJ must have made good time. We have yet to pass him.

"KJ will meet us at the truck," I say. The door to the garage swings open at my touch. I motion the girls outside, careful not to dislodge the sweatshirt that keeps the door from closing all the way.

Kimmi peers around the mostly empty garage. She's fully awake now, her face taut with questions. "Where are we going?"

"I told you—somewhere safe. Someplace where you won't have the Center telling you what to do."

Claire moves closer to Kimmi, linking her arm through her roommate's.

"Who will take care of us?" she asks in a voice just beginning to quaver.

I touch my forehead. The headache vibrates on the other side of my skull. I want to scream at the girls, to tell them that every second they delay might mean one less person I can rescue. I bite the words back. They're only eleven, and this is all new to them. I force myself to smile.

"Yolly will come with us," I say. "You'll see. We'll pass her on the way out."

Yolly's name seems to unstick the two girls. Arms still linked, they walk toward the mouth of the garage. I hurry ahead of them, scanning the space for KJ's thin frame. Has he gotten all the way to the truck? The garage holds only cars. We start up the ramp. I should have counted the seconds after we left the dorm room to see how long this trip takes.

Yolly still stands at the top of the ramp. I ease past her, barely glancing at her tense face, and duck under the still half-raised entry gate. The U-Haul truck hulks at the end of the block, a dark shadow in the frozen night. The sidewalk beside it is empty.

KJ is nowhere in sight.

26 ◄◄

I BREAK INTO A RUN, MY FEET HITTING THE PAVEMENT WITH uneven thumps. Yolly might have left the truck unlocked. Maybe KJ is already inside. I try the passenger door. It doesn't budge. Nor does the roll-up door in the back.

"KJ?" I hammer my fists against the hard metal. A useless gesture, since if he is there, he's frozen.

"What's the matter?" Kimmi asks. "Can't you get in?"

"It's locked," I say.

"Don't you have a key?" Kimmi sounds annoyed, as if she expected this lack of planning.

I fumble in my pocket with stiff fingers. Maybe the truck wasn't locked when he got here, but it locked when he went inside and closed the door. Somehow.

I slide the key into the handle and twist. The back panel rolls upward with a deafening rattle. Grabbing the lip of the truck bed, I hoist myself inside.

"No one's here," Claire says, after she and Kimmi have climbed in behind me.

I still the panic threatening to choke me. "I'm going to get the rest of the kids. When they get here, tell them to be quiet, OK? I'll be right back."

I melt time before they can protest, then refreeze and race toward the Center. Unburdened by the two girls, the freeze feels lighter, my headache less intense. I pass under the garage gate, scanning every shadowy recess as I run. KJ must have known time was going to melt before he reached the truck and hidden himself so he wouldn't be seen. My sneakers squeak against the smooth concrete with a noise that's as loud as a scream. I slow enough to search the dark spaces around the cars. No one. Inside the Center, the hall lies before me, wide and empty. Same with the cafeteria. And the gym.

My legs start trembling, and I put a hand against the wall. Where did KJ go? *I won't just do nothing!* he'd shouted at me. Did he mean he planned to confront Barnard? Threaten him somehow, demand he return Shannon? Pain lances my forehead. I don't think KJ could have entered Barnard's office without breaking my freeze, but he could wait until we leave and then face down his foe. I close my eyes and lean my cheek against the wall. I should have known KJ wouldn't have gone to the truck. KJ is too honorable to hide while others take risks. Especially since he blames himself for Shannon's capture. An image of KJ's hollowed eyes as he followed me around today floats behind my closed lids. Except for that blast of anger right before I told him to leave, KJ acted like a guy with nothing left to lose.

Another painful jolt shoots through my temple. I push myself away from the wall. I don't have the luxury of worrying about KJ. If I don't keep moving, everything we've both given up will be for nothing.

I manage to get all the spinners from the second-floor dorm rooms before my skills deteriorate. By the third room, the process falls into a rhythm, and by the fifth, I've honed my patter to the words most likely to convince quickly. There's one pair whose bodies are so small that I ask a couple bigger spinners to carry them downstairs still frozen. Emilio puts up a noisy protest until I tell him that every other spinner is already downstairs and he'll be left all alone if he doesn't hurry. Soon the back of the truck is crowded with slack-jawed children. From their perspective, new kids are appearing every few seconds, like some kind of wacky animation made real. At least their shock keeps them quiet. Or maybe it hasn't been long enough to start up a conversation. It's hard to tell how much real time is passing. After eight rooms, all I know is that I no longer have to duck when I get to the garage gate.

I'm stepping off the stairs onto the third floor when the dizziness starts. The third floor has four still-occupied rooms, only one of which has more than one person living in it. I start with the double. Aidan and Raul—Jack's closest friends. My head throbs when I bring them into a freeze with me.

"We have to go," I say into their confused faces.

"Where?" Raul asks. I recite my spiel. They're just words now, their meaning worn out through retelling.

"Where's Jack?" Aidan asks.

The room is starting to spin. I grab Aidan's hand, soaking in the pulse of his skills to keep from tipping over.

"I'll tell you everything soon, I promise, but please, if you want to be free of the Center, you have to come with me right now."

The two boys glance at each other and then, thankfully, reach for their shoes. I let go of Aidan so he can dress, then I take both their arms as we head down the stairs. The steps stretch on forever. Time swirls around me, straining to be free. I force my feet to keep moving.

"It doesn't make sense," Raul says when we finally reach the garage. "If we can naturally change things in frozen time, why hasn't anyone else been able to do it?"

The ramp from the garage must have grown steeper. Each step feels like I'm climbing a mountain. Concrete catches at the toe of my shoe. Aidan grabs me before I fall. How many more rooms are left? Three? The gate at the mouth of the tunnel blurs. I squeeze my eyes shut for a second to try to bring it back into focus. It doesn't work. KJ is right. I'm not going to make it.

"Alex?" Raul's face swims before me. The way he says my name, I'm pretty sure it isn't the first time he's called me. "You OK?"

"Yeah." I lever myself upright again. Raul's face is so blurry it's like he's underwater.

"You don't look OK," Aidan says.

I should go to the truck. Sit down. Rest. But there are spinners still left inside. Faces swim through my mind: Angel, Yuki, Simon, Calvin. No, not Calvin. KJ. The swirl of faces stops. How can I leave KJ?

"You can make it the rest of the way on your own," I mumble. Moving my lips takes too much energy. "Up the ramp and to the left. You'll see a U-Haul."

Raul's blurry face frowns. "Are these freezes harder than regular ones?" he asks. "It seems like they would be because . . ."

"Go! I'll be there in a sec. Hurry."

Raul opens his mouth to say something else, but Aidan grabs his arm and pulls him forward. With a worried backward glance at me, the two boys race past Yolly and out into the night. I stumble a few steps down the ramp. One more room. I can do one more. From a distance, I hear a rattle as the boys climb into the truck.

I let time slide from my grasp. The relief is so complete, I sink down onto the hard floor. I'll just rest for a minute. Excited voices drift through the night. Someone is crying. Someone else shushes them. I can't stay here. Concrete scrapes my palms as I claw my way up the wall to regain my feet. One more room.

I grab for time. The strands fight me, twisting like well-muscled snakes. Yolly's roller bag rumbles out into the street. The gate rattles as it begins its descent. I fight harder, dragging time under my control. The world seems to slow before it finally stops. Night stills. I push off the wall and force myself back down the ramp and into the Center.

I can do this. One more room. I'll get Yuki. I let her image fill my brain as I slog down the familiar halls. Dark hair swinging in a solid sheet behind her shoulders. The clack of bracelets sliding along her wrist. One more spinner. One more life.

The bannister creaks under my hand. I'm pulling against it, hauling myself up the last few stairs to the third floor. Another guard sits in the same kind of metal chair as his buddy on the floor below, except this guy holds a sports magazine in his lap instead of a phone, the pages bright with bulky men in gaudy uniforms. A few steps past him, the patrolling guard Yolly warned me about has started his rounds. I skirt both men carefully and search my pocket for the key.

Yuki lies in her bed, curled into a *C* beneath a pilled pink blanket. The last time I was in her room, there were pictures from movie magazines stuck up all over the walls, and a stack of well-thumbed thrillers by her bed. Everything is gone now, stripped clean —the dresser bare, the gaping closet holding nothing but empty hangers. I sink to my knees beside her bed. Time slips from my control with the ease of a loosened breath. I drop my head onto Yuki's mattress, letting the seconds tick forward.

Air drifts around me—not a breeze, just the natural softness of moving time. My eyes slowly shut. I'm so tired. It's a good thing Yuki doesn't have a roommate; I don't think I could manage bringing two people with me. Without opening my eyes, I burrow one hand under Yuki's blanket until I touch skin. Her arm feels warm and heavy. Sleep pulls at me like an ocean tide. A tiny rest. Surely there's time for that?

Something creaks. I jerk awake, adrenaline straining my eyes wide. Did the noise come from the guard's chair in the hall? Or was it the distant clang of a closing garage gate? A page of the guard's magazine shuffles. I squeeze Yuki's arm and wrestle with time until it stops. Only the adrenaline gives me the strength to manage it.

"Yuki?" I shake her. She murmurs something unintelligible. "Yuki, wake up."

Yuki's eyes open and almost instantly fill with tears.

"Alex!" she cries. "I thought you were dead."

"No." I touch my forehead. My skull is too small to contain the pain inside it. "I came to get you out."

Yuki sits up and looks around the unnaturally still room. "Why are we frozen?"

"Get dressed," I say. "We're leaving the Center. I'll explain later. I can't hold this much longer."

"Why not? Are you sick?"

I shake my head. Yuki gasps when I wince.

"You *are* sick!" she cries. "I'll call Yolly."

"She's downstairs," I manage. "And I'm fine. Or I will be, once I let time go. Please, Yuki, you have to hurry."

Yuki scrambles out of bed and grabs her clothes. I watch the dust motes hanging in a stream of moonlight and try not to think about anything at all.

"OK," Yuki says. "I'm ready."

Standing makes my head swim. Yuki sees me sway and hurries to put her arm around me. I lean my weight against her. A small surge from her power floats in to join mine. It helps, but only a little. Yuki has never been a strong spinner.

"Where are we going?" she asks.

"Basement," I mumble. "The garage."

We stagger to the stairs. The patrolling guard has made it to the end of the hall, his body half-turned as he makes his way back toward the steps. I grab the handrail, afraid to look down at the distance I might fall. I concentrate on my feet. One step. Two. Time pulls against me, a wild animal struggling to get free. I stop thinking about anything except keeping time under control. We reach the second floor and continue toward the first. Stairs—so many stairs—One, two. The stairway curves below us, bending around the guard station as it heads toward the lobby.

A faint wave from the zapper in Barnard's office drifts upward as I make the turn. I stumble, clinging to the bannister so I don't fall. The lights in the lobby burn my eyes. The roof of the guard station is just below us. What exactly did the man witness when I fought off Ross and Jack? Have the accumulated moments between freezes shown him anything else that might expose us? I rub my head. The buzz from the zapper is boring its way into my brain, unpicking the strands from my control, one by one.

"Alex?" Yuki sounds frightened. "What's wrong?"

"I need to sit." I drop away from her and collapse onto the stairs. "Just for a minute." More time strands evaporate from my grasp. "Try to stay quiet."

Time moves again. I can feel it brushing against me, invisible and insistent. Music from the guard's radio wafts up to us. It's a jazz station, the tune jaunty and full of horns. I reach out to grab time back. Nothing happens. My grasp is too insubstantial to close around the rushing strands. I lie back onto the stairs. Yuki stares past me, toward the guard station, her lips open in an *O* of concern.

"One minute," I mouth. She doesn't look reassured.

I squeeze my fingers against my temples. My head feels like a hollowed-out shell filled with nothing but thundering pain. How long will it take the patrolling guard to reach this spot? Will he recognize me or just think Yuki and I are two regular spinners on an out-of-bed jaunt? Will finding us make him check the other rooms? If he does, he'll see the empty beds. How long after that before they find the truck? I close my eyes and visualize the Center's network of security cameras, trying to imagine a way Yuki could make it to the basement without the guard seeing her. It seems unlikely. I reach for time again. It's like trying to grab a waterfall.

The hard edge of the stairs bites my cheek. It smells like dust. Yuki sits down beside me, one hand resting protectively on my shoulder. I want to tell her I'm sorry, but forming the words takes more effort than I can muster. I should have realized I wasn't strong enough to make it. Then, at least the others could have gone free. I don't deserve to be saved.

Heavy shoes clunk on the stairwell over my head. The patrolling guard is on his way down. Yuki's hand curls around my shoulder. With the last of my strength, I reach up and clasp her hand in mine. The guard's steps grow louder. A few more and he'll turn the bend and see us. It's over.

"Tired?"

Warm air brushes against my ear. Yuki shrieks.

I open my eyes. KJ kneels on the stairs at my side, one hand

293

wrapped around mine and one on Yuki's. The music is gone. Time has stopped.

"KJ!" Yuki throws her arms around his neck. KJ, knocked sideways by the force of her greeting, gives her back an awkward pat. I blink up at him. His cheeks are flushed, like he's been running. A smudge mars the tip of his nose. When he pants, the tendons in his neck show how gaunt he's grown.

He has never been more beautiful.

"KJ?" My voice is barely a whisper. "How . . . ?"

KJ holds up his leash-free arm. "Bolt cutters. I remembered there were some in the basement shop." He rubs the bare spot on his wrist. "It took forever to get there and cut them off. I was sure I'd end up running down the street after the truck. I hope you weren't too worried."

I sit up and rub my cheek. The stair left a dent in my flesh.

"Is everyone else gone?" Yuki asks.

KJ shakes his head. "I froze time as soon as I could and ran outside. The kids you rescued are there, and the garage gate is about halfway down. I melted time and waited a few seconds. When you didn't turn up, I came in to look for you." He grins at me. "You weren't hard to find. I nearly tripped over you heading up the stairs."

"You got here just in time," Yuki says. "We could hear the guard coming."

"I couldn't hold it anymore," I say. "I failed."

"Failed?" KJ disentangles himself from Yuki and picks up my hand. "Alex, you saved all but two of the spinners. What you've done is beyond amazing."

Something warm surges through me, filling the crater of my emptiness.

"Simon and Angel are still upstairs," I say.

"I know." KJ squeezes my hand. "I'll get them."

"OK." I lean my head against the bannister. "I'll just wait here."

"No, you won't." KJ slides his arms under my legs and scoops me up against his chest. I would protest if I had even an ounce of strength left. Instead, I curl my head against his shoulder and let him carry me out of the Center.

The back of the truck is packed with frozen spinners, some standing, others sitting on the hard floor. KJ sets me down on the lip of the truck bed. Time starts and he disappears, reappearing seconds later with Simon and Angel and then vanishing again. Conversations erupt behind me. My fogged brain manages to understand only one word in fifty. Someone says my name. Yuki responds with an angry, shushing noise. KJ reappears two more times, laden with armloads of pillows and blankets, which he tosses on the floor. In the next instant, he's standing in the middle of the mass of people and ordering them all to keep quiet. My backpack, the one I'd left on the sidewalk, rests in my lap.

I drop my head against the side of the truck. Through the cool metal, I hear the garage gate rattle back into place. I twist my head to stare up at the darkened Center, waiting for a light to turn on, or an alarm to scream a warning. Nothing happens. A minute later, Yolly's sturdy frame hurries down the sidewalk. She gives one anxious glance around the empty street, then veers over to the packed moving van.

KJ jumps out to meet her. Yolly hugs him quickly before hauling herself into the back of the van. A shout goes up when the kids see her. Yolly gazes around the crowded space, pressing a hand against her chest.

"They're all here?" she whispers.

I let my eyes drift shut again. Voices rise and fall. I hear KJ explaining what will happen next—that he'll freeze time, Yolly will cut the trackers out of the backs of the kids' necks while they're frozen, and then we'll all drive away. Some of the kids protest, and a few of the Youngers start to cry. When I pay attention again, KJ is sinking down next to me.

"You doing OK?" he asks. His voice is a gentle murmur under the jabbering voices. Yolly is soothing a crying Younger while everyone else claims blankets and pillows so they can settle into the cave-like space. The reality of our imminent departure seems to be sinking in. Kids huddle in groups of twos and threes, talking together and gingerly fingering the small bandages on the backs of their necks where their trackers used to be.

"I thought I'd lost you," I tell KJ. He pushes a clump of hair behind my ear, and I lean my face into his palm. "You said you couldn't just do nothing. I was afraid you'd gone to confront Barnard. Demand he give back Shannon."

"I meant I couldn't do nothing to help you. I know you." KJ traces his thumb along the edge of my bottom lip. "You're so willing to sacrifice yourself. I knew you'd risk everything to get the others out."

My whole face tingles in the wake of his touch. A few minutes ago, I'd been sure my life was over, and now, even with my total exhaustion, I feel more alive than I ever have. KJ's face is inches from mine—perfect, and so, so precious. I wish I could freeze this moment and hold it close to me forever.

KJ bends and brushes his lips against mine.

"I love you, Alex," he whispers.

I kiss him back.

"I love you, too."

Yolly stands up in the middle of the truck and waves her hands for quiet. "Everyone set?" she asks.

The kids nod, and Yolly turns to me.

"Where are we going?"

I dig Miguel's phone number out of my memory and use Yolly's cell to call him. He answers on the second ring, his voice gravelly with sleep.

"Miguel," I say. "This is Alex. We've decided to accept your offer. We have a car. Just tell me where to go."

Yolly nods as I repeat his directions out loud. They're simple: drive an hour east on I-84 to the Memaloose Rest Area. Miguel will meet us and take us from there. I hang up.

Yolly climbs from the truck and reaches up for the strap that closes the back. The glance she casts toward the Center's sleeping walls is nervous, but her hand remains steady as she pulls down the truck's hatch. A minute later, the engine rumbles to life and we start to move.

I curl against KJ's shoulder, feeling the hard lump of bone beneath the softness of his skin. The murmurs of twenty other spinners confirm what we've accomplished. They're safe. With every breath they take, the Aclisote will work its way out of their systems, changing their fate. I know I can't measure my actions on a scale—that I can't balance one life lost with one saved—but it still feels like I've finally gotten something right.

Sleep calls my name, and this time, I let it take me. When I wake up, we will be far away from everything that has been chasing us, away from threat and desperation and fear. Tomorrow our lives will start— real lives—with futures that shimmer with years of possibilities.

Tomorrow, we will be free.

Acknowledgments

I'm going to keep this one short. Vannessa McClelland, Mark McCarron-Fraser, Sonja Thomas, Joe Morreale, and Paul McKlendin critiqued every chapter of this book, sometimes multiple times. More importantly, they provided a community that kept me motivated to continue producing words. Mary Colgan, Rebecca Davis, and Suzy Krogulski at Boyds Mills Press all offered editorial insights, and together they made *Unleashed* a stronger book. Thank you. Without the support of each of you, this book would never have come to life. Finally, thanks to Sarah Stevenson and all the good people at Innovative Housing, who never complain about my working the kind of flexible schedule other writers only dream about.